POPULAR PUBLICATIONS · FACSIMILE EDITIONS

Dime Detective Magazine #10 (August 1932)

Dime Detective magazine was the flagship detective pulp in the Popular Publications stable, running for almost 300 issues over twenty years. The August 1932 issue contains stories by Westmoreland Gray, Carroll John Daly, Erle Stanley Gardner, Frederick Nebel, and Oscar Schisgall, and includes installments in the Cardigan and Vee Brown series.

Authors:

Westmoreland Gray, Carroll John Daly,
Erle Stanley Gardner, Frederick Nebel, Oscar Schisgall

Illustrators:

William Reusswig, John Fleming Gould

This *is* Fighting Talk

IF YOU'RE a quitter you won't read far in this advertisement. If you're not—if you have the courage to face facts—you want to know who is responsible for your not getting ahead faster. We'll tell you. It's YOU. The man who won't be licked *can't* be licked. If you're a drifter you'll always wish for success but never do anything about it. The earth is cluttered with that kind.

If you're a fighter you *will* do something about it. You'll get the special training that fits you for a bigger job and better pay.

In spare time, right at home, you can get the training you need through the International Correspondence Schools. Thousands of other men have lifted themselves out of the rut and into well-paid, responsible positions by I. C. S. study. Are they better men than you?

The time for action is *this minute*. Find out about this practical educational method that lets you learn while you earn. Check the subjects that interest you in the coupon below and mail it today. It doesn't obligate you in any way to ask for full particulars, yet that one simple act may be the means of making your entire life happier and more successful. *Do it now!*

EVERY STORY COMPLETE   **EVERY STORY NEW**

Vol. 3   CONTENTS for AUGUST, 1932   No. 2

Watch for the September Issue   On the Newsstands August 20th

Published every month by Popular Publications, Inc., 2256 Grove Street, Chicago, Illinois. Editorial and executive offices 205 East Forty-second Street, New York City. Harry Steeger, President and Secretary, Harold S. Goldsmith, Vice President and Treasurer. Entered as second class matter Feb. 26, 1932, at the Post Office at Chicago, Ill., under the Act of March 3, 1879. Title registration pending at U. S. Patent Office. Copyrighted 1932 by Popular Publications, Inc. Single copy price 10c. Yearly subscriptions in U. S. A. $1.00. For advertising rates address H. D. Cushing, 67 West 44th Street, New York, N. Y. When submitting manuscripts, kindly enclose sufficient postage for their return if found unavailable. The publishers cannot accept responsibility for return of unsolicited manuscripts, although all care will be exercised in handling them.

Please mention MAN STORY MAGAZINES (POPULAR PUBLICATION GROUP) *when answering advertisements.*

JOBS FOR 300 MORE

Money Starts at Once

Astonishing New Kind of "Chain Store System"

Pays Men and Women up to

$70 a Week!

Even in Times Like These

ABSOLUTELY New—Nothing Else Like It—Sweeping Country Like Wildfire—Thrilling—Lots of Fun Running Business—Lots of Money Easily Made—No Wage Cuts—Not Affected by "Depression"—Housewives Wild About This New Kind of "Chain Store"—Chain Managers (Men and Women) Cleaning up—Now Expanding and Offer Work to More Managers Who Have Ability to Recognize a "ground floor" Opportunity—Who Have Ambition Enough to Work for $70 a Week.

IF YOU want work—if you'll be satisfied with $7.50 to $10 a day to start—with more as you make good—here's the most surprising opportunity you ever heard of. You know what a Chain Store is. Chain Grocery stores and Chain Drug stores all over the country are making money hand over fist.

Go to Work at Once

Now comes an Ohio man and invents a kind of chain store system so new and different from anything you ever heard of that it is sweeping the country and spreading like wildfire. If you are honest and ambitious, you can start one of these "chain stores" right in your neighborhood—be owner-manager—and keep all the profits for yourself.

Earnings Proved

Already Local Managers are reporting unheard of success. Korenblit, $110 in a single week. Lennon, $39.63 in 7½ hours. Mrs. McCutchen, $26.55 first day. Mrs. Hackett, $33 in 7 hours. These big earnings of a few managers show the wonderful possibilities, and right now a similar opportunity is offered to you.

30 Customers — $15 for You

Housewives are "wild" about this new system. It's like bringing two "chain stores" right to their homes. Saves time, trouble, money. You simply call on regular customers every two weeks by appointment, set up

your "Chain Drug and Grocery Stores," take orders, handle the money and deliver the goods. You keep a big part of every dollar taken in as your pay. Only 30 calls a day should easily net you $15 cash —regular and steady. If you work only half time, only on a 15 call "Chain," you should earn $7.50 a day or $45 a week.

Get the Facts

Space here doesn't permit giving full details, but if you'll mail the coupon to the man who started this amazing new system, he'll send you a remarkable free book that explains everything and shows why *now* is the ideal time to get started. Don't fail to investigate the newest, big-money plan introduced in years. Fill in and mail the coupon today —before someone else gets your location.

A. L. MILLS, President
369 Monmouth Ave., Cincinnati, Ohio

A GOOD THING TO INVESTIGATE IF YOU'RE OUT OF WORK

Why do you want $3,500.00 CASH RIGHT NOW?

I WILL PAY $250

For the Winning Answer to this Question

I am going to give $3,500.00 to some deserving man or woman who answers my announcements. *You may be the one to get it!* But, before I give it to anyone I would like to know why you want $3,500.00 cash *right now.* Just answer this question—tell me in a sentence of 20 words or less, and in your own way, why you want $3,500.00 cash right now—*nothing more to do toward the $250.00 cash prize!* Sounds easy? It is easy! The first answer that comes to your mind may win the prize. No selling—no soliciting. There are no strings at all to this amazing prize offer of $250.00 cash. ALL persons 16 years of age or older owe it to themselves to enter this contest.

20 SIMPLE WORDS WIN $250.00 FOR SOMEONE, MAYBE YOU!

Nothing More for You to Do!

$250 Prize given just for the winning answer to my question

There is no way you can lose. Simply tell me why you want $3,500.00 right now. The prize for the winning answer is $250.00.

The mere fact of sending in a few words for this big $250 cash prize qualifies you for the greater opportunity to

WIN $3,500 CASH

Or a Studebaker-8 Sedan and $2,000 Cash

This huge prize is extra and separate from the cash prize offered for the best answer to my question in only 20 words or less. No wonder we say that here's your opportunity to win a fortune. Just imagine! $3,500.00 cash besides . . . all coming to you at once. Think! Why do you want $3,500.00 cash right now? Do you want it to start a business of your own, pay off a mortgage on your home, buy new furniture or clothes? Maybe you want it to help you get an education. Consider all the things you could do with such a huge sum. Plan now—then write your answer—rush it to me at once. Yours may easily be the winner. All replies become the property of Richard Day, Manager.

BE PROMPT! I Will Send You a $100.00 Cash Certificate AT ONCE!

To make it worth your while to be prompt in sending in your answer to my question, "Why do you want $3,500.00 cash right now?" —if you will see that your letter is postmarked not more than three days after you read this offer I will send you a Cash Promptness Certificate entitling you to an extra $100.00 in cash should your reply, in the opinion of the judges, win the $250.00 cash prize offered above, making a cash prize of $350.00 in all.

Hundreds have won

Throughout the past year we have given financial help to hundreds of deserving people in all parts of the United States . . . we have given away hundreds and thousands of dollars in prizes. Beemer won $4,700. Harriet Robertson won $1,100. Hundreds more made happy with huge prizes and cash awards. Now is YOUR opportunity—ACT TODAY!

Rules

Only one answer accepted from a family. Use your own name. $250.00 given for best answer to my simple question, "Why do you want $3,500.00 cash right now?" Answers must be postmarked not later than September 15, 1932. Judges will consider answer only for practical value of the idea, construction and spelling. Neatness or ingenuity of submitting answer not considered. Duplicate prizes will be given in cases of duplicate winning answers.

RICHARD DAY, Manager
909 Cheapside, Dept. H-400-H Cincinnati, Ohio

Just Sending Answer Qualifies You for Opportunity to Win $3,500.00

Some say I am wrong. They say that giving money to people will not help to bring back prosperity. They say that the people who get money from me will spend it foolishly. Now I want to find out. I am going to give away $6,000.00. Someone is going to get $3,500.00, all cash. If I gave you the $3,500.00 why should you want it right now? Tell me in 20 words or less. Just sending an answer qualifies you for the opportunity to win $3,500.00. If you are prompt I'll send you a $100.00 Cash Certificate AT ONCE! Here is an opportunity of a lifetime. Costs you nothing to win. Rush your answer today. Send no money—just tell me why you want $3,500.00 cash RIGHT NOW—If I gave you the $3,500.00 that I have promised to give to some yet unknown deserving person.

Richard Day

Use Coupon or Write Letter with Your Answer

The Beast in Black

by
Westmoreland Gray

Gaunt, hideous, clad in somber garb, it stalked the sleet-cold countryside on murder bent. While high above the howling wind each night a shrieking siren heralded the kill. What was this dread thing, this horrid Beast in Black? Why had it laid upon the town its curse of doom?

The grotesque form on the trellis began its descent.

CHAPTER ONE

Siren of Doom

THE wind-whipped sleet danced in weird, eddying whirls in the dull darkness of the village street. It blew in grayish-white sprays around the corners of the gloomy store buildings. Straight out of the north the wind shrilled its high, eerie chant. No soul stirred in the street, nor huddled in the doorways of the buildings; no lights broke the gloom of the town. It was half an hour after midnight and the temperature was six below zero. Pinehurst had long since taken itself to bed under pounds of covers piled high. Even the lone night watchman had sought refuge from the bitter storm. The place was given over to an awful solitude and the screaming night wind.

Only in front of the Pinehurst National Bank was there any other sound, any life whatever. Before its closed doors a dog crouched and shivered—and howled disconsolately in rising and falling tremolo. The animal's thick coat

9

bristled in the frosty night and its eyes glittered like fire.

Inside the darkened bank, in the cashier's partitioned office, a man lay slumped across the desk. There was a small hole in his temple. A little trickle of blood ran down from it and stained the papers under his face. A flat thirty-two automatic pistol was gripped in the nerveless fingers of his half-extended hand. And though the office was fireless and bitter cold, the man felt no chill. He was dead.

Suddenly on the outside another sound arose. Arose above the shrill cry of the wind, above the dolorous howl of the dog. It was high, unnerving and all-pervading, a dread sound that filled the night with hideous, strident warning. It was the village fire siren, wailing like an awful banshee over the cold-stricken town. For long moments it screamed and screamed. The flimsy siren tower beside the pine fire station shook with the siren's vibrations.

The old night watchman, bundled in many antiquated garments, came from his refuge in the depot waiting room, flashlighting his way up the block-long board walk toward town. He stared all around at the dark, leaden sky for a tell-tale red glow—but saw none.

Reluctantly the more willing of Pinehurst's citizens kicked off the covers. Lights came on in half a dozen dwellings. Muttering curses, volunteer fire fighters jammed shivering bodies into icy-stiff garments, slammed out of their homes and made for town. Others augmented their number.

A huddle of men and one or two hardy and curious women gathered about the front of the fire station, mumbling, staring dully about. The siren had stopped screaming now. The night watchman was clumping toward them, preceded by the feeble cone of light from his electric flash.

"Where's the fire, Uncle Joe?" a stalwart volunteer demanded. "Gotta hustle —but gotta know where to!"

"I dunno, Zim." Uncle Joe's teeth were chattering. "Been by the telephone office—that's where this here siren is blowed from, you know—but the night gal was just wakin' up from everybody callin' in at once. She never knowed nothin' about the blowin' of the siren!"

"Guess it's a false alarm," Zim muttered. "But who coulda blowed the whistle?"

The crowd shook its collective head, as did Uncle Joe.

"It might a been," said the village mechanic, "that ice getting on the wires or wind blowing 'em, made a contact and set off the whistle."

One old, bent man with a dull, lined face, tapped his cane on the wooden ramp of the fire station. "Ye mark my words, it's an evil sign. 'Tain't no plain happen-so that that there whistle blows on a night like this. It means somethin'—somethin' turrible, I declare."

The crowd laughed a little uneasily. Old Ab Briggs was given to superstition and dire prophecies. But then—it was an unholy night, and the siren had never sounded of its own volition before. Ab's words struck a vague, chill fear in their hearts. They shivered and were silent for a moment.

"What's that?" Zim Bates cried out sharply. "Listen!"

But they had all heard it. The howl of a dog, borne to them on the biting night wind. The howl of a dog raised in a crescendo of misery.

"Huh!" grunted one of the more practical. "'S only a hound howling."

"That there," Ab Briggs said stoutly, "is the wail of death. Dorgs know when death's in the air. I mind when Mellie Sanders died all by herself in her shack on the edge o' town. She kept a whole caboodle o' hounds. They howled two days 'fore the old 'oman's corpse was found."

"Shut up, Ab Briggs!" one of the women cried. "Want to frighten a body to death?"

"Anyway we can go see about it," Zim said. "Sounds like he's howling over near the bank."

They found the shivering, miserable animal there.

"It's Charley McMain's dog!" Zim exclaimed.

They tried the door to the bank and found it locked. Then stood about, teeth chattering, wondering what to do. Ab Briggs grimly maintained that there was "death in there, I can smell it. I knows the odor o' death, I tells ye!"

But they did not find the body of Charley McMain, the cashier, that night. They dispersed, Uncle Joe leading the dog away on a leash. Pinehurst took itself back to bed again. But the dog escaped from the watchman and slunk back to the bank, to howl throughout the night. It was still there, still at its post, when the bookkeeper, Willis Buford, opened up the next morning.

And it was then that Charley McMain's body was found. And with it was found a note—a confession. It was typewritten on a sheet of paper which was still in the typewriter on Charley's desk.

My back's to the wall. I'm taking this way out. I'm $300,000 short. Lost it in speculations—

The tragedy struck a note of indescribable horror in the hearts of Pinehurst's inhabitants. Coupled with the mysterious night blast of the siren, the howling of the dog, the unprecedented winter storm, and the inevitable closing of Pinehurst's only bank, people took it as an almighty curse on the little town. Nearly everybody lost their life's savings in the bank failure, even to the farmers for miles around.

Two bleak and leaden days followed, with the cold unabated. People went about their work dully and with a feeling of despair. Auditors had taken charge of the closed bank. Officers came and went, their cars skidding on the icy roads. It was as if the whole town moved in an awful sort of nightmare.

And then another shock came to Pinehurst. It struck fear still deeper into the hearts of the already sorely tried villagers. They awoke on the third morning after Charley McMain's death to find the street placarded with ominous warnings. Warnings printed meticulously by hand on black-bordered white cards.

"Pinehurst is under a curse," those warnings read. "A hideous wrong has been done. The people of the city have been ruined. The Almighty calls now for vengeance. Each night, as the siren sounds, a man of Pinehurst shall die!"

The people were in such a mood that this warning struck the last note in hopelessness for them. Charley McMain's father, always a recluse and something of a fanatic, was prostrated, and it was rumored his mind was unstrung. Terror gripped the little town with icy fingers. It was reflected in the dull faces of men, in the quaver of their voices even, as they spoke to each other in low tones.

Verily Pinehurst felt that it was doomed.

CHAPTER TWO

Behind the Door

WHEN Ruth Kimberley had left Dalshire, the metropolis a hundred and fifty miles north of Pinehurst, to take the McMain case, her fiancé, Collin Windsor, the well-known private detective, had slipped a small automatic in the pocket of her brown pony coat.

"I'm not trying to scare you, Ruth," he said, "but I've been reading about that Pinehurst thing and there are some points that don't look good to me. At the first sign of danger wire for me. Will you?"

And now Ruth Kimberley sat in a gloomy, half-lighted room assigned to her on the lower floor of the old Mc-Main home, a large and somber building of antiquated architecture. Something of the fine courage with which she had taken the case was ebbing. Ruth was a proficient nurse, but she was young and vital and impressionable. First she had sensed a hostility in the gaunt, almost cadaverous old man who was her patient. Ruth feared Ezekiel McMain, though strangely she feared no bodily harm for herself. Sitting now outside the door of his bedroom, with only the small blaze of the gas stove to keep her company, she recalled her meeting with the old man on her arrival that afternoon. Recalled his prodigiously long frame outlined under the bed cover; his thin, slender, knotty, but restless and strongseeming hands; his parchmentlike skin stretched over sharp, high cheek bones. And particularly she remembered his deep-sunken eyes with the bright, maniacal fury burning in them; his high, querulous voice as he insisted that he needed no nurse and "didn't want a strange female hanging around ministering to him." Then he had given vent to low, vague, ominous mutterings as he spoke of his son's death.

Nor had Ruth's first impression of the village itself been conducive to high courage. Arriving on the southbound 3:13 at a time when the storm had just commenced again with a blast of new fury, she had seen the look of hopelessness and terror in the faces of the villagers about the station. She had seen one of the "curse" warnings that was still tacked to a weather-beaten pine pole. She had seen the desolate, sleet-encrusted street and the stores with crepe on their doors. Only the little doctor was cheerful in his busy, fussing way and Ruth had sensed that most of his cheerfulness was a mask.

As Ruth sat there now she could hear the whine of the high wind outside, could feel the old house lurch with its changing pressure, and hear the walls and ceilings creak.

Ruth stirred uneasily, rose and turned to McMain's door, with the idea of looking in to see that he was resting, responding to the medicine. Silently she turned the knob. She pushed gently against the door—but it did not yield.

Ruth's hand dropped to her side and she stood there momentarily puzzled, surprised. The door had been bolted on the inside. She raised her hand, knocked lightly on the panel. "Mr. McMain!" she called.

No answer. Outside the wind shrieked in a high moan. A loose piece of roofing rattled ominously.

"Mr. McMain! Let me in! You must not lock me out like this!"

Fear began to grip the girl. She cried out. She pounded the door with her fists. When this brought no response she turned and ran from the room. She made her way down a long, cold corridor, then through the dining room to the room in the rear of McMain's bedchamber. She grasped the knob of his back door and shook it with all her might. It too was locked!

And then a dread sound arrested her. It froze her in her tracks, momentarily paralyzed her. It was the wail of the village siren, that rose and rose into a wild, blood-chilling plaint. That warning that death was about to strike in Pinehurst! Its keen-cutting sound overrode the howl of the night wind and struck horror to Ruth's heart when it came to her in that cold, gloomy, half-lighted room.

Ruth took a new and firmer grip on herself. She deliberately shook off the fear that was taking hold of her, moved herself to action.

First of all she must find out what was happening, what had happened inside that locked room! She would get Pompey, the old negro servant who lived in a little house at the rear. If need be, he could break down the door. And she must phone into the village for help.

Back in the long hallway she went swiftly to the phone. She twirled the crank briskly, placed the icy receiver to her ear. She waited a long moment, but there was no response. She rang again and again, jiggled the receiver hook. There was no click, no buzz on the line. The telephone was evidently dead. Suddenly Ruth knew. The wires had been cut!

She jabbed the receiver back on its hook, caught her pony coat from the old-fashioned hall-tree and threw it about her. Through the dining room and kitchen she went and threw open the rear door of the old house. The blast of the wind nearly took her breath away and the wail of the siren still rode on the gale.

ON THE step she stared out into the darkness, across the somber and shrubbery-shadowed yard. There was no light in Pompey's quarters, but soon she made out the outline of the little house. Gathering all her courage, she ran across the yard toward it.

She found the old darkey there. On his knees, beside his rumpled bunk, he was moaning a terror-stricken prayer.

"Get up, Pompey!" she ordered sharply. "Come to the house and help me. I'm afraid something has happened to Mr. McMain."

"Oh, no, miss!" Pompey quavered.

He rolled his frightened eyes and their whites gleamed in the dark. "Don't nebber tempt providence by movin' erbout on a night like this! Don't yo' hear that banshee of death a-screamin'? It's the curse ob death on Pinehurst!"

Ruth shook him roughly but he wouldn't budge. He just rolled his eyes wider and moaned louder.

She left him finally and made her way around the corner of the big, grim old house. She came under the two windows of McMain's sick-room and stared up.

She gave a little gasp at what she saw. Though both of the windows had been tightly closed because of the cold weather, one of them, the front one, was open now! She stood there looking up, with the sound of that siren in her ears, with the hungry wind whipping her garments —stood there in the cold, staring, wondering.

At last she moved briskly toward the trellis work under the windows. Small interlacing tentacles of dead vines covered the ground beside the house. As Ruth stepped through these something tripped her and she fell. She got to her feet again, stooped and felt through the vines for the obstruction. Her hands encountered it—the handle of an ax. Apparently it had been shoved under the dead foliage to be hidden, to be out of sight.

She lifted it in her hands, stared at its vague outlines there in the dark. At last, carrying the ax, she hurried around the corner of the house, reentered the rear door.

All was quiet in the house. The wailing of the siren subsided to a low moan, then died out. Ruth passed through the kitchen, dining room, corridor, and into her own small room outside McMain's.

Not until she stood before the locked door and was about to raise the ax did she look at it in the light. Her stroke was arrested in midair. She gave a little cry of terror and her gaze fastened on the shiny metal of the ax. The butt of it was stained with blood—fresh blood!

The sight of that blood, together with all that Ruth Kimberley had been through in that gloomy old house, was too much for her. She fainted. The handle of the heavy weapon slid from her hand, and she slumped to the floor beside her couch. The flickering light of the gas fire was in Ruth's eyes when she came to finally. She lay inert, a little dazed for a moment. Then got resolutely to her feet and pushed the gruesome bloodstained ax under the couch to stand considering her next action.

She turned to make one more trial at McMain's door. She twisted the knob and pushed against it.

The door gave in easily, almost threw her off her balance! She caught herself and stared into the room.

The gaunt sick man lay under the dim glow of the shaded bed lamp. His feverish, malevolent eyes stared at the girl in apparent puzzlement. "Do ye always enter a sick-room head foremost, miss?" his querulous voice demanded.

He spoke as if nothing had happened, as if his nurse had not been locked out of his room for the past hour or more, as if no siren had blown.

Ruth did not wish to alarm him. She glanced at her watch. "I'm sorry I disturbed you, Mr. McMain. I tripped on the edge of the carpet. It's time for your medicine. I'll bring it in."

"Be quick about it then," the old man said sourly. "And begone! I tell ye I won't have a strange female about, soon as I get a chance to have a word with Doctor Green."

NOTHING else happened that night. Ruth slept but little, and that fitfully. Morning came, bleak, bringing no surcease from the gloom. The little doctor came at nine. There was nothing cheerful about him this morning, affected or otherwise. The lines of his haggard face were deepened with care and his eyes showed loss of sleep. He was nervous and jumpy and greeted Ruth non-committally.

"How's Zeke, this morning, Miss Kimberley?" he asked.

"Resting nicely," Ruth said. "And seems to have done well during the night."

Doctor Green spent only a few minutes with McMain. When he came out he sank down on the edge of Ruth's couch and passed his hand over his eyes with a gesture of resignation.

"Mr. McMain?" Ruth asked anxiously.

"Oh!" the doctor said, as if coming out of a bad dream. "He's doing as well as could be expected. But—well, I guess I might as well tell you. You will hear anyway, child. There was a murder in Pinehurst last night."

Ruth's heart stood still. Her hand went to her throat.

The doctor went on more rapidly. "I thought it was all balderdash, that business about a curse on Pinehurst—and the wailing siren."

"Who was killed?" Ruth asked almost breathlessly.

"Jonathan Wilson, one of our most prominent men," Doctor Green said with some return of dignity. "Owner of a great deal of Pinehurst property. He was a director of the closed bank. I've just come from his place— Good God! Would you believe it? He'd been dead about eleven hours—killed right about the time that siren was blowing!"

Evidently the little doctor was quite shaken. He licked his lips, mopped his forehead and stared before him.

Ruth leaned forward. "How—how was he killed?" she asked in a small voice. "That is—what kind of a weapon?"

"His head was bashed in," Doctor Green answered. "Something heavy and blunt. Like the butt of an ax, for instance."

Ruth sank into her chair. The doctor glanced at her, noted the deathly pallor of her face.

"Why, what is the matter, child? Er —damn me—I'm a blundering old fool! I could have told it a little less bluntly."

Ruth smiled and her color came slowly back. "It's all right, doctor. I guess it just gave me a turn. That and hearing the siren last night."

She turned her gaze from the doctor's haggard face. She did not tell him about that bloodstained ax nor of her harrowing experiences. She would wire for Collin Windsor and save it all for his arrival.

Ruth sent her telegram at ten, though the operator at the station accepted it subject to delay, as the storm was playing havoc with all lines of communication.

The day wore on, Pinehurst still in the grip of the storm—the coldest and longest that the little town had known in forty years. All day Ruth went about her duties mechanically, avoiding as much as possible any contact with the grim old man who lay in his bed in the side room. She tried to force from her mind the continually recurring thought that Ezekiel McMain was a murderer. She kept her hopes up by sheer will power.

When darkness began to gather, however, and another night crept over the village with no word from Collin, courage began to desert her. Was she going to have to spend another awful night in that house of tragedy with a man who might be a murderer?

IT WAS nine-thirty when a large roadster skidded perilously around the corner of the Pinehurst bank building.

and drew up with a screech of brakes in front of the drug store, the only lighted spot in the village. Two men got out, muffled in heavy coats. They blew plumes of frost into the air and slapped their gloved hands together.

"Whew!" cried Jimmie Bolton, the shorter of the two. "I hope I never have to make another drive over roads like that." He stared up and down the street. "So this is Pinehurst! The town with a curse. It looks to me like it's been cursed for the last forty years."

"Let's see if we can find out in here where the McMain place is," said his companion.

The keeper of the drug store was a wispy little man with a shiny bald pate, weak eyes and thick-lensed glasses. He stared at the two men from the city with frank curiosity as they entered the shop. He saw Collin Windsor, a tall, well-knit man just under thirty, a man of quick step, alert mien and athletic build, handsome in spite of his slightly acquiline features. And Jimmie Bolton, prone to chubbiness, with a youthful, innocent face, and eyes that saw interest in all things.

"We're looking for the McMain place," Windsor told the druggist. "Can you direct us to it?"

"Also," said Jimmie briskly, "we're looking for the latest news on this here, now, Pinehurst curse. I'm with The Dalshire Times-Herald covering the story. Telephone wires were down when I left Dalshire this afternoon and ever since then we've been skidding this way over hellish roads. What's the latest lowdown?"

The storekeeper had plenty to tell them; about the murder of Jonathan Wilson and the second sounding of the siren of doom; about the sheriff and three of his deputies from the county seat being in town on the case; about the auditors verifying Charley McMain's shortage of over three hundred thousand, Windsor listened to the voluble account, though he was anxious to be off to find Ruth Kimberley, to be assured of her safety.

When the druggist had finished Windsor and Bolton drove east as directed. It was easy to pick out the McMain place from the druggist's description. It was cheerless enough to look at—the big, rambling antiquated structure amid its somber cedars and the dead foliage of entangling vines and shrubbery.

"Lord, what a spooky-looking dump!" Jimmie exclaimed. "Imagine a nice girl like Ruth Kimberley working in a place like that."

They walked up the long gravel walk bordered by soughing cedars. Windsor's hand caught the brass knocker and he pounded stoutly. Nothing but echoes of the knocker came back to him.

"I don't like this," Windsor said shortly. "That was loud enough to wake the dead. Surely somebody's here."

"Try the door," Jimmie suggested. "Maybe it's unlocked."

It was. Windsor and Jimmie pushed into the vestibule, which was dark.

"Ruth!" Windsor called. "Where are you? It's Collin!"

There was no answer.

With rising apprehension Windsor fumbled around until he found the door to the corridor. He peered into this tentatively. It was dimly lighted with a small shaded globe at the rear. He called again and again. But got no answer.

Windsor spun on his heel, clipped out: "On your toes! We're going through this place!"

In the hallway they opened other doors. The first looked in on the great, cavernous living room, dark, ghostly-appearing in its desertion. The second was to the dining room, equally forbidding, equally deserted.

It was Windsor who flung open the third door. A faint light greeted them and with it a pungent and sickeningly sweet odor.

"Chloroform!" Windsor cried.

He pushed into the room, stopped and stared. The only light came from the small blue flame of the gas stove. But that was enough to show Collin Windsor what was there. Ruth Kimberley, disheveled and with her uniform rumpled, lay on the floor by the couch. The doorway beyond her was open. Windsor gave one cry, strode across and knelt over her.

"She's been chloroformed." Windsor's words were thick. Jimmie sensed the hurt in his voice. "Quick! Find the phone and call the doctor!"

Windsor lifted the girl up in his arms and placed her on the couch, straightening her out to a comfortable position. He began rubbing her wrists. He heard Jimmie twisting away viciously at the phone in the hall. Seconds later Jimmie stuck his head back in the door. "Phone's dead," he said.

"Then ride for the doctor. Get a move on! Hurry!"

"Which way do you ride for a doctor in this damn forsaken burg?"

"How the hell do I know? But get the lead out of your feet. Find him!" There was a sharp edge on Windsor's voice.

He heard the clash of gears as Jimmie got the car in motion. He sat down to stare at the girl and some of his first excitement passed. After all, it was only chloroform, and Ruth's pulse was good.

He drew off the girl's shoes and placed a light blanket over her. Then he peered into the open doorway nearby. The only light in the room beyond was a small bed lamp and from this vague illumination Windsor could see that the rumpled sick-bed was empty. Also that one of the high windows in the east wall was open, its dingy curtain billowing in from the wind outside. He stepped into the room to look about.

"Poor Ruth!" he said aloud. "Looks like she was set here to nurse a madman —and a murderer! Guess she watched him so closely he had to chloroform her to get out to commit his crime!"

He stood up from his inspection of the bed, turned, and was about to retrace his steps to the girl's couch when a sound stopped him dead in his tracks. The night air was filled with it. The piercing wail of the village fire siren. Pinehurst's banshee of death!

CHAPTER THREE

Piano Wire—and Precautions

COLLIN WINDSOR tried to laugh off the fears that beset him. It was absurd to believe in such rot. To believe that each time a mechanical banshee howled a villager died! The thing was impossible.

But his eyes were grim as he moved toward the doorway. There was Jonathan Wilson, now a corpse, to attest to the validity of the villagers' belief. He had died while the siren howled. You couldn't laugh that off! Was death striking again tonight while that unnerving wail sounded across the storm?

There, waiting in that old house, Windsor could almost feel the buzz of excitement that pervaded Pinehurst, the terror that struck the town with the wailing of the siren. He could hear the sputter of motors as cars moved along the scant, gloomy residential streets; checking over from home to home; grimly visiting each house to see who of their number would be missing now! Windsor felt a great wave of sympathy for these humble folk of the stricken little village—and especially for Ruth, who had been drawn into the awful thing.

He waited five minutes longer and Jimmie did not return. Collin turned on his heel, stalked through the corridor to the front doorway. He listened. The siren was silent now, but he could hear cars moving back and forth about town. He walked rapidly down the gravel walk to the curb and looked up the street toward the village. No car was in sight. What the devil was keeping Jimmie and the doctor?

He turned impatiently back toward the house. As he retraced his steps sudden fear overtook him. Something might happen to Ruth while he was out. He quickened his pace, reentered, and walked rapidly the length of the hall to her room. She was there, just as he had left her.

But there was something different, something changed since he had left the room. His trained, observant eyes darted about. What was it? His glance fell on the door to Ezekiel McMain's room. It was closed now—and he had left it open!

On tiptoe Windsor crossed to the door. Gently, silently he turned the knob and pushed it open—peered in.

Two burning eyes glared at him from the sallow, skeleton-like face on the pillow under the bed lamp.

"Who be ye?" Ezekiel McMain demanded in a rasping voice. "Get out! Ye don't belong in my house. And I won't have ye peeking about, spying at me. Get out!"

"Sorry, Mr. McMain," Windsor mumbled. "Didn't mean to disturb you."

"Keep that female outta here, too," McMain shouted after him as he closed the door.

Windsor smiled grimly. "Nice sociable company for Ruth. Poor kid!"

With a sigh of relief Collin heard his car grind to a stop out front, heard Jimmie's and the doctor's feet crunching up the walk. Presently the door opened and Jimmie's round face and Doctor Green's harassed, wizened one, looked in.

The little physician took things in at a glance. He had understood only in part Jimmie's excited explanation. "Where's McMain? And what's happened here?" he demanded as he hurried across and bent over the girl.

While Green worked with her, Collin explained all he knew. The doctor nodded, but was surprised obviously to learn that McMain had left his bed and now had returned.

"I didn't think he had the strength. But people develop unnatural strength in delirium. Might have been so in Zeke's case."

Jimmie Bolton said: "Had a devilish time finding the doc. He was cruising around with some others, calling at every house."

The doctor paused in his work. "Trying to learn if the killer had struck again," he explained. "You see—we believe in that siren now when it blows."

"Has there—been another murder?" Windsor asked.

"We haven't found a body yet. They're still looking. The thing's got me. I'm saying they'll find one."

The little man shivered. He looked at Collin. "So you're Collin Windsor. I've heard of you. This Pinehurst affair ought to be a case that'll test you, young man."

"It begins to look that way, doctor."

IT WAS a quarter of an hour before Ruth was revived enough to be able to talk. She clung to Collin's arm as he sat beside her couch, and Collin read in her eyes some of the horror she had gone through.

"I don't know for sure just what happened," Ruth said. "I had given Mr. McMain his medicine at nine-fifteen. He was quiet and showed no more than his usual resentment toward me. He watched me closely though, and I thought his eyes were crafty." Ruth shuddered. "I was sitting in here, trying to read. I didn't

even hear his door open. Suddenly I felt someone hovering over me, back of me. I tried to scream—I guess I did. Then a hand clasped my mouth. Another covered my face. I smelled chloroform! I struggled—as long as I could. Those were strong hands!"

"Hands of deliriu.n," Doctor Green averred.

"I didn't know any more after that."

Doctor Green turned to Windsor. "McMain's mind is unstrung, Windsor. Charley's suicide and disgrace, you know. He got a bad head blow several years ago, in a car accident. He resents Miss Kimberley being here."

Doctor Green left after looking in on McMain. Left to join again in Pinehurst's gruesome search.

When the doctor was gone Ruth told her story in full to Collin. Her brown eyes looked on him with confidence as she talked. She told about McMain locking her out of his room and how, apparently, he was absent from it at the time of the murder the night before. She told him in a constricted voice about finding the red-stained ax, and about hiding it under the couch.

"If there was another murder tonight," she said with remorse, "I am to blame! If I had told about the ax and about last night, the county officials could have restrained McMain immediately, maybe arrested him—or at least put him under heavy guard. Collin, I was saving all the information for you."

Windsor's face had gone very grim but now he forced a smile. "Don't go blaming yourself for anything, Ruth. You have been a very brave girl. I got here as soon as I could after receiving your wire, dear. You see the train had already left and the drive took a long time over those slippery roads."

"I know—I know," Ruth said dully.

Windsor drew the ax from its hiding place under the couch. Turning his back to shield it from Ruth's view, he and Jimmie stared down at the gruesome weapon. Windsor turned it over in his hands. The blood-stains on it had dried and darkened now.

Suddenly Jimmie pricked up his ears. "I hear a car chugging down the street," he exclaimed. "Maybe it's one of the search cars. I'll run out front, hail 'em, and see if they've learned anything yet."

Windsor nodded and continued to study the ax. Finally he shoved it under the couch and turned to talk to Ruth. Presently he heard Jimmie Bolton returning and sensed something ominous in the very precision of the boy's tread.

With a reassuring word to the girl he arose and went to meet Jimmie in the corridor.

Ruth looked up as he came back into the room and saw the gravity in his face, in spite of his forced smile. "Don't try to fool me, Collin," she said. "It's—happened again?"

Collin came over, sat down beside the couch and took her hand. "There's no use trying to lie to you, Ruth. Yes, a man named Junius this time—William Junius—a prominent merchant here in Pinehurst. He was found strangled in his bed. A piece of piano wire was twisted about his throat."

THE abyss of gloom and fear into which Pinehurst was plunged was indescribable. Three times the siren had blown and each time a man of Pinehurst had died—just as the placard on the little village street had prophesied. Scoffers who had laughed at the warnings were now gray with fear. Old-timers and superstitious ones shook their heads and made still more dire prophecies. Men in the street stared at each other with horror in their eyes. They moved from place to place in their daily rounds with faltering steps. Some said the killer was human, a madman. Others averred that the victim had died by other than human hands, hands which nothing could stay, that Pinehurst was truly under a curse. And all wondered who would be the next to be struck down?

Shortly before eight that morning a farmer who lived several miles out, came in town with word for Sheriff Simms. He had been riding out from Pinehurst between nine and ten o'clock the night before, he said, and saw a strange-looking figure leave the grounds of the Junius place.

" 'Twas a uncommon tall feller," the farmer said. "And he run with a funny step, sort of crow-hop. He was dressed in black, and I couldn't see no face—like as if he had it covered up with something black. His clothes was floppy like. He was a queer sight and sure give me a turn. But he heard my hoss and ducked into some shadows. Never thought nothing of it just then. But when word got round that Will Junius had been killed, I thought there might be, well—some sorter connection."

News of this spread over the mystery-ridden town. The doctor spoke of it to Windsor at McMain's a little later. "That farmer drinks a little," Green said. "But —that description sounds too familiar to be taken lightly."

"Familiar? Whom does it suggest to you?" Windsor inquired.

"Zeke McMain," Doctor Green said with conviction. "He wears a garb like that, or did—long capelike overcoat. And he walks with a birdlike hop."

There was a meeting in the mayor's office over the defunct Pinehurst National Bank that morning. It was called by Mayor Thompson, and Collin Windsor was there by request. Others at the meeting were Sheriff Tom Simms from the county seat and two of his deputies; Doctor Green, Constable Sam Dimmer, and the town marshal, "Bud" Grimes. There were also Simon Winters, who owned the big general supply store, and Victor Burgess who was a retired merchant.

Windsor had turned over to the sheriff the ax that Ruth had found. He had also informed the sheriff of another clue that he had found that morning. Windsor had searched the old grand piano in the living room of the McMain home, and found a length of wire missing from one of its strings. Careful measurement proved that this missing piece exactly fitted the strand which was taken from around the throat of William Junius!

Sheriff Tom Simms, a big heavy man with carefully creased trousers and a heavy gold chain across his chest, cleared his throat. "As I see it, gentlemen, there's nothing for us to do but make a move against McMain. Arrest him and put him behind bars! Evidently he's a madman."

There was a vague chorus of approval at this. Mayor Thompson, a small, stocky man of forty, with thinning blond hair and an expressionless face, spoke. "What do you say, doctor?"

"I say no!" Doctor Green said with emphasis. "Zeke McMain's a very sick man and his sanity teeters in the balance. Imprison him in his room, if you wish —but do not confront him with an accusation just now. If you do I shan't be responsible for the consequences!"

"Professional integrity!" the sheriff said airly, gesturing with a fat hand.

Thompson turned to Collin Windsor. "We'd like to hear from you, Mr. Windsor."

"I favor the doctor's plan," Collin said quietly. "Certainly there's a possibility that McMain is the killer. If so, as long as he is at liberty he is a menace. But— there is a decided shade of doubt in my mind whether McMain is the killer or not."

"Blazes!" the sheriff growled. "What more proof do you want? Haven't we found and seen enough? And as to motive, McMain had plenty of it. Plenty! Everybody knows that he believes that his son Charley was framed in that bank failure. Zeke McMain has always been something of a fanatic—queer. Many folks think he's been crazy since he got that lick on the head. Now he's gone in for wholesale murder, looks like!"

COLLIN WINDSOR smiled. The whole meeting listened for his words. "A lot in what you say, sheriff, and I'm not denying it. Each man killed so far was a director in the failed bank. Yes, it may be that McMain is doing this because he believed his son was framed, wronged by those men. And the killer is going about this in exactly the way a man of McMain's turn of mind would. The blowing of that siren each night, the careful picking of victims with regularity. All that appears to be the work of a madman, an unstrung fanatic."

Windsor drew a cigarette from his case, lit it, and looked over his little audience. "Yes, if I had been a director in that bank I would certainly be looking to my safety now!"

"I guess they are," Sheriff Simms said with a grim chuckle. "I reckon Thompson and Sime Winters and Vic Burgess are shaking in their boots this minute!"

Windsor continued. "On the face of it it looks as if McMain is the guilty man. So don't let us leave him unguarded one moment. But the whole atmosphere of the case suggests a well-wrought piece of fiction to me. It appears as if someone else were committing these murders—and doing everything in his power to make it look like Ezekiel McMain's work!"

Thompson spoke. "Will you explain more fully, Windsor?"

"First, Ezekiel McMain is a shrewd man, even if he is a mentally sick one. If he had escaped from his room that first night and killed Jonathan Wilson with an ax, would he have hidden the weapon just outside his own window on his return, with many better opportunities of disposing of it along the way? Then on the second night would he have chloroformed Miss Kimberley, when probably he could have slipped from his room between her calls and never have been missed? And again would he deliberately have taken a piece of wire from his own piano to strangle William Junius when the strand was sure to be missed at the first search? If I know anything at all about incipient insanity, gentlemen, an acute shrewdness, a craftiness, I might say, is one of its symptoms. And that does not fit in with what McMain has done."

The little doctor was on his feet. "Windsor is right!" he cried.

The meeting broke into a hum of individual discussion. Thompson quickly called it back into order. "Something has to be done, men! We know there is a killer abroad in town and that another fine citizen may die tonight. We can't let that go on!"

"Let's have another suggestion from Mr. Windsor," somebody said.

Thompson turned again to Collin. Collin said: "I suggest something in the nature of martial law. Have everybody stay indoors tonight except men of the law. Put a heavy guard around the home of Ezekiel McMain. Have a man stationed at the fire-siren tower to see if it really is the village siren which sounds, or a counterpart of it hidden somewhere nearby. We may be able to trace the killer through that siren. Also I suggest some protection for the remaining directors of the bank."

After much discussion it was decided to follow Collin's suggestions. The meeting broke up in a little more cheerful frame of mind than it had begun.

And that was how things stood on the third night. People of Pinehurst stayed close by their hearthsides. Four men patrolled the grounds of the McMain place. A fifth, one of Simm's deputies, had his post in the vestibule at the head of the corridor inside. Constable Dimmer was stationed as a sentinel at the siren tower. Marshal Bud Grimes was on guard out at Simon Winters' home. A deputized citizen watched over Victor Burgess' safety.

But with all of these precautions Pinehurst shuddered with the rise and fall of the wind, and listened with apprehension for the first eerie note of the siren. All wondered if these man-made protections could stay the murderer's hand tonight?

CHAPTER FOUR

Killer's Covert

DOCTOR GREEN came at eight-thirty that evening and was alone for some time with his patient. When he left he reported that McMain was sleeping.

Windsor and Jimmie Bolton, the latter all aquiver with excitement over the affair and the big story it would make in The Times-Herald, lit a fire in the great living room, drew up chairs to it and talked over the case. Collin Windsor always found the chubby reporter a good foil for his wits, when he was working on a case.

"What do you make of it, Jimmie?" Windsor asked him.

Jimmie grinned. "You're asking me so you can show me where I'm wrong, Collin. But I'll be the goat. Maybe you hit the nail on the head when you said some palooka was doing this and framing it to look like McMain's work. If so, he's sure accomplishing his purpose!"

"There's one possibility we don't want to overlook, Jimmie. The directors of the busted bank have plenty of enemies now. People both here in town and in the country all around have lost heavily in their bank. Naturally they're outraged —and blaming everybody connected with the bank."

"Good gosh, yes!" Jimmie exclaimed. "I hadn't thought of that. A disgruntled depositor! That furnishes plenty of motive if we look for the killer in someone other than McMain."

Windsor was silent for a long time. He puffed meditatively on his cigarette and stared at the gas fire. Presently he shook his head. "It doesn't fit in though, Jimmie. This affair doesn't look like a case of revenge to me. It's too coldly plotted, too machinelike. Good Lord, it looks as if some person had set out to kill a certain number of men for a certain purpose! The siren and the curse warnings are psychological clap-trap to camouflage it, make it look like the work of an unbalanced person—McMain, for example."

Jimmie Bolton stared at Windsor in wide-eyed surprise. "Do you mean—"

Windsor stood up. He paced back and forth several times. Finally he stood before Jimmie. "I mean," he said, "that the Pinehurst killer wants a certain number of men out of the way. That his victims are already picked. That he is simply capitalizing on the fear and superstition of the inhabitants to throw a smoke screen around the real purpose of the killings. The man is shrewd, calculating, and he is not a man of unbalanced mind. Unless we can stop him the murders will go on until that certain number of men are eliminated—and not until then will the Pinehurst curse die out."

Jimmie Bolton shivered. He looked at his watch, then forced a smile—but it was a grim one. "It's about time for the devil to start doing his stuff, then," he said hoarsely. "Cripes, I listen to hear that hell whistle start tootin' any minute."

Collin Windsor did not smile. "So do

I, Jimmie. But if the killer stalks tonight, he's going to have to step warily. The village is well patrolled."

"But what is the motive, Collin? If we eliminate McMain with his revenge motive and the possibility of the disgruntled depositor with the same motive—"

"Frankly, Jimmie, I don't know."

"Money?"

"Possibly. There may be some loot that we don't know is in existence."

Jimmie was about to answer when the corridor door opened. Ruth Kimberley stood in it. She was a little pale. Repressed excitement was in her face. "Mr. McMain, Collin," she said. "He's locked his door again!"

Windsor jumped up. "The devil!" he exclaimed. "You stay here in this room, Ruth. Here by the fire! Understand?"

He drew the girl into the room, stepped through the door—Jimmie at his heels—and closed it. In the corridor the deputy joined them. Collin strode quickly to the rear of the corridor, into Ruth's room, and made for the door of the sickroom. He stopped and the two of them brought up behind him.

Windsor raised his hand, knocked. "Mr. McMain!" he called. "Unlock this door!"

There was no reply.

"McMain!" Windsor shouted. "We're coming in. We'll break down the door! Do you hear?"

A WEIGHTED, dramatic silence followed Collin's words. For the space of two watch-ticks there was no sound whatever.

And then an awful sound arose. But it did not come from within the room or even from within the house. It was the rising cry of the siren high above the wind outside, high above every other sound. The noise grew in volume, died down, grew again.

Windsor whirled on both of them. "Get on the phone, Jimmie." The wires had been fixed during the day. "Hang on it! Get hold of Sheriff Simms. Have him check up at once on Burgess and Simon Winters and Mayor Thompson—as well as every other house in town. Come on, Jackson," he said bruskly to the deputy. "Lend me a shoulder—we're gonna break in this door!"

Jimmie Bolton made for the telephone as the other two men backed off and flung themselves in a concerted assault against the locked door. It was not until the third attempt that it gave way. Wood splintered; the door flung wide. Momentum threw the two men into McMain's room.

They brought up and stared at the bed. The old man was there. He moved restlessly but did not speak. Under the dim glow of the bed lamp they saw that his sunken eyes were closed. He was asleep. Even their noise with the door had not awakened him!

"Stay here and watch him," Windsor ordered. "Don't take your eye off this room until we've heard from the check-up and know whether that siren was a false alarm or not."

Reports came in slowly from the search. Windsor stood at Jimmie's shoulder at the telephone, avid for each bit of news. They learned that Mayor Thompson was safe, then that Simon Winters was safe; and finally—that Victor Burgess was safe.

Some time later a car slid to a stop at the McMain place. Sheriff Simms and Doctor Green got out. They came into the living room to warm their frosted hands and feet at the gas fire.

"I reckon we can rest easy for tonight," the sheriff said cheerily. "We've checked every house in town and I'm certain there hasn't been a killing."

"Well, if there has," the man Jackson stated stoutly, coming in from his vigil in McMain's room, "old McMain never had anything to do with it this night. He locked his door, but he never left his room—and he's sleeping as sound as a log."

"What about the siren, sheriff?" Windsor asked. "Have you heard from Constable Dimmer? Was it really the village siren blowing?"

"That's a funny thing," Simms answered. "You know, Dimmer says the sound didn't come from the siren—but from the roof of one of the nearby buildings. Dimmer's searching roof tops for it now."

"Good work, sheriff," Collin said noncommittally.

"Come on, doc," Simms called. "Let's go turn in. I think the danger's all over for tonight. Jackson, tell the boys they can take it kinda easy now."

Plainly the sheriff was optimistic about the affair. Evidently he felt that the sentinels need not remain on guard any longer.

"Funny, Jimmie," Windsor said, after the sheriff and doctor had departed, "that the murderer would sound his siren when he had failed to make his kill."

"Maybe he just enjoys giving the town a scare," Jimmie said. "A man who had done what he has would have a ghoulish sense of humor, no doubt."

Windsor shook his head. "Looks more as if he were trying to mislead us—to throw us off guard. Now that the siren has sounded—with nobody being turned up—naturally the killer may expect that the patrol will relax. Now is when he could strike unhindered!"

"Gosh," Jimmie breathed. "And Sheriff Simms fell for it like a ton of brick."

Windsor nodded. "We can't relax our vigil, Jimmie. I want you to take up your post in McMain's room. Don't be surprised at anything that may happen, though. The old man may not give you any trouble, but keep your automatic handy and don't leave your post before daylight!"

Jimmie looked hard at Collin Windsor.

"As for me," Windsor continued, "I'm going out and check up myself on the possible victims. Keep your eyes open, Jimmie!"

WINDSOR got information as to the way to the residences of Mayor Thompson, Simon Winters and Victor Burgess from the man patrolling the front of McMain's. At Thompson's place, just across the wide expanse of shrubbery-loaded lawn from McMain's, Windsor found the mayor a little alarmed, but preparing to retire. After a brisk walk eastward, Collin came to Victor Burgess' home, a somewhat pretentious two-story affair.

Burgess was safe with his wife, but much more alarmed and excited than Thompson had been. Collin gave them a few encouraging words and departed further on his grim expedition of check-ups.

He headed north toward Simon Winters'. A premonition, an ominous hunch, spurred his steps. The night was still bitter cold, but the sky had cleared partially overhead. The clouds had gathered in an ugly bank on the west, and a white, brilliant moon hung in the east quarter of the heavens. Its weird radiance threw trees and shrubbery in bold, black relief and made Collin's shadow a long, grotesque, writhing thing beside him.

Winters' place was on a lonely spot just beyond the edge of town. The road that led up to it was a shadowed, tree-bordered trail. Collin stopped at the front and looked at the gloomy, unlighted house. There was no guard. Probably the man stationed here had been released after the sounding of the siren.

Collin's sense of impending disaster was stronger now. Somehow a spell of tragedy seemed to hang over the house. He shivered and gently pushed through the gate.

Then he saw something that made him dart aside, into the shadow of a bush. From the black outline of a small outhouse—apparently a tool shed—a furtive figure ran toward the big house. It was an awkward, grotesque figure, more like an apparition than anything real, anything human. It was tall and ungainly, with flopping black garments, and ran with an odd, jerky, birdlike stride. Collin got but half a glimpse of it before it disappeared in the darkness at an angle of the house.

Collin slipped his gun from its underarm holster and moved swiftly to the nearest cover, a small cedar. He didn't want to alarm his quarry, yet he knew that sinister figure was on murder bent. He must stop him at any cost.

From tree to bush, from bush to tool shed Collin ran with swift stealth. He now had a view of the back of the house and the entire rear area. He paused there waiting, watching. But the black figure was nowhere in sight. Precious, vital seconds ticked by and still there was no sign of it.

Had the man already gained entrance? Was it possible that even now the murderer was stalking inside that gloomy, unlit house? Collin ran his gaze around the east facade of the building, gleaming white and spectral in the moonlight. He must find Winters, quick, before the killer struck.

Risking discovery Collin moved in a stooping run to the side of the building. He crouched under a window. Gradually he raised his head so that his eyes were above the sill. Moonlight streaming through the window somewhat illuminated the interior. It was a deserted dining room. Collin swore and darted to the next window.

HE peered in—cautiously, warily. The gray light that fell inside showed that this was Winters' bedroom. There were the rumpled covers, the huddled bulk of Simon Winters' body under them. As Collin stared closer he could make out the man's face against the pillow.

There was a vague shuffle of movement in the dusky gloom beyond the bed. And Collin knew! There was someone in that room with Winters.

Now he could make out the outline of a gaunt, black figure. He could not discern substance—just form—the black hat, the loose, ridiculous, funeral garments. The figure came closer and moonlight fell on it. It bent over the sleeping man. Collin could not see the face, but he did see what was gripped in the skulker's hands. An ax! A moonbeam struck its glinting edge and Collin saw the weapon being slowly raised! When it fell, no doubt, it would be aimed to drive through Winters' heart!

For half a second Collin was incapable of movement, spellbound, fascinated with horror. A man was being murdered before his eyes! Then he flung himself free of the spell holding him and was electrified into action.

He jabbed the window viciously with the nose of his gun and yelled in a thunderous voice: "Don't move! You'll die!"

But the figure did move. It spun around like a top, garments billowing out from it, even as Collin fired.

Collin sensed something coming toward him and ducked. The thrown ax shattered the remnants of the window, flew over his head to land in the yard, sent falling glass all about his ears. Collin jerked back for another glimpse and another possible shot, but the figure was gone. Only Simon Winters was there, sitting up in bed, yelling at the top of his voice, and threshing wildly with his arms.

Collin ran around the rear corner of the house. If the man came out this way he would be ready for him. But he didn't. With chagrin Collin heard a front door slam. He raced back in that direction. The hopping, queer-running, black-garbed man had attained the front fence, was vaulting it.

Winters was in the front door, blasting away with a shotgun. Collin did not stop to see if Winters were aiming at him or the man ahead, but ran on after the fugitive.

It was a losing chase for Collin, however. Already his quarry was in that maze of mingled shadows which was the lane toward town. When he reached this Collin had to advance slowly, cautiously. Any dark shrub might conceal an ambush.

He went through the whole length of the lane and then beat back through the shadows along it. He spent an hour searching that entire section only to be forced at last to concede that his man had evaded him. Finally, acutely disappointed, he turned toward town and headed for the McMain place.

CHAPTER FIVE

The Beast in Black

THE McMain place had a quality of quiet somnolence about it when Collin reached it. There was a dim light in the vestibule. Collin entered to find the deputy, Jackson, snoring in his chair, draped with a great red-and-yellow quilt. At least this was reassuring. If there had been any sort of turmoil certainly Jackson wouldn't have been sleeping so soundly. Collin passed him by on tiptoe and pushed on to the interior of the house. He opened the door to Ruth Kimberley's room.

Ruth lay on the couch in a tired sleep, for which Collin was glad. The girl had

had more than her share of fear and worry in the last three days. She needed the rest.

The doorway to McMain's room was closed. Windsor turned the knob and pushed it open. It was gloomy in there. For a moment Collin could not discern just what had happened. A groan from the floor brought him to quick realization. With an oath Collin whirled, snapped on the room light. Jimmie Bolton's chubby form lay sprawled on the floor, his chair overturned beside it. There was a welt, an ugly, blue one, on Jimmie's forehead. But even now, as Collin looked down, the boy mumbled and stirred.

Collin dropped to his knees, grasped Jimmie's wrist. His expression relaxed. Jimmie's pulse was O. K. Relieved, Collin stood up.

Windsor's glance flew to the sick-bed in the middle of the room. Ezekiel Mc-Main lay there as if in deep slumber, his head thrown back, his mouth open.

Collin turned quickly, strode out of the room. He paused at Ruth's couch, shook her gently. "Something has happened to Jimmie, Ruth! I need you to help me with him."

The girl sat up quickly and reached for her negligée.

"Jimmie's had a blow on the head. Look after him. I'm going out and wake up Jackson."

Windsor left her and moved on rapidly to the vestibule, where he shook Jackson roughly into consciousness. "Wake up, man!" he snapped, his voice on edge. "A dozen people could break into this house while you snore!"

Jackson yawned widely and rubbed his eyes. "I ain't had no sleep in three nights," he grumbled. "I reckon I couldn't be blamed for dropping off when things seemed quiet."

"Go back and see if you can help Miss Kimberley," Collin ordered. "I'm going

out to check up on the boys patrolling the grounds."

Windsor found the man out front stalking his post, but asleep on his feet. How vigilant he had been was attested to by the fact that Windsor, returning from Winters' place, had just slipped by him without being challenged. Together they moved around the house to investigate the other guards. Two of them were on the job, the man on the west side and the one at the rear. But the man who had guarded the east side—the side opposite McMain's window—was not to be seen.

"I ain't seen Bill in a couple of hours," the man from the rear post admitted. "I reckon I would have thought something about it sooner, if I hadn't been so near dead on my feet."

"Come on!" Windsor said sharply, repressing the angry words which came to his lips. "Let's beat through the shrubbery and look for him. I'd certainly hate to have my life depending on you fellows. A freight train could slip by you without being seen!"

It was Windsor who found the missing guard. The man was unconscious from a blow on the head, a blow similar to the one Jimmie Bolton had received. His body had been rolled under a small, shadowy fir.

After an examination of the man's wound and pulse, Windsor decided that he was not dangerously injured.

"Pick him up and bring him inside," Collin ordered two of the others. "I'll get Doctor Green on the phone and have him over. He'll certainly have a house full of patients this time."

AN hour later Jimmie Bolton was sitting up with his head bandaged, and feeling groggy, but able to tell, so far as he knew, what had happened to him.

"I'll need some excusing," he said sheepishly. "But please remember, Collin, that I didn't have any sleep last night and darn little today. Ruth was sleeping on her couch and resting easily for which I was glad. I guess Jackson was asleep up in the vestibule. Looks like the thing had kind of got in the air. I suppose I dozed off a little too. I know I came alert suddenly with a jerk. I thought I heard a door open—but I looked up too late. There was a huge, tall, black something in front of me. I just had time to glimpse it, when it dissolved into a blur of movement—and something smashed my head. After that I didn't see anything but stars. The next thing I knew was Ruth and Jackson bending over me, pouring ice-cold water in my face!"

The thing seemed incredible! Apparently McMain had been asleep when Collin Windsor had left for his trek across the village, and, certainly, he was sound asleep now. But it appeared that the old man had awakened in the interim, slugged Jimmie, gone out through the east window, slugged the guard on that side, walked hurriedly over to Simon Winters', tried to murder Winters in his sleep, returned home, entered his room again—and again gone to sleep! Doctor Green, whom Collin had called along with Sheriff Simms, expostulated at the impossibility of the thing.

As for Windsor, he was a little dizzy from loss of sleep. Things were beginning to look fuzzy to him. Doctor Green looked at him shrewdly before he left the McMain place in the early morning. "Man, you're out on your feet," the physician said. "You've got to get some sleep. I'm going to see to that."

Collin protested, but the doctor opened his case and stirred up a powder in a glass of water. "Take this," he ordered, "and get to bed! No back talk, understand?"

Collin slept over six hours. It was nearly ten o'clock when he awoke. Ruth was there with his breakfast on a tray but Collin lay for a long time without moving. His head was clear now and he was thinking with machinelike precision, groping through the maze. And he was beginning to see through the thing, beginning to see a motive for it all. And with this realization he was able to make a very definite plan. It gave him a feeling of power. Collin smiled reassuringly at Ruth and ate his breakfast with relish.

The doctor had ordered that McMain be undisturbed, and now the old man was sleeping soundly in his bed. With Jimmie Bolton, Collin went over the house carefully searching for clues. Especially did he examine the east windows of McMain's room, using a stepladder to climb up from the outside. There were scratches on the window sill and something that vaguely resembled a heelprint on the trellis beside it. Jimmie Bolton seemed to consider these clues valuable, but apparently Collin attached no importance to them. Continuing their search inside the house, they were rewarded by finding, in a musty, obscure closet in one of the bedrooms, a worn old black broadcloth suit with a capelike greatcoat of similar material. The suit was worn and somewhat shiny, but was neatly pressed and showed meticulous care.

"I understand these are the kind of clothes McMain has been addicted to for the past several years," Collin said. "Wonder if this is the only suit of this type he owns."

Ruth, who had joined them on their search, looked the clothing over. "I don't know, Collin," she answered doubtfully. "Of course he has been confined to his bed ever since I've been here. But I'm sure Pompey will know."

"I'll go get him," Jimmie offered. He was gone but a few minutes and returned with the old darkey retainer shuffling behind him.

"Yessuh," Pompey said. "Dat's Mr. Zeke's Sunday suit."

"What we want to know, Pompey, is whether Mr. McMain owns another suit like this."

Pompey nodded his head with emphasis. "Sho did! He had a old suit which he nebber wore none much, on account of it was too shiny. It ortto be hangin' right in de closet where yo' found dis one."

Collin's eyes snapped. He turned to hang the clothes back on their hook in the closet.

"That means," Jimmie Bolton said, "that he's got the other suit hid out somewhere—maybe in his own room—so he can use it when he sneaks out!"

Collin smiled tolerantly. "Smart boy, Jimmie. I'll give you the job of finding it, eh?"

Jimmie grinned ruefully. "I know that tone of voice, Collin. You're only doing that to get rid of me. Oh, well, once the goat always the goat."

THERE was another meeting in the mayor's office that morning. But Simon Winters was not present. He had stated that only fools would remain in Pinehurst to be murdered—and had left on an early morning train.

The sheriff immediately took the bit in his teeth. He confronted Collin Windsor. "Young man," he said, in an accusing voice, "I hold you personally responsible for what happened last night. Inexcusable—even if you did save Winters' life! Yesterday I wanted to arrest McMain, put him behind bars, and you objected. Last night in spite of all our precautions he got past our guard and would have killed another man."

"I'm not convinced, sheriff, that McMain is the murderer," Windsor announced stoutly.

The sheriff's face puffed and turned red with anger. "Convinced! Convinced!" he stormed. "While you're trying to make up your mind—he goes about killing—or near killing—Pinehurst citizens!"

Little Doctor Green pushed forward, fire in his eyes. "Get quiet, Simms!" he expostulated. "Or you'll wake up to find you are making a fool of yourself. Windsor is right. McMain—"

"Doctor!" Windsor called sharply.

The medical man shut his mouth suddenly, looked about him in confusion. He sat down and subsided into vague mutterings.

Windsor cleared his throat, stood up and faced the ring of anxious faces with a degree of defiance. "Gentlemen," he said quietly, "I still stand by what I said yesterday. Consider—if McMain is *not* the murderer—would incarcerating him have saved the attempt on Winters? Now! I'm going to make an extraordinary request, the consequences of which I'm willing to stand the entire responsibility."

He paused. The sheriff made a queer snorting noise but the others were tensely quiet. "I want to ask for complete abolishment of all surveillance and patrolling. I ask the sheriff and his men to withdraw from the chase—just for to-night. I ask especially that there be no guard or watch over Ezekiel McMain. I have a plan to catch the killer and only by complete freedom can I hope for it to succeed."

An uproar of dissent came from the whole meeting.

"What!" cried the sheriff. "Give the killer a free hand? He might murder the whole town!"

The little doctor stepped forward and stood beside Collin Windsor. "You men act like a pack of wolves," he accused. "Listen to Windsor. Have a little confidence in him. . I personally, as Ezekiel McMain's physician, guarantee that no one in Pinehurst will suffer from his hands."

Windsor smiled and sat down as the little doctor talked on. He was something of an orator and those villagers had confidence in him. He finally won them over. A grudging promise was given by the sheriff and Mayor Thompson that neither McMain or any part of Pinehurst would be under surveillance that night.

So when evening came no hollow-eyed and fidgety men patrolled the grounds around McMain's house. No one sat guard over the old man himself. Deputy Jackson was no longer in his arm chair in the vestibule. Indeed, there was no one in the house with Ezekiel McMain, other than Jimmie Bolton and Ruth Kimberley, who sat in tense and restless vigil in the girl's room adjoining the old man's.

As for Collin himself, no one knew where he was except those two. And they had been forbidden to tell.

In the shadow of a ragged fringe of hedge on the east side of the McMain grounds, Windsor crouched close to the ground and stared out into the gloom. A glance at the luminous dial of his wristwatch had just told him it was a quarter to ten. It was bitter cold; fine sleet whipped his face with stinging pinpricks of pain. Windsor had been waiting there since nine o'clock.

Cedars and bushes and other shrubbery loomed black and mysterious in the gray, ghostly night. The dry rustle of the wind, whispering through the trees, and the movement it gave them, lent a sinister suggestion of living, spirit-restless things. Tensely Collin waited.

HALF an hour dragged by. Collin's position was painfully cramped. His mind wandered longingly to the warmth of the gas fire inside the house. He began to wonder if his vigil was to be in vain. Then suddenly he jerked alert. All foreign thoughts fled his mind.

The sash of McMain's east window was slowly, silently raising. Fifty yards from that window, secure in his hiding place, Windsor stared up.

There was the vaguest suggestion of a figure in the window, though Windsor's eye could detect no substance to it. Presently a leg came over the sill, an oddly long leg. Then a tall black figure was balanced there, one arm reaching out, groping for the trellis work. Then the entire grotesque form was outlined against the gray-white of the house, as it swung to the trellis and began its descent.

From sheer excitement Collin held his breath until his lungs ached. Silently as a cat, almost ghostlike, the black shape in the wind-whipped, flapping garments came to the ground. It stood there for a fraction of a minute poised like a huge, ugly, sinister bird, peering—peering about. No white oval showed where the face should have been. Covered by a black mask, Collin guessed.

Then the black thing moved. It strode away toward the east in fast, hopping strides, darting from shadow to shadow across the grounds. Abruptly it turned then, and made for the street.

Collin forgot his aching muscles. Silently as his quarry he shifted, stood to his feet. Inside his overcoat pocket his gloved hand gripped his automatic, finger over the trigger. This time he would be tuned to shoot surer, quicker, more deadly than before. And not once did he let his eyes leave the swift-moving figure now at the sidewalk.

Fleet, in spite of its awkward stride, the figure in black was walking eastward. Collin took up the trail warily, keeping as close as he dared without risking discovery. It was important for Collin to know the figure's intended destination. On that hinged everything.

The street was dark, ghostly, deserted—

looking. No light broke the gloom in any direction. Not even starlight, for the sky was now leaden. Collin trod as silently as possible. The form ahead veritably seemed to walk on wings.

The black figure stopped suddenly, whirled about. But Collin had been alert, warned by some sixth sense. He pressed himself in the shadow of a bush that bordered the walk. The man moved on.

"He's making for Victor Burgess'," Collin decided.

They had come several blocks. A tall scraggly line of hedge fringed the sidewalk and Collin had kept himself in the edge of its shadow as he walked. But now he decided on action—a quick forward rush, a gun in the man's ribs and sudden surprising capture.

Then abruptly, startlingly, the black figure ahead stopped, whirled as if glancing back, then darted into the hedge. One moment he had been there where Collin could see him—the next moment he was gone!

For an instant Collin was possessed with sheer frenzy. He must not let this man get away! Murder was on his own hands if he did! He leaped out in the clear and ran rapidly toward the spot where his quarry had disappeared. He broke through the hedge and glared about him. The figure was nowhere to be seen. Collin swore and turned about. A sound came to him, a quick sibilant rustling sound. He spun on his heel—too late. That tall black form was over him, one long arm swinging in a wide arc. Collin dodged, threw up his arm to shield the blow.

But the blow had too much momentum. It crashed down on his head with appalling force.

Collin staggered back, vainly trying to bring his gun up. But he had no control over his limbs. His muscles had gone limp. The hedge and the sleety ground

spun around him. The dark world seemed to tilt high on one end. It settled back and then went black.

Collin Windsor sank groggily to the ground.

CHAPTER SIX

Death in the Dark

COLLIN fought desperately against unconsciousness. Some cell in the back of his brain kept vividly alive, told him over and over that if he surrendered to insensibility the Pinehurst killer would stalk unhindered in the village. Certainly one murder—maybe more—would be laid at his feet because of his utter failure. He was struggling in a half-world of confusion, thoughts muddled, vision blurred.

Then he realized someone was with him, tugging at his shoulders. Was it the killer, back to finish him? Blindly, viciously, Windsor struck out.

"Collin! Collin!" It was Ruth, calling to him, pleading with him. Slowly the dizziness receded. "I couldn't help but watch—and see you when you left," she was saying through chattering teeth. "I slipped away from Jimmie and followed you."

"Ruth! The siren—has it blown?"

"No. You've been out only a minute or two."

"Thank the Lord!" Collin gave a sigh of vast relief. His brain cleared. "Then it still isn't too late! Ruth, wake up the people in this house. Have them phone Simms to send officers to protect Burgess and Thompson! Quick—a carload of men to each place! The killer is free—roaming Pinehurst!"

"All right," Ruth said shortly. "But then you're going back to McMain's and see the doctor. You've got a bad head wound."

Collin grunted, struggled to his feet,

stood there swaying. Dimly he saw Ruth running toward the house, heard her awakening the inmates, saw lights come on, heard excited voices. Then nausea swept over him again and he staggered, almost fell.

After that Ruth was walking him along the street, supporting him. She was talking to him but he hardly knew what she was saying. Block after block along the gloomy way.

And then suddenly Collin was possessed of his full senses, jarred alert by what he saw. They were passing Mayor Arthur Thompson's home, were at the corner of his grounds, when a tall ungainly figure darted from a bush in the yard up to a small side porch.

Collin's fingers gripped the girl's arm, bit into her flesh. "Look, Ruth!" he said hoarsely. "The killer's going in Thompson's now!"

The girl muffled a little scream. "The officers will be too late! "We must warn Mr. Thompson."

"No! We mustn't scare away the killer—he'd escape again. I'm going in after him," Collin said.

Ruth caught at him, held him back. "No, no, Collin!"

But he gently freed himself. "You go straight to McMain's and wait with Jimmie, understand me?" he said, then turned and sprinted toward the side entrance. Ruth stood rooted, eyes wide with horror. Her throat felt as if a tight band were about it. Collin—going in there to face a madman, a murderer!

Windsor did not look back. He moved swiftly, silently, and disappeared in the darkness of the side porch.

Ruth waited, eyes riveted on the spot where she had seen Collin last. Her breath came in little gasps. As the seconds passed they seemed like hours, like eternities.

Then she moved, ran swiftly toward the porch. Inside the pocket of her pony coat her fingers were gripping the butt of the little gun Collin had given her in Dalshire. The side door was unlocked. It swung inward at her slight push, with the tiniest of squeaks. And she was enveloped in the pitch-black void of the silent house. She stood just inside for a moment, listening. Then she moved ahead, forcing herself into that unknown, forbidding gulf of blackness.

Gradually her eyes began to discern substance. Outlines, vague and bulky, loomed out of the darkness. Chairs, tables, doorways—doorways leading further into horror and lurking danger!

Her little gun was in her hand now, as she moved slowly forward. Once she had a scare that made her heart stand still, then pound like a hammer. She had walked toward a mirror and her own grim, set, white face came staring at her out of the inky gloom. She almost screamed out for Collin, but caught her breath, and moved on.

Now she was in the hallway. It seemed empty except for the furniture and the things with which her imagination peopled it. Then she groped ahead, wondering. Where was Collin? Where was the sinister black figure?

Now she was in a wide room, a sort of sitting room, she guessed. Her repressed breathing, to her, sounded loud, almost thunderous. She stood there, torn between flight and advance, awful fear holding her tense. For suddenly she knew there was someone else in that room! She felt his presence there, across that narrow space of blackness. She raised her gun, ready. Was it the killer —the man in black? Or was it Collin?

SOMETHING stirred, half heard, unseen, somewhere beyond Ruth's vision. She moved farther into the room. She dared not turn on the light—that would alarm the murderer, wherever he was in the house. But she had to know who was in the room. Her left hand, clenched and icy-cold in her coat pocket, found a match.

Hardly realizing what she did, Ruth drew the match out. Her gun held ready, she reached out, struck the match against the back of a chair.

Weird, jerky shadows danced in the wavering light. Familiar things momentarily took on twisting, grotesque shapes. There was a venomous curse and then Ruth saw the thing at the opposite doorway.

The tall, awkward, black-garbed figure! He had been listening against the closed door—listening for Collin, surely —and now he whirled, glared balefully at Ruth, who held the match with shaking fingers.

But most of all, Ruth saw that he was unmasked. His face was revealed to her in the ghastly light. And she knew him!

The match went out and Ruth fired just as the figure leaped aside. The darkness was utter, abysmal. Again and again Ruth fired wildly. She was backing away, groping behind her for the doorway. Her back brought up against the wall.

She knew he was creeping toward her, that he meant to kill her. She had seen his face, she would betray him. She must die!

Hysteria overwhelmed her. She screamed, she called out to Collin. She blazed away before her with the automatic until it clicked empty. Still the thing was closing in on her. Soon she would be smothered in black garments. Strong fingers would entwine her throat.

She cried out once more, just as horrible arms grasped her. She turned faint, but above the drumming and ringing in her ears she heard Collin pounding on the door at which the killer had been listening. Then suddenly the arms relaxed, left her. And she heard the man

padding swiftly across to that door.

Now Collin was in danger! Immediately Ruth's reason and courage returned. Her hand groped for the light switch, found it. She flooded the room with light.

Across from her, the door was splintering under the blows Collin was giving it with some heavy object. Pressed against the wall, poised, waiting for the door to fly open was the figure in black. A fiendish grin was on his face, which was stained now with a trickle of blood from one of Ruth's shots. His arm was uplifted, hand gripping a gleaming *machete* —a relic from the wall of the room— ready to cleave Collin's brain with one blow!

"Not that door, Collin! Don't come through! He'll kill you!" Ruth's voice sounded strange, shrill—foreign to her.

She saw the man come toward her. She leaped aside, snapping out the light. Then heard the man brush by, through the door. There were rapid footsteps, first in the hall, then ascending a stairway.

Collin had not heeded her warning. The door crashed open and in a moment he was with her.

"I was locked in the room!" he panted.

"He's gone up the stairs," Ruth whispered.

"Good!" Collin exclaimed. "There's only one stairway to the upper floor— you see, I've been all over the house following him, until he locked me in. If he's upstairs we've got him!"

Collin, gun out, moved to the foot of the stairs. For a long moment there was nothing but silence. Then, unnerving, from out in the night, came the scream of the siren! The awful sound of it almost froze Ruth's blood.

"Grandstand stuff!" Collin muttered. "Trying to break our nerve. All right—"

There was a movement at the head of

the stairs. In the gloom Collin was shifting, catlike, from side to side of the stairway. Then suddenly from the upper darkness flame leaped in vicious spurts and the roar of shots reverberated in the dark hall. The killer was coming down through the gloom, gun blazing before him!

Collin's own automatic was speaking its piece—lancing out jabbing fingers of flame. There was a screech and the black thing flopped, lay sprawled there at the foot of the stairway.

There were shouts and poundings at the front and back doors. The questioning voices of men. Ruth was fumbling for the light switch. Then the place was illuminated.

The hallway was crowded with men. Sheriff Simms, Doctor Green, Deputy Jackson and half a dozen others. They stared down at the spread-eagled figure on the floor, then at Collin's drawn, haggard face and at his smoking gun.

The fallen man was face down. The crowd could not see who it was.

The sheriff stepped forward. "It's—is it McMain?"

"No," Collin said. "I knew it couldn't have been McMain—tonight or last night. For with Doctor Green's aid and permission, I've had McMain kept under a powerful sleeping drug both nights—merely as an added precautionary measure in case I had guessed wrong."

Collin stepped forward and turned the body over so that the light fell on the blood-streaked face.

The man was Mayor Arthur Thompson!

High on the night air the siren was still wailing. The murderer had gone out to the tune of his own death music.

THEY finally found the switch controling the siren, in the closet of an upstairs back room. Everybody breathed easier when the thing was silenced. Doctor Green examined the body and pronounced Thompson dead. Collin raised the cuff of the dead man's trousers and showed the stilt-like contraptions Thompson had built into his shoes to give him a height equal to Ezekiel McMain's. It had been these which had caused Thompson's queer, hopping gait, which was not unlike McMain's.

"You see," Collin explained later, when the doctor was dressing his head wound, "Thompson wanted his every move to look like McMain's. This was done to deceive not only the law but also his intended victims."

"But why?" the sheriff demanded. "What motive did Thompson have?"

"The bank loot," Collin announced. "Charley McMain was not short and he didn't commit suicide. The directors looted their own bank, murdered McMain and planted that suicide note. I suspected the plant almost at once, because the confession was left in the typewriter unsigned. They would not risk a forgery."

The doctor gasped. "Then Wilson and Junius and Burgess and Winters were all in on it?"

Collin nodded. "At first it was a conspiracy. The stolen three hundred thousand is hidden somewhere. The thing to do now is arrest Victor Burgess—or Simon Winters if he can be caught—and force the secret from him."

Eager voices were questioning Windsor, begging for more explanations. "My guess from the first was that McMain was not guilty," Collin continued. "No man, even a madman, would plaster himself with guilt by spilling his clues around like those that were found. But tonight and last night, for absolute safety, in case I was wrong, I persuaded Doctor Green to give McMain a powerful soporific. I can assure you McMain did not move from his bed either night.

"You can see how Thompson conceived the plot and worked it out," Collin said. "By killing off his co-conspirators he not only destroyed those with guilty knowledge, but retained all the loot for himself. God, what a plan! Don't you see the cumulative value of each murder? First five to split with— then four—then three—then two—"

Collin shuddered. "The sirens and the 'curse' warnings were probably suggested by the mood the village was in. Of course that first siren—the night Charley McMain was killed—was accidental, set off by the wind or ice on the wires. But it gave Thompson his idea.

"No doubt Thompson's original plan was to lock McMain in each night while he prowled to make his kill. He'd lock both doors of the sick-room and crawl out of the window garbed in a stolen suit of McMain's."

"But what about the night Junius was killed—the night I was chloroformed?" Ruth asked. "McMain *was* gone from his room that night."

"Old McMain is shrewd. He only pretended sleep when Thompson came to lock his doors. He saw Thompson chloroform you, then followed him. No doubt McMain found out what Thompson was about. But he kept his mouth shut. As long as Thompson was killing bank directors—whom McMain hated—well and good.

"Tonight I think Thompson started out to kill Burgess. But when he found he was followed he lost his nerve and turned back. He was coming home to cast off his disguise, call it off, when Ruth and I saw him enter and followed."

Victor Burgess, arrested, broke down and confessed to the directors' looting of the Pinehurst bank. Later Winters was arrested to face charges with him. Burgess told where the loot was cached, in an old deserted house in Pinehurst, and every dollar was recovered.

The search for the hidden siren earned its reward early in the morning. Cleverly concealed wires were traced from Thompson's house to where the siren was located, hidden in the hollow of the chimney on the roof of the mayor's office.

Ezekiel McMain was much improved that morning and Doctor Green released Ruth to return to Dalshire with Collin and Jimmie Bolton.

"It looks," Jimmie said happily, as they all three piled in the roadster to head for Dalshire, "like the Pinehurst curse is over. I'll sure have to hand it to the village. It was certainly a right smart curse for a small town!"

Brown bent low and swung.

Murder at Midnight

A Vee Brown Story

by

Carroll John Daly

Author of "The Death Master," etc.

"One hundred thousand dollars to the man who gets Vee Brown!" That was Mandozza's offer for the kill. And now, all through the danger ways of the underworld, the murder masters set their traps—set them to stop the grinding wheels of the Crime Machine.

CHAPTER ONE

"He Dies Tonight!"

VEE BROWN finished his lunch and smoked innumerable cigarettes, snuffing them out in his coffee cup and staring vacantly over my shoulder. For the life of me I couldn't tell if he were contemplating running down some criminal or planning the words or music to another of his numerous sentimental song hits. For Vee Brown, as well as being a first-grade detective assigned at present to the district attorney's office, was also the unknown Vivian, composer of music and lyrics for Tin Pan Alley's biggest song hits.

I never knew, nor could even guess, what his income was as a song writer. But it must have been enormous, for he had a penthouse atop one of Park Avenue's most pretentious apartments, a fifteen thousand dollar car with a liveried chauffeur, and a bank account that seemed limitless. And I did know that in the apprehending of criminals he spent many times, for information alone, the amount of his yearly salary from the city.

Now he sat facing me, drumming on the table top with slender, tapering fingers. Fingers that strummed the notes that made him Vivian—Master of Melody; fingers that moved a gun so quickly and pressed a trigger so accurately that he was known as Vee Brown—Killer of Men.

He must have caught interrogation in my glance for his clear black eyes sparkled and he gave me that twisted, whimsical smile.

"I'm thinking of Mandozza," he said. The fingers of his hands closed slowly until they bit into his palms. "And I think I'm going to get him."

"Mandozza!" I started. For it was Mandozza who had laid plans to trap me through a girl, Una Coles; trap me so as to get Vee Brown—get him for Ernie Slawson to kill.

"Mandozza," Vee Brown repeated. "But never mind, Dean. The thing's over and forgotten. Slawson is dead. You still think the girl tried to save my life. I still think she tried to take it."

"But, Vee, she didn't try to knock your gun up. She jumped between you and Slawson in the hope that—"

"Nonsense, Dean! After all, it's only one man's opinion. How drab life would be if everyone thought the same!" Then suddenly, "You haven't seen her since?"

"No," I said, "I haven't."

"Nor thought of her?"

"Yes—" slightly defiantly, "I have thought of her."

"You would. And you'll see her soon, Dean. I'm sure of that." And when I would have questioned him, "Don't look now, but the third table from the door—the man with his back against the wall. Mandozza's right-hand man in New York. His name is Curry—Frankie Curry. He rather fancies himself with a gun, I understand. He's been following me for three days."

"Why?" I asked, but I did not turn.

"He has orders from Mandozza to kill me. Oh, I'm not trying to belittle the man. He's ambitious, willing; has even taken a couple of shots at me. I will say that it was not to his discredit that he missed. It was under the most unadvantageous conditions. So we'll put him down as a good gunman who misjudged the opportunity."

"Good God, Brown!" I sputtered. "It's as bad as that?"

"Just as bad as that. Mandozza chooses his men well, but he lacks patience. That, Dean, is the undoing of his hired assassins. They get nervous and try to create the opportunity instead of waiting until the opportunity presents itself."

"But, Vee, you don't think that here—that he might try it in the restaurant and hope to get away in the confusion, counting on Mandozza to—"

Vee Brown cut in with a wave of his hand. "Frankie Curry is not exactly an idiot. His chance of getting away in the confusion would be good. It's not that which stays his hand. You see, I'm facing him, Dean; and I hope I can say without conceit that he would be dead before he could draw his gun halfway out of its holster. He's bright, ambitious and eager. But his orders are to be sure. And the only way he can be sure, Dean, is to shoot me in the back."

"Vee, can't you have him taken in—make some charge against him? Concealed weapons, the two attempts on your life."

Vee shook his head at me and smiled. "I couldn't clutter up the city prisons with all the gunmen who would like to take my life. No. Mr. Frankie Curry is a menace to society," his lips set grimly in a single straight line, "and as such should be removed." Then suddenly, "We won't discuss him further. I am on the verge of the greatest scoop of my life, of my career as a detective. Mandozza, the biggest racketeer the city ever produced! Other public enemies sink in insignificance in the enormity of his activities."

"But it's impossible to convict him. He has big official friends. Hires the smartest lawyers, and pays thousands for protection to—"

"And that is just it." Vee Brown's black eyes shone as he leaned across the table. "He hired one lawyer who was just a bit too smart. He's got letters, papers, proofs. I can't get Mandozza for murder this time, but he's done an 'Al Capone.' It's his income, Dean. Federal government. I can hand him a jolt for at least seven years."

"And the lawyer? How did you work it?"

"The district attorney, the police, the federal government! They all centered their attack on Mandozza, and failed. I didn't. I was tipped off, and paid well for my tip. I centered my attack on this lawyer. Nothing to do with Mandozza, you understand. I caught this mouthpiece on an entirely personal matter. And when I had the evidence—when I was sure—I went straight to him and presented my case. Then I gave him his chance. 'Deliver me Mandozza,' I said, 'and the evidence against you goes in the fire.' The lawyer's offense was jury fixing, Dean, and I had him right. 'It's Mandozza or

you,' I told him." Brown shrugged his shoulders. "The answer was Mandozza, of course. I'll have the evidence in a couple of days." He came to his feet. "I'll be on my way. It's Mandozza's birthday, you know, and in fairness I should give Mr. Frankie Curry a chance to make good."

"But wait, Vee; I'm coming along with you."

"No—" he said. "You sit here for a bit, and tell me if you get a message from the girl."

I didn't fully get that, yet I knew he wouldn't explain. But I did grab him by the arm and ask: "Just what did you mean when you said I'd—I'd see her again soon?"

"Nothing." Brown shrugged his shoulders. "Nothing at all. But Frankie Curry was talking to a lady when he came in. Good-by for a bit, Dean." And as he passed down between the tables he called back to me: "I'll be back at the apartment at six."

I ordered another cup of coffee, then I turned slowly, indifferently. I wanted to get a look at Frankie Curry. But the third table from the door against the wall was vacant. The gunman had evidently followed Vee Brown from the restaurant. My eyes knitted slightly. Why didn't Vee let me go with him? At least, trail behind Curry? I was armed; I could use a gun. Why had he wanted me to stay there in the restaurant? And the answer to that question came almost the very moment I asked it.

THE waiter brought my coffee, held it in his hand as he leaned over and spoke to me in a low voice. "The lady in the rear booth would like you to have your coffee with her, sir," he said.

And I was on my feet. Maybe I paled slightly; maybe the hand I laid upon the white cloth trembled a bit. But I was not confused, not uncertain. I knew just as well as if the waiter had spoken the name, who the lady was.

I followed the waiter down the room, watched him place the coffee upon the long table partly hidden by the high-backed seats, saw him move the sugar and cream carefully and methodically. Then I was in the booth, sliding along the seat, pushing myself far into the opposite corner across from the table—across from Una Coles.

She didn't hold out her hand in greeting; she didn't smile even. She just eyed me coldly with those deep black eyes. As she turned her head and looked out into the dining room I caught the fineness of that profile. Sharp—very sharp—it seemed now. Her thin lips were set tightly. There was nothing of the softness, the goodness that I thought I had seen behind the fear in her eyes. The fear was still there, but there was a hard cold determination that downed it. She was still beautiful; there could be no two opinions about that. But her beauty was different. It was a cold, hard—maybe even a sinister beauty. She was being swept up in the life that she lived. She had fought against it before, I thought—now was fast becoming a part of it. I shuddered slightly. Maybe Brown was right. She was a girl of—I toned my thought down somewhat, a girl of the half world.

She was the first to speak, and her voice was hard; forced, it seemed to me. But then, maybe I wanted it to seem that way. "You hate me, don't you?" she said.

"No, Una—I don't."

Her eyes knitted; the black lines below them became suddenly very pronounced. "Do you still want to marry me?" she asked.

I didn't smile. I couldn't. This girl—this woman—had taken something out of my life. "No, Una—I don't," I admitted.

"I'm glad of that." She nodded vigor-

ously. "It wouldn't have been very flattering to have had such a proposal from a fool." And looking straight across at me, "Vee Brown! Am I free to walk the streets, or will he arrest me on sight?"

"I don't think he'll arrest you," I said. "You see—well—after all, he's my friend. The truth of that story—of my stupidity and gullibility—has never been told. He kept your name out of the Slawson kill."

"For me?" Her eyebrows went up.

"No—for me." And suddenly, "Una, you did save his life that night? You did jump in front of him to save him from Slawson?"

"What do you think?" she asked.

"I want to think you saved him," was the best answer I could give her.

"You can think that." And for the first time she put emphasis into her words, life into her voice. "But if I did it for Vee Brown or for you or for myself I don't know. You see—maybe I jumped between Brown and Slawson because I wanted to die. I did want to die—"

For a moment I thought she was going to cry. At least, her eyes grew misty and she dashed the back of her hand across them with an angry, digging motion.

"Do you still want to die?" I don't know why I asked it, but the words came out.

"No—no." She leaned on the table now and those black eyes flashed with a dangerous light. For a moment the sinister aspect was gone from her; the girl of the half world was missing. I was looking at—well—at class again. Fineness—breeding. I don't know the exact name for it. And she was talking rapidly.

"I want to live so you will know, so Vee Brown will know. I want to face both of you, but most of all I want to face myself—and know that I'm not yellow, that I've got the blood, got the character—yes, got the guts to pull out. That's all." She was on her feet. "I'm going to pull out if I have to resort to—to murder."

And here was a different Una. Not the frightened and horrified girl whom I had wanted to save from Slawson—from Mandozza—from some unknown thing that they held over her head. She was sliding along the seat of the booth, leaving me. I stretched out a hand and grasped her wrist.

"Una," I said, "tell me what it is, what has changed you so. And—this talk of murder!" Vee Brown was right, but I wouldn't admit it even to myself then. I loved her. I must have loved her.

"What has changed me?" She jerked her arm free and turned on me. "What has made me talk of murder? You— you, with your talk of marriage to a girl like—like you must have thought me." She paused a moment, her lips set tightly. "Vee Brown kills. They haven't got a chance when they draw on him. It's as if he stood them up against a stone wall and shot them through the back."

"That's not true." I was on my feet now too, defending my friend. We were talking in a hoarse whisper. "He never kills like that. He kills only—"

She cut in viciously on me. "Well—he kills, and his picture goes on the front pages; his name goes into the editorial columns. They want more like him. Well —they'll get one more. I only want to kill once; kill the man who's arranged for the death of many. I don't want to be lauded in the papers. I want to kill just one man and find my way back to respectability."

"Una, you can't do this. You mustn't talk like this."

"No? And why not? Is it better that I stay the slave of a murderer, and through my actions—actions that I kid myself I don't understand—kill others, cause them to kill themselves, drive them to insanity—watch homes broken? Isn't

it better that I kill once—strike once— and be done with the brutal, inhuman man who controls me?"

"You mean," I barely whispered the words, "Mandozza?"

"I mean," she said, just as low—but her voice was hard, "Mandozza."

She stood at the end of the table now. A few were watching us—speculatively but not suspiciously. I fell back in the seat and tried to look at ease. But my voice shook when I spoke to her. "You didn't ask me here to tell me this, Una."

"No," she said, "I didn't. But I don't wish to recall the words. I only hope you won't repeat them. I asked you here to warn you. Mandozza knows more than you think, more than Vee Brown thinks or could even suspect. He knows about Quinley, and—and—well—I wanted to tell you that Vee Brown is to die tonight. Those are Mandozza's orders. Frankie Curry has been following him for days."

"Vee Brown knows that," I said, and then wished that I hadn't. After all, was the girl simply sent to feel me out, to find out if Vee Brown suspected? Was the line she had been giving me all rehearsed? But I looked at that flushed face. Every word that she had told me was the truth. Or she was the world's greatest actress. No. It was impossible not to believe her but it would be foolhardy to trust her. Yes, I wished I hadn't spoken out. I watched her face for the telltale light that would let me know that she had learned what she had been sent to learn. But it wasn't there. Then she spoke.

"Of course Vee Brown knows. He is no fool. But what he doesn't know— and you don't know—is that Mandozza is to strike at him today—must strike at him today. There's your warning."

And she was gone; gone while I sat there gaping and without the chance to ask a single question.

CHAPTER TWO

The Man With the Gun

MY COFFEE grew cold. I ordered another cup; sat over it until it was also cold. Then, getting my check and taking the perplexed look off the waiter's face with the size of my tip, I left the restaurant. Vee Brown knew that Mandozza was out to get him. Vee Brown knew that Frankie Curry was sent to kill him.

But Una had said that Mandozza was to strike at him that day. She hadn't mentioned Curry. If only I was with Brown! I was on my guard and armed. I tapped the Colt automatic I carried in my hip pocket. I never could learn to carry a gun under my arm, as Brown did—under both his arms for that matter.

I crossed over to Broadway and went to a movie. And the picture did not help my already shattered nerves. Gangsters; racketeers; gunmen. Gunmen with hearts of gold beating beneath steel vests. The people liked it. I didn't! It was unreal. I had been associated with Brown for some months now and had met many gangsters, but had found no hearts of gold. In fact, no hearts of any kind.

Then other thoughts — disturbing thoughts. Jack Ferris, editor of The Globe, for which I had done many features about Brown, had warned me of a rival in the field. The Sun-Standard was hot on the trail of Brown. They had discovered he lived on Park Avenue; saw the high-priced car, and doubted politely that all this was paid for with my money. The lease was in my name; the car licensed under my name. They were checking up on it now. But Brown wasn't worried. Before the panic I was a rich man—known as a rich man. No one could tell to what my resources had fallen— that is, no one but myself.

It was about a quarter to six when I reached our apartment house. I was growing cautious—or just nervous. I looked up and down the street. Many people passed. Each one my jumpy nerves suspected; each one no doubt was a respected citizen.

The door was held open; the doorman smiled at me. I passed between the potted plants, turned toward the elevators; the ones nearest the door, that had an operator. The corridor was empty; the elevators all above; one descending. The dial showed it to be passing the twelfth floor.

I had turned to pass down to the automatic lifts, hesitated, and finally decided to wait for the operated car to descend. It would be only a minute or two—probably less.

There were footsteps across the marble floor; a tall, broad-shouldered man came out of one of the little writing rooms. He had a letter in his hand and did not look at me as he approached, going toward the mail chute by the main entrance.

He reached me, stopped suddenly, and something hard and round jabbed against my side.

"It's a gun, buddy." The man smiled. At least, his lips parted and he showed his teeth. "Walk down the corridor. The cars you run yourself will suit me. Come on—move! Or I'll put a hole in you."

I had often wondered what I would do in such a situation. And now I knew. I obeyed. Mechanically I walked down to the row of self-operating lifts. One of the automatic elevators was just reaching the ground floor. A man and a woman in evening dress stepped out. The gun in my side slipped easily into the man's jacket pocket; then it was against my side again, boring hard.

They were an elderly couple. The man wished me "Good evening." The woman smiled. A voice answered them; it said

"Good evening." It sounded clear and calm. It was my voice.

The man beside me spoke as we entered the car. "There's no cause to be alarmed, buddy. I'm a private dick and I'm working for The Sun-Standard. We know Brown doesn't get his money honest. We know you don't pay this rent. I'm going to find evidence up in that apartment—that penthouse of his."

I got my voice back, and some of my dignity. I said: "You'll find no such evidence there. You haven't any warrant to search the apartment. You're going to get into a hell of a lot of trouble for pulling this kind of stuff."

The man closed the door with his left hand, pulled over the iron grating, pressed a button—and said: "We always get in trouble. But Brown's covering up crooked joints, protecting a certain fence. He got his pay-off today. We're going to get him."

And I laughed. He wouldn't find anything in the apartment that would give Vee Brown's source of income away. I could claim that the music room was mine, that music was my hobby. There was nothing to connect Brown up with the writing of songs. The man was a fool. I told him so.

"Maybe," he agreed with me as the car shot up. "But I'm paid to be a fool. It's a little irregular—illegal, maybe. But Vee Brown will understand. He's not above a little thing like 'illegal entry' himself. Besides, if I can get something on him— There, there—stick in the corner; this cannon might go off."

For the first time I got a good look at the gun in his hand. And it was a cannon. A 45 Colt automatic. I could see beneath the man's coat too. There was a badge. The man himself was a brute of a fellow. His features were flat; the nose particularly giving the impression of flatness. There seemed to be no bone in it, and it looked as if a horse might at some time have kicked it, spreading it over his face. His eyes were blue, a watery, foggy sort of blue, but with sharpness in the center of them when he looked at me. Hard, steady, appraising, cruel, yet with a sort of intelligence. His mouth—well—maybe I didn't notice it particularly, but it was twisted slightly at the right corner.

We reached the top floor, passed to the end of the corridor and paused before the entrance to the penthouse.

"Well—" the man shoved a gun against my back, "stick a key in the hole and open the door. I know it's tricky and made special, else I wouldn't of bothered to bring you up with me."

"You'll regret this—" I started, and stopped. The gun dug into my back, driving me against the door.

"Listen, brother. I don't fancy this job any more than you do. But if you say the word I'll knock you on the head and use the key myself. Why not play ball?"

This man wouldn't shoot, wouldn't dare to shoot. It was one thing to search an apartment with his crooked agency behind him. But another thing to—

And I staggered slightly. The man raised his gun and brought it down on my head. Not hard enough to knock me out, but hard enough to give me a few very unpleasant moments while I searched frantically for my key and shoved it into the lock. Any minute I expected the gun to crash down again, and this time with the full force of that big muscular right arm behind it.

WHY play the fool and get myself a broken head in the bargain? Brown had told me something about these so-called private detectives. No harm could come of his searching the apartment. Vee Brown would be along in a few minutes and would laugh at the whole thing. I felt a hand under my arm, down my jacket. My gun was jerked from my hip pocket.

And the door was open—we were inside. I was holding my head. The man had shut the door behind us. We were alone in the apartment, for I remembered that it was Wong's day off. Wong was our only servant.

"Keep going, brother," the man said as he pushed me along the hall, through the foyer and into the huge living room.

"Remember. You'll pay well for this, and—" I started.

"Close your pan!" He pushed me into a chair. "Now I'll tell you the real reason for my visit. Vee Brown was paid off today, paid well. And the lad who drew the money out of the bank and paid him doesn't know that the numbers of the bills were kept. I've got a list of them. I don't know how deep you're into it, but if you want things to go easy with you, don't act up. Just sit there in that chair." He looked at the heavy curtains before the open door to the music room and nodded in satisfaction. "Here's the ticket. Brown's mighty quick with a gun and will be wanting to use it if he knows I'm onto his racket. Now listen, buddy, and maybe save yourself a bellyful of lead. He'll be along soon, because I got a guy to make a date to phone him here at six."

"You're crazy," I told him. "Vee Brown has no connection with criminals or crooks. I pay for the apartment. He lives here with me. You can find the lease in my bank; the landlord has one, and my lawyer—"

"Enough. Enough!" He shoved his left palm against my face. "Now get a load of this. I know as well as you know that Brown is poison with a rod. I don't intend to get shot and I don't intend to shoot anyone unless I have to. You're to sit in that chair. I'll go behind the curtain. When Brown comes in he'll face you, or should. That'll put his back to me.

That's all I want; just his back to me. If you stay quiet and don't give the show away I'll stick him up from behind and search him for his crooked money. If, as you say, he ain't got it—O. K. I'll fade and take my chances on the squawk he'll make later. If he has got it, then he can talk turkey to The Sun-Standard. But I know Brown, and I ain't aiming to pass out. So be careful and don't tip my hand, or I'll shoot him down from behind the curtain.

"Remember!" he warned me again after he had examined the curtains a bit. "It's almost six o'clock now. I'm going behind that curtain. I'll be covering you and I'll be covering Brown from the very moment he enters this room. And, so help me God, if you warn him in any way, peep in any way, I'll shoot him through the back."

"You're a fool—" I started, but he stopped me.

"Fools are dangerous when they're armed. If you've got nothing to fear by my frisking Brown, then don't take a chance on getting killed. And if you have something to fear—why—figure out if it's worth death."

THERE were footsteps in the hall—across the marble floor. I heard them distinctly, heard the soft whistle too, knew it to be a new tune that Brown must have running through his head.

The man was gone, slipping behind the curtains, parting them slightly. For a moment I saw the snub nose of the automatic. Then that too was gone. Just the slightest, maybe imaginary bulge against the drapes. But I did know there was a slight crack in the curtains and that watery blue eyes were looking into that room.

What should I do? One sensible thing, of course. Let the man cover Vee, search him and go on his way. Then—well—it wouldn't make a bad feature for The

Globe. Jack Ferris would get quite a kick out of it. But would Brown—would he fancy being held up in his own apartment this way? The detective was a fool. Maybe I would even have to save his life. At the first command to stand still, Brown might turn and fire. To stick up Vee Brown! It might be done, of course, if the man with the gun was behind him. But—

The key clicked in the lock, the door opened and closed—and Brown was coming down the hall.

"I've got a tune, Dean," he called as he crossed the foyer. "A tune that might suit you—or a friend of yours. Listen to the title. I say—you're there, aren't you?"

"Yes," I said, "I'm here." And Vee Brown strode into the room, his back already to the curtains. He was coming toward me, walking swiftly—his black, keen eyes flashing about the room, taking in every part of it, every detail but the curtains he had passed—the curtains that hung before the open door to the music room.

And I saw the gun. It was coming slowly from behind those curtains, raising slightly, drawing a bead on Brown's head —the back of his head. Then I saw the eyes behind that gun, the blue, watery eyes —water that seemed to have frozen now and turned to ice. I read it in those eyes just as if it were in print. The thing that Brown said you could read in a man's eyes. The lust to kill. And I knew the truth. The man was going to kill Vee. The man was—

And Brown suddenly bent low and swung. I didn't see him move his right hand but he must have, for there was a gun in it, a smoking gun. It seemed as if there was only one roar, but it was too loud for a single shot. It was two shots— two shots that came as one. For plainly I heard the picture above my head crash to the floor behind the chair.

I sat straight and stiff with horror. There was a dead silence. Then two hands stretched up from behind that curtain; fingers grasped the thick drapes and a face appeared.

I saw the blue eyes. And they were frozen still. Dead eyes! And the man stood there, his fingers twisted in the curtains; stood there on his feet, his knees sagging and lifeless. He was dead. I knew that. I felt that. Good God! I saw that. Then the curtains ripped from their rings, and the dead man crashed straight forward, out upon the living-room rug.

"Brown! Vee!" I cried. "You killed him."

"I did." Vee Brown stood there looking down at the silent thing on the floor, the curtains draped about it. "Yes—I did, Dean. And if I do say it myself, it was damn pretty shooting."

I WAS on my feet, talking in a confused way, telling Brown that the man had said he was a detective from some private agency; paid by The Sun-Standard, and simply wanted to search him for "incriminating evidence." I didn't think Brown was listening, for he was pushing the curtain beneath the man's head and talking.

"The curtains are expensive, of course," he was saying, "but the rug! It set me back close to twenty-five hundred dollars. There—" he straightened, "the curtains saved it. Not a spot upon it, not a trace of blood. Now then, Dean—this story about his being a detective!"

And I told him all that the man had said quickly—fearfully. I finished.

And Brown smiled. He went to the wall cabinet, opened it and poured me out a stiff drink, but took none himself. "It was true that he wanted to search me. He thought perhaps I'd have that evidence about Mandozza on me. Somehow Mandozza must have found out, to act so quickly—and almost successfully. He took you in with that story of being a private dick."

"That wasn't true then!" I gasped.

"Of course not. The man intended to shoot me in the back the moment I faced you. You see how it was. He lost his nerve when I swung, though he fired first. Lost his nerve completely when my gun flashed. Just ten feet between us. And though I crouched, I might have remained standing and he'd have missed me by a good foot." Brown jerked a thumb toward the spot where the picture had hung —well above my head.

"But why did he bother to tell me that he was a detective? He had a gun on me. I would have had to come here anyway. He would have had the same opportunity to kill you."

"Ah! But if you had suspected that man was going to kill me you'd have called out a warning the moment I entered the room. Yes, you would, Dean. You're built that way. I know that, and Mandozza guessed that. You may think that you wouldn't. But you would. You couldn't have helped it if you'd died for it the next second."

It was the finest compliment I ever had, yet I denied it vigorously. I don't know. Perhaps Vee was right. I hope he was right.

"Come and have a look at him." Vee Brown turned to the dead man.

"How—how did you know?" I asked him. "How did you know he was behind the curtains?"

Brown hesitated a moment. Then: "I always cover a room when I enter it; eye it very carefully, perhaps unconsciously— or maybe 'automatically' is a better word. I did it this time. And if there was danger I knew it could come only from one place—one possible place. Behind the curtains to the music room. And then, I saw it in your face, Dean. You suddenly understood that it was death, I think.

Well—I had looked the room over and I knew where death must come from."

"And you fired blindly?"

"Not blindly, Dean. It might have seemed like that to you. But I held my fire, just a split second maybe—and look! Right between the eyes."

I looked down quickly, then turned my head away. "Who is he?" I hardly whispered the words. They choked in my throat.

"Can't you guess? Don't you know? Why, it's Mandozza's right-hand man, who rather fancied himself with a gun. It's Frankie Curry."

CHAPTER THREE

Gift for a Gangster

VEE BROWN paced the room. And he made me tell him of my meeting with Una Coles and of what she had said. I didn't think he was paying attention, but he was. For when I mentioned the name Quinley, that the girl had used, he stopped.

"That's the lawyer, Dean. Mandozza suspects then—more than suspects."

"And the—the body, Vee. Shall I call the police and—"

"And have them tramping all over the place? Flatfeet—the coroner—Inspector Ramsey! Photographers and the newspaper boys. And The Sun-Standard with its criticism of my—my activities." He used the final word in the place of "killings," I thought. "No, there's another way. He was Mandozza's man. If it were outside—in the park or in some deserted alley! Mandozza always takes care of his own dead—his—his—"

And suddenly: "By God! I have it. It'll shake Mandozza for once. And they say that nothing can ever phase him— cause him the slightest emotion. He prides himself on—" And Vee Brown went toward the music room, stepped over the body of Curry and closed the door behind him. For some time I heard the rasp of his voice as he used the private phone. When he came out he was humming to himself.

"It's the song—the new song. Shall I dedicate it to you or Una Coles? Listen!" He hummed softly, a catchy, sentimental melody with a touch of sadness to it. "And the name of it, *You're a Wonderful Girl—For Somebody Else.*"

"Brown!" The significance of the title made me sore. I changed the subject. "What of the body there?"

"It's all arranged," he told me, and his voice was grim. "They say there are no coincidences in life, Dean. Well—here's one. They're giving Mandozza a dinner tonight. It's his birthday. I'm going to send him a present he won't forget. We'll use that old trunk of yours, Dean. I'm going to send Mandozza the body of Frankie Curry."

For a moment I couldn't speak, and then: "My God! Vee—you can't. It's too horrible!"

But he dragged in the trunk, and—God help me—I don't know how I did it, but I did help him fit the body into it. And he was talking all the time.

"It's safe as safe can be. Mandozza won't squawk, for that's not his way. And the man I'm using! Well—he's a crook, of course, but I can trust him. For an hour, only, he'll be in the express business, and the wagon that comes will be so labeled." Vee Brown was at the desk, writing something on a card. Then he opened the lid of the trunk, held the card a moment, started—I think—to drop it in the trunk, and changing his mind presented the card to me. "Read it," he said, and his eyes shone.

And I read it—and it fell from my hand. It's message was ghastly.

Happy Birthday,
Vee Brown.

He picked the card up as I remonstrated. "You can't do that. It's too horrible—too gruesome. You can't—" I clutched at his arm. He drew the hand that held the card behind him.

AND my hands fell to my sides. Vee Brown had changed. He swung on me suddenly, viciously.

"So—it's too gruesome!" His eyes fairly glittered with anger—hatred—maybe a touch of bitterness, that I had never seen in his face before. "And what of me? For three days Mandozza's man dogged me day and night. For three days I expected and waited for a bullet in the back. They call me a killer, even a murderer—and I let him live, with my own life in the balance. And then I killed him—killed him when I had to kill him. A slimy, hired murderer, whose only interest in my death was the fifty grand that Mandozza placed upon my life—my death. And now what? One man dead, who tried to kill me. One man, in the hundreds that Mandozza controls. One man, in the thousands who walk the streets with guns in their pockets and murder in their dirty souls. Curry has failed. What now? I know what now. I'm to be on the spot, open sport for any hopped-up, cheap gunman who wants to shoot me in the back. Mandozza let it out. If Curry failed, he swore to let loose an open offer in the underworld. Fifty grand to the man or woman who kills me. Fifty grand for the murder of Vee Brown. On the spot, for every gunman in New York, every man who's got a gun and is willing to use it."

Vee Brown glared viciously at me, dropped the card into the trunk, and slamming down the lid clicked both the catches and fastened the single strap across the top.

"Now what?" he went on, less viciously if not less vindictively. "Mandozza has two guards with him, day and night. They'll be with him when he opens the trunk. They'll see the feared gunman, Frankie Curry. They'll read the card when

Mandozza drops it to the floor, just as you dropped it. And they'll talk. The thing will run over that grape vine of information in the underworld. And I tell you, Dean—fifty grand won't be enough. Double it and treble it, and it won't be half enough. That even a cop would dare to kill Mandozza's right-hand man seems impossible to the underworld. That the one who killed him would announce it and so defy Mandozza as to ship him his body will shake the underworld, shake its faith in Mandozza. But the card— the whispered word of that card! I tell you, Dean—it's a masterpiece. Mandozza won't be able to live in the same city with me, and live it down."

"But," I stammered, "you're—you're forcing his hand. He'll have to have vengeance. He'll have to have you killed, or—"

"Or kill me himself." Brown gave the strap a final pull. "He was something of a gunman in his day and has kept his hand in, I understand. Now I've called that hand. He'll have to make good. You see, Dean, Mandozza is the greatest menace to our city, to our fine police force. Judges, public officials, and crime itself take his orders. The new man on the force soon realizes that to arrest one of Mandozza's men is a waste of time, and sometimes more than that—a deterrent to promotion—perhaps even the pacing of a lonely beat, and eventually a bit of lead in the back. No—it sounds fantastic, I know. But Mandozza is getting stronger, not weaker. He hopes some day to hold the greatest city in the world in the palm of his hand."

"But you, Vee. Can't he get to you through bigger people, those who could take your job from you?"

Brown went right on. "I work for the district attorney. His record has been searched from his first political job as assemblyman at Albany. And it's clean and the mayor's behind him; and con-fidentially, Dean, they're both behind me. I have a free rein, just one order. Get Mandozza!" And very slowly: "Some day I'm going to get him, Dean—shoot him straight between his mean, shrewd little pink eyes, as I did—"

He stopped. The doorbell rang. Vee moved a gun from a shoulder holster to a jacket pocket and opened the door. Two husky men were there for the trunk. A third was behind them. He was a wizened little old man. I recognized him. It was Irving Small.

I don't know how much money changed hands. But I do know that twice Vee Brown went to the little wall safe in the music room.

Five minutes later the trunk was gone. Vee Brown was shaking himself up a cocktail. "Get your hat, Dean," he said, as he brought me a Martini. "I'm sorry Wong isn't here to ice the glasses. But hurry. I'm hungry enough to eat the proverbial ox."

THE very first words Brown spoke after the oysters came took away what possible appetite I might have had. "Seven o'clock," he said, and smiled. "Just about the time Mandozza is viewing his birthday present. Not the most pleasant he received, maybe, but I'll wager you—the most expensive. It cost a pretty penny for cartage and—"

I pushed aside my oysters and said nothing.

"All right! That subject's taboo. Tell me about the girl again, and this determination of hers to kill Mandozza."

We had just lighted our cigars when the message came by a uniformed telegraph boy. Brown read it and passed it over to me.

"We must give Mandozza credit for meeting a situation the moment it arises. Read it aloud, Dean. I want to get the sound of it."

I did what he asked.

"Dear Mr. Brown:—

I will do myself the honor of calling on you at your penthouse at eight o'clock sharp. Since a banquet is being given me later, I hope you will find it convenient to see me promptly.

Let me assure you that my visit will prove greatly to your advantage.

Very truly yours,
Louie Mandozza."

"It sounds like an advertisement." Vee grinned across at me. "It sounds, too, as if Mandozza is getting just a bit high hat. But after all, he's a remarkable man, Dean. Twenty years ago he sold fruit from a pushcart on the East Side. They say he reads a lot—especially the lives of history's great men." And again that twisted smile. "But he won't take a bath, Dean. At least, that's the gossip."

"You won't see him, of course."

"But I will, Dean. I will indeed. I have many failings, but discourtesy is not one of them. He'll have his two body-guards with him. He never travels without them."

"Two guards. You'll see him after—after the trunk! Three to one."

"Three to two, Dean. You forget that you'll be with me."

"But what good would I be against three trained, expert gunmen?"

Vee smiled. "You could lean out the window and holler for a cop. But honestly, Dean, I don't think he means trouble. If he does—I'll shoot him to death of course."

"The other two—the bodyguards. They'd get you, Vee."

"And if they did, what a glorious way to die! The greatest racketeer in the city and the greatest— The sentence is for you to finish, Dean. But seriously; I've spent my life studying guns. There's a thing that makes all men equal, Dean— at least, physically. It's the gun; the eye that looks along the shining barrel; the finger that closes tightly upon the trigger, and the willingness of man to use it.

There's no man who's as quick as I am— as accurate as I am, as—well—as willing to close a finger upon the trigger. Mandozza knows that. His hired thugs know that. If I can't handle the three of them —which I dispute—the man who reaches for a gun first, dies with it still in its holster. It won't be a pleasant thought for those hired gunmen to have when they wish to feel for a rod."

Conceited? I never was sure about that. Maybe Vee was. Maybe he wasn't. It would be hard to judge a man like Vee.

It was close to eight o'clock when we reached the penthouse. Wong was back and opened the door.

VEE smoked cigarettes and looked over the evening paper. Indeed, he acted much as he would any night he intended to spend quietly at home. As for me—I tried to read the papers, tried to stare out the window at the millions of lights in the great hustling city. But I made no go of it. We were about to have a visit from Louie Mandozza, the most feared czar in the criminal world today. I couldn't get that out of my head. And I couldn't get out of my head the fact that he was coming with two bodyguards, two gunmen— and that Vee Brown had killed Mandozza's right-hand man.

The service phone rang in the hall. Wong came from the back of the apartment toward it.

"Wong—stop!" I called out nervously, and then to Brown: "Let Mandozza come up alone—don't let the guards in. He won't expect that. It's too much for any man to ask. The most natural thing is for you to—"

Vee Brown stopped me. "Take the phone, Wong. If it's Mr. Mandozza, tell the boy to send him and his friends up."

And it was Mandozza and he was coming up. Brown gave me that twisted smile.

"We are not afraid of Mandozza or his

guards—or his hired assassins. We know that, Dean. We must let Louie Mandozza know that. It will bother him and it will worry his guards. But the very fact that Mandozza announces his arrival assures— or should assure us that his mission is peaceful. Being a detective, Dean, I will hazard the guess that Mandozza makes first an offer, than a warning—and last, a threat."

And as I paced the room nervously: "The whisky and soda, Wong—and caviar. And, Wong—" Wong stopped in the doorway, "on toast, I think, with a slice of olive."

It was five minutes later that the bell to our private door rang. Wong slipped unperturbed across the foyer. The door was opened and a deep voice spoke.

"Mr. Mandozza. And you might tell Mr. Brown I have two friends with me. If he prefers it so, they can wait in the hall, and—"

Brown was on his feet, crossing to the foyer, into the hall which led to the door. I could hear his voice plainly—low, calm and pleasant. "In the hall? Certainly not, Mr. Mandozza. Drafty—I've complained about it several times. But that's the price one must pay for a penthouse, I guess. Why—I'd never forgive myself. They'd catch their death of cold, even in this mild weather."

Then the voice of Mandozza, low and husky. They were in the foyer, across it. I was facing the three of them there in the living room. Brown brought up the rear.

The three were in full evening dress. Mandozza, an imposing figure, wearing his clothes easily and naturally. Not so the two bodyguards. They were hard, unimaginative, brutal-looking men. They reminded me of the singing waiter and bouncer of the red-light district in the pre-prohibition days. They looked exactly as they should look, as you would expect them to look. The armed bodyguard of a big racketeer.

CHAPTER FOUR

Louie Mandozza

LOUIE MANDOZZA! Big, certainly, but not tall. It was the breadth of his shoulders that made him so huge; the length of his thick arms, hanging down so that the ends of his fingers reached his knees. Then the huge, strong, hairy hands. I think it was the hands and the forward bend of his shoulders that first gave me the impression of a huge gorilla. It was in his walk too; a sort of swaying motion to his body. I raised my eyes and looked at his face, his head. It was a large head with a high forehead and jet-black hair smoothed straight back behind it. Sleek, oily hair that shone in the light.

There was nothing of the gangster in Mandozza's face, unless it was his mouth. Thick, cruel, coarse lips that turned out slightly, like a negro's. A big, yet sharp beak of a nose and hard, staring, peculiar-colored eyes. No, they weren't pink, as Brown had said. At least, I don't think so. The pupils themselves were just two tiny points, and the balls of the eyes behind them were slightly tinged with a dull red streak which, coming and going as it did, gave one the impression of pink— like a Persion cat's eyes. Soft and kind the eyes seemed until he set those black points in the center on me. But they were hard and cold and steady and maybe cruel, like his mouth—but I couldn't be sure.

But Brown was introducing us and Mandozza was talking. "Dean Condon, eh? I have read your articles in The Globe and enjoyed them." He took my hand in one of his great hairy ones, and though I'm a strong man and rather proud of my grip, I felt my fingers give; go limp under his grasp just before he dropped my hand.

Brown motioned the three of them to the long, low couch—so low and soft that it was difficult to arise quickly from it.

Mandozza eyed it a moment, showed his white even teeth in a smile and dropped into the center of it. His men grunted, and sat one on either side of him. He made no effort to introduce them.

Wong brought the whisky and soda. The two guards smiled, stretched hands toward the bottle of Scotch as Mandozza spoke. "My friends don't drink," he said crisply, and reached for the bottle as the hands of the two guards dropped back on their knees. It was funny how they sat so. It was quite apparent that they made a point of keeping their hands plainly in view.

"I never drink during business hours myself," Vee jerked his head toward me, "but Dean will join you of course."

Mandozza took a generous dose of the whisky, poured the soda into the glass and held it in his hand as he watched me mix my drink. He waited, too, until I drank before he put his own glass to his lips. Mandozza was a careful man.

"That's not bad liquor for these times." He ran a tongue over his huge lips. Then he took another drink of it. "Mulligan must supply you." He nodded. "So you don't drink during business hours. And you're right, Mr. Brown; this is a business call."

"I suspected that." Brown dropped into a chair by the long table, facing the three men. His hands fell easily upon the smooth surface of the table. I stood to his left, hesitated a moment, sank into a chair, laid my glass upon the table, crossed my legs in what I flattered myself was easy indifference, and lit a cigarette with fingers that must have trembled visibly. Mandozza's little black darts of eyes, with the semblance of pink behind them, flashed from Brown to me.

"Your friend," he said to Brown, "is not a very good actor. You," huge shoulders shrugged, "have no cause to act. I think I could do business with Mr. Condon very quickly."

"It is too bad then," Vee smiled, "that your business is not with Mr. Condon— but with me."

"Partly with you. Perhaps a bit with Mr. Condon. He's your friend. He glorifies you in the paper. And—" Mandozza turned his big head, slowly raised a ham-like hand and swept it about the room, "these swell diggings—the big car, the servant. All this cannot be bought with a detective's salary. Oh, I know a lot about you, Mr. Brown. If there's anything irregular you've taken good care of it. So— I must presume that Mr. Condon puts up for the information you buy and the stool pigeons you use. I may say then, without fear of offense, that you should be and undoubtedly are very grateful to Mr. Condon."

"It remains, of course, to be seen to what extent my gratitude would reach."

MANDOZZA leaned forward, pushed his huge body with some difficulty to the end of the couch and tapped gently upon the table. "You are clever, Mr. Brown, and I never resent or criticize a man who protects his own life, even at the expense of—of my closest associate." And although Mandozza's face was calm, I felt certain that he was seething inside; only by great control holding back his anger—his hatred.

"But after all," Mandozza went on, his voice steady, "your humor was a trifle gruesome. Yet, perhaps it served its purpose. You sent a message to me, and that message was—the city is not large enough to hold us both. Unfortunately my connections are such at this time that I cannot leave."

"So you open with a threat," Vee Brown said.

"Not at all. You will ask for and are entitled to six month's leave of absence. There is a ship leaving Monday; a cruise around the world. I will pay all the expenses of that cruise and place in your hands now one hundred thousand dollars in cash. You need fear no—no retribution."

"And you, of course, will circulate the story that you drove me from the city."

"Certainly," said Mandozza. "We understand each other perfectly."

"And the alternative?"

Mandozza set his thick lips tightly. His eyes knitted to two slits and his hand upon the table became a fist. "The alternative is quite simple. I can't break you. I've tried. You'll be a dead man in twenty-four hours."

"I've heard that line before. So I'll accept the alternative."

Mandozza removed his hand from the table and sat straight and stiff upon the edge of the couch. His voice never changed when he spoke. "There is more. Something for your friend, Condon. He loves a certain girl; he has even asked her to marry him. She was quite proud of that. If you accept my proposition I send the girl to Mr. Condon—alive."

I jerked erect. The cigarette fell from my fingers upon the Oriental rug. The word "alive" had startled me, alarmed me—yes, horrified me.

Vee Brown leaned quickly down, and lifting the cigarette from the floor snuffed it out in the ash tray. "I am afraid that Mr. Condon no longer wishes to marry the girl."

"Marriage is not necessarily stipulated in the agreement."

Vee said quickly as he looked at my face: "We refuse, of course." And as Mandozza started to speak, "I am afraid you can no longer interest us, Mr. Mandozza."

"And the alternative to that is that I will send the girl to you, Mr. Vee Brown." He leaned forward now and his lips curled, and the pink of his eyes was lost in the icy pin point of black. "Two can play at the same game. I shall send you such a present as you sent me. I shall

return your trunk, Mr. Brown—shall make you a present, Mr. Brown. Mr. Louie Mandozza will not be under obligation to any man."

"I'll go!" The words just shot from between my lips without much sense. "I'll take the trip. The girl—"

But Brown cut in on me, crisp and calm and clear, as my nervous fingers reached for the bottle upon the table and raw liquor cut far back in my throat. "It's simply bluff, Dean. Mr. Mandozza likes the girl, has use for her in his side line. Blackmail, I believe that is."

"I never bluff." Louis Mandozza was talking. "The girl interested me. She was from a different world. She was useful. But now—" again the massive shoulders shrugged. "She was playing with a gun this afternoon." He stretched a hand up to the top of his left shoulder. "I am sure you will be glad to hear that the wound was very slight. So you see, from an asset she has become a liability, a menace; a very slight menace, of course, to Louie Mandozza—but still, a menace. If you know your history, Mr. Brown, you will recall that Marat was killed by a woman. Killed in his bath."

Vee Brown smiled. "Killed in his bath, eh? If the stories about town are true, Mr. Mandozza, you have very little to worry you there."

Mandozza's face grew red with anger. He struggled to his feet. The two guards followed him. The hand of the man on the right crept up over the white bosom of his shirt, toward his left armpit. Brown was also on his feet. I half came to mine. Things looked bad.

Brown spoke sharply. "I warn you, Mandozza. Your guard to the right! A further movement of his hand means—death."

MANDOZZA swallowed hard. The guard's hand dropped to his side. The red receded from Mandozza's face.

For a moment things were tense. Then Mandozza spoke.

"Time passes and we get nowhere. The alternative to my proposition is simply this. I will make an offer that will race through the underworld." He stuck out a finger and pointed it at Vee Brown. "One hundred thousand dollars to the man or woman who gets you, Vee Brown. One hundred grand for your dead body, and no questions asked. You'll be on the spot. On the spot for every criminal, every gunman, every sneak thief and hop-head in the city of New York. What do you say to that?"

"You're too late." Brown shook his head. "There's another story racing through the underworld tonight. A story that will be whispered from table to table while they wine and dine you at your own party. I don't think, after hearing that story, there will be many who'll care to put me on the spot. You know the story, you know how such news travels. You realized the truth before you sent your message. That's why you came with your offer of money. That's why you came with your bluff about the girl. You're through, you're washed up. Soon you'll get your first jolt. Oh, not a very long one, maybe, but long enough for the boys on the Avenue to forget Louie Mandozza."

"All right." Mandozza fairly snarled the words as he backed toward the foyer, his two gunmen following him. "I'm no coward. No one ever called Louie Mandozza yellow. If what you say is true; if your gruesome bit of humor has stumped the underworld, then—Louie Mandozza will make it a personal matter."

"Louie Mandozza won't be around in a day or two to make it a personal matter," Brown answered, while I simply stood there gripping the arms of a chair, trying to think; trying to figure things out, and finding simply chaos in my mind.

"You mean the Quinley evidence for the federal government!" Mandozza was having hard work now to control his rising temper. The red was creeping into his face again. "That will be attended to by tomorrow. There will then be no evidence —and no Quinley."

Brown threw out his hands in a gesture of indifference, but there was that tiny flicker in his eyeballs which always warned me that he was worried.

"You can't beat the rap this time." And although Brown spoke with great assurance I felt that he did not fully believe his own words.

Mandozza was down the hall and at the front door now. The door was open; the guards were in the corridor. I was just behind Brown in the foyer when Mandozza spoke his final words.

"I'm giving you twenty-four hours to change your mind. Then—" and very slowly and with a certain satisfaction, I thought, "then I'll return your trunk." And in a louder voice, and to me over Brown's head: "She's a neat piece of goods, Mr. Condon. A neat piece of goods—alive."

The door closed with a bang; heavy, steady feet beat for a moment on the marble corridor without. Then silence. Mandozza had come and Mandozza had gone. But he had left something—something terrible behind him. Something that tore down deep in the pit of my stomach.

I WAS at Brown the minute he returned to the living room. "What about the girl—what about Una Coles? Are you going to let her die—let her be killed? It's your fault, Brown. That trunk—that horrible, gruesome, deadly trick! Now— what of Una Coles?"

"Well," he demanded, "what of Una Coles?"

"She saved your life. She—"

"Good God! Are we to have that over again? Has the death of Curry got anything to do with the girl taking a pot shot at Mandozza? She told you herself that she was going to kill him. Am I a hunter of criminals or a squire of dames? Do I accept the responsibility for every woman who smiles at you and—and—"

He had me by the shoulders, shaking them gently. "I'm sorry, Dean," he said. "It's tough. It's hard. You're in love with the girl, of course. But buck up. We'll see that she lives to ruin your life. There's twenty-four hours yet."

"But Mandozza—the trunk! It's too horrible."

"Death is the same no matter where death lies. Twenty-four hours! That's an eternity in the game we play, the police play, the criminal plays. What do you want me to do? After all, I'm a cop, Dean —just an ordinary cop who's been taken out of his harness. I—" And suddenly he stopped, whistled softly. "The girl knew about Quinley, and Mandozza knew about Quinley. And Mandozza didn't seem worried about that evidence. Why —why? Well—he explained that, Dean. Now—Quinley's got the evidence. It's ready. He's simply holding out on me to give himself time to leave the city. He practically told me that. And I didn't kick. Why should I? Every man wants to live. Mandozza would get bail, of course. They couldn't refuse him that. And five minutes after he was out—yes, five minutes after he was arrested, Quinley would be dead."

Brown crossed the living room, was in the music room, was getting a number on the private phone. Part of the conversation I heard, but Brown explained it to me ten minutes later, when he entered the living room again.

"Quinley didn't want to do it at first. And the fear of prison couldn't influence him as it did before he thought Mandozza knew the truth. So I put the fear of Mandozza into his crooked heart. That was a real fear, Dean, for he knows, as I know, as every crook in the city knows—Mandozza doesn't bluff. He—" and stopping suddenly as he saw the fear in my face and remembered, probably, his statement that Mandozza was bluffing about Una, "Well—Quinley is to give me the evidence tonight. I named a dozen safe places but he would have none of them, and perhaps he's right. It's a room below the cellar in a deserted Greenwich Village house. I tell you, Dean, if I'd gone deeper into Quinley's affairs I'd bet my royalties on my last song that something far more sinister than jury fixing would have showed up. But there!" He tapped the envelope he held in his hand. "That's the evidence of Quinley's little crooked work. I'm to exchange it at midnight tonight for the Mandozza evidence of false income-tax return."

And a few moments later, when I didn't speak: "We have about two hours and a half, Dean—then big things. Don't bother about the girl." He snapped out his watch. "In another few hours Mandozza will have other things to worry about besides Una Coles. And, now—" he stood still and hummed softly a minute. "I was joking just before dinner about the song I was going to write for you— *She's A Wonderful Girl—For Somebody Else.* But while Mandozza was talking it got running through my head. The lyric—everything seemed there. By tomorrow it may be gone again. So—" he turned toward the music room, "call me in two hours and a half. That'll be eleven fifteen sharp."

"Vee!" I started, and stopped. The door of the music room had closed, the key had turned in the lock. I shuddered slightly. There were times when I didn't believe that Vee Brown was human; other times when— I looked at the Scotch upon the table, turned to the little wall cabinet, and taking out a bottle of rye drank a good three fingers of it, straight. What was running through my head? Just this.

What of Una Coles? And did I love her?

For two hours and a half I paced that room. For two hours and a half I glanced almost constantly at the clock above the fireplace, and every couple of minutes even checked it up with my watch. The hands moved so slowly!

I came out of my half trance with a jump. It was eleven fifteen. I raised my closed fist and hammered upon the music-room door.

CHAPTER FIVE

Sub-Cellar Set-Up

TWENTY minutes later we were speeding downtown to the Greenwich Village section in a taxi.

"Buck up, Dean. There'll be so many things occupying Mandozza's mind that he won't have time for thoughts of personal vengeance. These federal boys are tough customers to fool with. Once I have the evidence, we'll have no trouble in getting a search warrant and can comb out the many places controlled by Mandozza. We'll have a list of them all, Dean."

"Brown," I said, "there's something about that girl that haunts me. Something that tells me she's been caught in the maelstrom of crime by Mandozza and dragged into a life she hates."

"Maybe." Brown seemed rather disinterested. "But, after all, in the next hour it's a man we must think of—not a woman. It'll be a great thing for the city, to give Mandozza his first jolt." He shook his head. "But I'm not satisfied. I wanted to pin a murder rap on him. I dare say I could name ten murders off-hand that I know he's responsible for; that every cop on the force, to the newest rookie, knows he's responsible for. Yet, I can't prove it; they can't prove it. I'd like to

be able to put the finger on him—to fry him, Dean."

He hummed a bit and tossed half-smoked butts out the window. And, as was his habit, he had the taxi stop nearly a block and a half away from our actual destination.

"Quinley is in a blue funk, Dean," he told me, when we stood on the curb and watched the taxi drive away. "I'll bet Quinley has more things than just evidence of Mandozza's little play against the government. He was desperate when he planned to meet me. He must own the house. Our meeting is to be in a subbasement, as he called it—below the cellar. A smart lawyer, Dean, who's gone crooked. I don't blame him for being frightened, but I guess he'll be careful enough about being followed." He looked toward the blue of the sky a moment and seemed to be thinking aloud more than speaking to me. "The evidence must be in that sub-basement, of course; else why meet me in such a place? Why let me know of this private hideout?" He chuckled as he led me down the street and around the corner. "A wise bird, this lawyer. Who would suspect the fastidious Quinley of having a private office below a cellar in an empty house?"

Silently we walked down the side street, Brown's head ever turning; his sharp black eyes peering into areaways; searching the hidden shadows of vestibules to brown-stone fronts.

"We weren't followed," he said emphatically. "I'm sure of that. If I didn't see a 'shadow' I'd feel it. And here we are—the sixth house from the corner. It looks empty enough. We are to slip through the alley and enter by the back door. Quick—so!"

Brown pulled me suddenly into a narrow alley between two houses, hustled me down it until we were hidden in the shadows of the houses on either side. Then he held me there, our backs flat against the wall.

"We must be sure." He spoke in a low voice. "Quinley's life depends upon that, and I promised him his life and his freedom. He'll be leaving the city tonight and the courts will have heard the last of his golden voice. At least, until Mandozza is safely behind the bars."

For five minutes we stood there. It was not late. Perhaps half a dozen people passed, all moving quickly, evidently with some definite destination in mind. Once a policeman passed. Slowly, methodically he went on his way, his footsteps heavy in the silence—to die away finally down the block.

"Now—Dean." I saw Brown's right hand move quickly, then sink in his jacket pocket, and I knew that one of his guns had gone from a shoulder holster to a side pocket.

Silently we reached the end of the alley, climbed worn wooden steps, passed into an outside pantry, the door of which hung perilously open on rusty hinges.

THE moon crept in and shone upon a dilapidated ice box; and to the left of it a door that, though old and needing paint, gave the impression of substantial protection. On this door Vee Brown knocked—knocked but once—and the door swung quickly open. Muttered, nervous words from within; a calm, reassuring reply from Brown—and we were in the musty kitchen.

The door closed without the expected creak of rusted hinges.

"Here—" A trembling voice spoke as a pencil of light cut across the kitchen floor. "I'll have to take your hand. I didn't know you were to bring a friend. I thought you would come alone."

"He always goes with me," Vee said. "Has written me up a bit, when the others criticized my shootings. You must have read the papers and—"

"But this! It's not to be written up; not to—" And the words were lost some place back in the man's throat as I heard him swallow suddenly.

"Of course not." Brown took my arm and evidently Quinley's as we moved slowly across the kitchen, through a door and to some steps.

We were down those steps and in the cellar; across it. There was an open trap and a dark hole below it; the outline of steps much the same as the wooden stairs we had descended from the kitchen. Brown stopped at the head of those stairs.

"Surely," he said, "you can have a light down there. It's below the cellar—can't be seen from the outside."

"There's an electric light below." Quinley's words all seemed to stick in his throat. "I'll light it as soon as we get down. It's just a wire from the ceiling."

"Good." Brown held my arm at the top of those steps. "Dean and I will wait here until we can see our way better."

"Yes—" said Quinley. "I lifted the trap when I first came, but I didn't go down. It's a retreat—a sanctuary. It always gives me a feeling of security to be down there alone. But tonight—God! It seemed like death lurked there below. I don't know why. No one could possibly be there. Yet, I'm afraid."

"The stuff is there? The evidence against Mandozza?"

"All of it, in the safe. I kept it as a protection against him in case—in case— Well—sometimes he misunderstands the actions of his friends, and—and—you know. They die suddenly."

"Sure—I know." Brown's voice was impatient. "But this time he won't misunderstand. We won't let him. Go down and show a light—a real light. You're safe. I'll be here above, with a gun."

"Yes, yes—of course," the man's voice broke again, "it's safe. I'm protecting myself in every way. I—" And his feet seemed to stagger a bit on the stairs. I wondered if Brown had pushed him. Anyway the circle of light from the small flash shone on those steps and the shadow of a man followed it down.

A damp, dank air seemed to creep slowly up from the place below.

"Damp and musty," Brown whispered.

I shook my head, forgetting that he couldn't see me in the darkness. To me the air seemed cold. A queer sort of coldness that seemed to settle inside of me rather than outside. I could feel it in my throat, in my chest—even down in my stomach. As if it seaped out from inside my body and—

The light snapped on below. Vee Brown said: "I'd like to put my spotlight around this cellar, in case—" Then in the darkness I saw his shadow shrug its shoulders as he started down the stairs. "But we can't change Quinley's life. It's rather a new experience for him—or for anyone else—to betray Mandozza to the law."

We reached the room by plain, wooden, open steps that might be found in any cellar. The room was poorly furnished. A flat old oak desk, a chair behind it, two other straight-backed, common kitchen chairs with their backs against the wall. In the center of the room was an oil heater, but it was not lit. In one corner was an old-fashioned safe; high up on the far wall a calico curtain that looked as if it hid a window. But there was no window, for as Brown lifted the curtain only solid brick showed.

"I had to have it that way," Quinley said. "It seemed like a tomb without it." He shivered slightly and looked at the oil heater. "I didn't light it. It didn't seem worth while; we won't be here long."

FOR the first time I got a good look at Quinley. He was a tall, lanky man, with a pronounced stoop to his shoulders. His dark hair was graying at the sides,

and blue eyes that might have been keen and piercing were now feverishly bright, with a shifty uncertain look to them. He struck me as a man who had not slept for several nights. And I didn't wonder at that.

Brown was saying: "No, we won't be here long. If the stuff is in the safe, get it out. Yes, yes—I have the envelope with the affidavits you want in my pocket. Once I get the hooks into Mandozza you'll never be bothered again by me."

And as Quinley knelt by the safe and nervously fiddled with the combination, Brown stepped to a long bit of calico hung on the far side of the room. It was much larger than the window one, stretching to the floor—and might have hidden a door.

But like the one at the window—it didn't. This time, instead of plain bricks, there was a row of long and fairly deep wooden shelves. Papers were on the shelves—law briefs, and the dust upon them was more like dirt—soft and damp.

The safe was open—and closed again. Almost eagerly Quinley spun the dial. Then he was on his feet again, with a long envelope in his hands. He spoke. "The trap above. I had better close it. Someone might—"

Brown stopped him with a wave of his hand as he took the envelope, and placing it upon the desk proceeded to take the papers from it.

"We'll leave it open," Vee said. "If anyone wishes to come down, his feet will show first—and so give us little trouble." He looked at me and looked at Quinley, and understanding, I gripped my gun the tighter.

There, directly under the hanging electric light, Brown went over those papers. Quinley watched him, nervously clasping and unclasping his hands, looking from the bent head of Brown to his own twisting fingers.

It was close to fifteen minutes before Brown sat erect, placed all the papers back in the envelope, folded the envelope carefully, smoothing out the crease with the heel of his hand. Then he took a small envelope from his inside pocket, put the one Quinley had given to him into that pocket and handed the other to Quinley.

Eagerly Quinley grasped it, tore open the flap, ran fingers quickly through its contents and looked at Brown.

"Great!" Brown tapped his inside jacket pocket. "Better even that I expected. A few months out of the city, Quinley, and you can come back. You're a good lawyer—not too old yet—and have a brilliant future if only you'd stay on the level."

"I can never come back," Quinley said in a far-away voice. "As far as the city knows me, I will be dead. Mandozza or his associates will be waiting for me."

"Nonsense." Brown came to his feet. "With Mandozza away for seven or more years it will be simple to break up his gang—his racket. An army without a general is quite as bad as a general without—" He straightened suddenly and his hand shot to his pocket. "What was that?" Keen black eyes were centered on that flight of wooden steps.

I had heard nothing and I started to tell Vee so.

He raised his hand and stood listening, his head held high—like a hunting dog. But strain as I might, I heard nothing.

"It's not the police—the police!" Quinley cried out hoarsely. "You didn't double-cross me and—"

"Don't be a fool," Brown cut in. He jerked a gun into his hand and went toward those steps. "Keep an eye on 'His Nibs,' Dean." He nodded toward Quinley as he stood at the foot of the stairs and looked up. "Probably nothing more than a rat, but I wouldn't like that trap door to bounce down on us."

I watched Quinley. He faced the stairs and watched Brown. Three—four—five

steps Brown climbed. His body from the waist down was in the light; from the waist up it was in the shadow. I could see the flash in his left hand now. One more step he took, and stopped dead on those steps; stood frozen to the stairs, I guess. Frozen—just as I was frozen to that floor. I half swung my body toward the tiny squeak which came from the curtained shelves almost directly behind me.

Brown was helpless to defend himself. Those shelves were a fake, they covered a door that led to another room—or a hall of some kind. Anyway, Mandozza and his two bodyguards were in the room with us. Two men leveled guns at Brown's back.

A gun was jabbed against my side. A harsh voice spoke. It was Mandozza. "Don't move, Brown. Don't turn. Drop that gun and flash! Three men are covering you, all anxious to fire the first shot into your back."

My head turned slightly so that my eyes were glued on Brown's back. I heard rather than saw his gun tumble from his hand. It struck one step, then bounced down to the floor below. The flash had fallen between two steps and rolled back beneath them as it hit the floor.

CHAPTER SIX

Murder at Midnight

THINGS happened quickly after that. My gun was taken from me. I was thrown into a chair; my hands thrust roughly behind my back. I felt the cold steel against my wrist, tried to pull my arms from the strained position and realized that I was manacled to one of the thin round supports of the back of the chair.

"Now, Eddie—" Mandozza was talking to the bigger of the two guards, who was on the stairs now, his gun planted directly in the center of Vee Brown's back. "Don't make a move. Let Capollo search Brown and put the bracelets on him. I'll cover Dean Condon."

"I put the cuffs on this mug, Condon," Capollo explained as he crossed toward Vee Brown. "Listen, boss——" when Mandozza started in to curse him, "Condon's the athlete of this party. Brown couldn't hold his own against a tom cat without his rods. Maybe he has a pair of bracelets of his own, that'll fit."

"Maybe." Mandozza nodded as Capollo started in to search Vee, while the man called Eddie kept his gun pressed against Brown's back—and then to Brown, "No funny work, now. There's a hundred grand to the man that kills you. Be a sport and don't start trouble. I want to save that money and snuff you out myself." Things are clear and they aren't clear. I know that they found no bracelets on Brown. I know that Mandozza was particular about that search. And I know that I gave up all hope when they found and took the little sleeve gun that Brown was carrying.

I know that Brown was searched so thoroughly that he could not have concealed even a nail file, and I know that when the search was over and the envelope containing the income-tax-fraud evidence against Mandozza was laid on the desk beside him, Mandozza ordered Vee Brown to raise his hands in the air.

I know that, because I saw Vee's arms go up, saw that his two hands were just lost in the well of blackness above the trap.

Even with Brown helpless and unarmed they kept him so, standing on the wooden steps, his hands high above his head. Capollo, the more vicious of the two guards, held the gun now, the muzzle of which was stuck deep into Vee's back. Then, for the first time, Quinley, who had remained crouched in a corner, spoke.

"I did it, boss—I did it! Eh?" He was bent far over as he slowly and ingratiatingly moved toward the desk behind which Mandozza sat, examining that evidence against him. "I even gave him the papers—as you said to. They are all there—all there."

"All there—yes." Mandozza looked up and his eyes snapped, and the pink behind them turned to a blood red. "You were a smart lawyer, Quinley—smarter than I thought. They wouldn't have much trouble getting me with this." And with an oath, "I wouldn't have believed it possible."

"But I trapped him for you. He telephoned me, like you thought he would. And I went through with it—and you've got him. I've paid the price, and now— The door there, to the garage. I can go? Yes—that's it, isn't it? I delivered Vee Brown to you and I can go. You're a real man, boss. You'll let—you'll let——" And he raised his eyes and looked straight into the eyes of Mandozza. Then he shrieked—shrieked and backed away, his arm raised across his face as if to protect himself.

"You're not going to let me go? You're—My God! you can't—you wouldn't——" And in a piercing scream, "You're going to kill me!"

Mandozza spoke through tightly pressed lips. "You're a rat—a lousy, dirty stool pigeon. If you had failed in this trap tonight I'd of had you on your knees—begging me to kill you. You want to live now, but you'd of prayed for death then. As it is, Quinley, I'm going to be easy with you. But you're a rat." Mandozza came to his feet, walked easily across to the foot of the steps, and drawing a gun jammed it hard into Brown's back.

"All right, Capollo—I like your work. I'll cover Brown, here. You give it to the rat."

I REMEMBER, of course, as one might remember some parts of a nightmare. A thing that gets you for some time afterward, at night, but doesn't seem real enough to bother you when you're awake. It's not a pretty story and I'll make it short.

I know that Capollo crossed that room. I know that Quinley fled, shrieking, into a corner. I know that Capollo raised his gun and fired, and that Quinley's arm dropped from his face and his hands clutched at his stomach. I will carry with me for a long time Capollo's laugh, and his twisted lips and the blood lust of his green eyes. I guess Capollo stood so for a full minute, though it seemed like an hour to me and must have been eternity to Quinley. And then, when Quinley sank slowly to his knees, Capollo fired once again, shooting him through the head.

"I'm sorry, Brown, you couldn't see the little display. But we'll have another for you." Mandozza went back to his desk when Capollo returned and stuck his gun against Vee Brown's back.

Burnt powder got into my throat. It irritated my nostrils but I could not move my hands from behind my back. And in the corner lay—lay the thing that had been Quinley. And Capollo—Capollo! I shuddered. Was he going to kill Vee Brown and me—like that?

"And now," Mandozza spoke to Vee, "you had your chance. An offer of one hundred thousand dollars, which would have meant ease and comfort—a chance to see the world. A chance to repay your friend, Dean, for all that he—"

Heavy steps beat across stone. Mandozza was on his feet, facing the doorway that the shelves covered. But Capollo never moved his gun from Vee Brown's back or took his eyes off him. I turned my head. A man was in that doorway. He spoke.

"It's the girl—Una Coles. She's gone. Tied a sheet to the bed and dropped out the window." And in a voice that trembled, "I swear to God I never left my place in the hall, by the door. It ain't my fault, boss. You never let her know you knew she meant to snuff you out when she pretended to be fooling with that gun. Remember I wanted to tie her and search her for a rod? She didn't believe your story about just wanting her to spend the night here. She got suspicious you were going to put her out and dropped from the window. Maybe she had a gun!"

"Maybe she did," Mandozza said thoughtfully. "It's not exactly pleasant to kill a woman. I sort of hoped she'd take the hint I gave her and save me the trouble. How long ago was it that you missed her?"

"Just now. She's been gone only ten—fifteen minutes at the most. Maybe only a minute. I looked in less than a quarter of an hour ago and asked her if she wanted something."

"I had a hunch," said Capollo, from the foot of the steps, without even turning his head, "that she was listening in when we planned this little cold-meat party for tonight."

"She isn't much use with a gun if she's got one," said Mandozza. "Take the outside of the house. Eddie, you go through the yards behind, to the street beyond. Benson's back there with the car. She would go that way, I think. Benson knows, and will grab her."

The man in the doorway departed. Eddie, who had been standing beside my chair, looked from me to Brown and back to Mandozza.

"It's all right." Mandozza grinned. "It'll be over in a few minutes. Go ahead!" And Eddie also left us.

"All right, Capollo." Mandozza came to his feet. There was a gun in his hand now. "Turn Vee Brown around—and keep the gun in his stomach." And I saw Vee turn slowly, his arms still in the air; the whiteness of his hands lost in the blackness above.

Mandozza turned in the middle of the room and looked at Vee. "I'm not given much to speeches," he said, "and I have to get back to a dinner tonight and make another speech, but—"

The telephone upon the flat oak desk rang suddenly. Capollo straightened slightly, but his gun only bore the deeper into Brown's stomach.

"What the hell!" Mandozza exclaimed, went to the desk and lifted the receiver. "Yeah—Mandozza. That's right. That's fine." A moment's pause—then, "Dragged her into the car, eh, and got her at forty-seven? Good boy! Bring her right over. It won't take but a couple of minutes. Eh—a cop? Well!" Mandozza looked up and spoke to Capollo. "Benson picked up the girl and has taken her to forty-seven. She raised hell when he grabbed her and a cop spotted them. He don't think it's safe to bring her over. I guess not, too."

"That dame," said Capollo, "knows too much. He'd better knock her over."

"Sure!" said Mandozza, "I guess that's the way it'll have to be." And into the phone, "All right, Benson. The girl's full of words she wants to talk to wrong people. You better—" he hesitated a moment —then, "if you don't hear from me in ten minutes take her for a ride and leave her up in the park."

He listened a moment, and then, "I know, I know—but that's the way it is. Ten minutes!" And the receiver went back on the hook with a click.

"Cripes!" said Mandozza, as he came to his feet again and walked over toward me, with his gun dangling in his hand. "It's a mess." For a moment he seemed almost human—had seemed almost human when he hesitated about killing the girl. Then he changed, suddenly swung toward Vee Brown and hatred glared from his eyes.

"You killed my friend," he said. "I'm going to kill yours—kill him before your eyes. Let you watch him die, as Quinley

died. And he could have lived—but didn't because of you. Because you thought you could get Mandozza. Are you watching, Vee Brown? Are you—" He swung toward me, raised his gun and pointed it straight at my stomach.

Maybe I cringed slightly. Maybe I didn't. But I'm not ashamed of it if I did. For a moment later I raised my head and looked straight into the jet-black eyes of Vee Brown. Did I see sorrow there, fear, overpowering remorse, for the terrible death I was to die? I didn't. I saw that peculiar look in his eyes. The flash that was there when he was on the hunt. And I—I was trying to tell Brown with my last look that I didn't blame him. That—

Mandozza's gun shoved close against my stomach. I set my lips tightly and never took my eyes off Vee Brown. But Brown wasn't looking at me now. He was looking at Capollo. And Capollo didn't turn his head, but he let his eyes slip sideways, toward me. Evil, green eyes—eyes that were gloating—eyes that wanted to see death, murder. My God! I think the man enjoyed it.

"Now, Brown," Mandozza was saying, "your friend, Dean—like my friend, Curry. Dean first and then—"

I didn't hear any more. I braced myself to take it, to die like Quinley died, with his hands—with his hands— And I straightened there in my chair, my eyes bulging. What I saw was unthinkable—impossible!

VEE BROWN'S right hand swept suddenly down from the blackness. A white hand, that seemed black, that held something black. But I didn't know then. Just that downward motion of Brown's hand as Capollo turned his eyes back and looked straight into the eyes of Vee Brown.

There was a roar of a gun, the sudden dart of flame—and Capollo was hurled from those steps as if struck by a battering ram. It was ghastly—it was terrible. Capollo had been there; his white face was visible; his green eyes were glaring, living things—and now he lay dead in the corner, shot through the top of the head by the gun in Vee Brown's hand. Capollo never even closed a finger upon the trigger of the gun in his hand. He never had the chance. He died with the single downward motion of Vee's right hand.

Mandozza seemed to jerk back on his heels. His gun hung at his side. His eyes blinked, and the pink was plainly visible. He half raised his gun. He knew and he didn't know. Then he spoke, even before he turned his head.

"You shouldn't have done that, Capollo. Not yet—not until—"

Vee Brown came slowly down those steps. I saw his gun drawing a bead smack on the side of Mandozza's head. And he was smiling and his lips were a single straight line, and there was death in his eyes—the lust to kill in his eyes. The same lust to kill that might be in the eyes of any gunman. And he spoke. "It wasn't Capollo, Mandozza," he said softly. "It was me—Vee Brown."

Mandozza raised his hand and swung. And the lust to kill seemed to go out of Brown's eyes, and a softness that was new to me crept in. The muzzle of Vee's heavy black 45 automatic dipped slightly and the gun belched lead.

Mandozza shrieked once with pain; his gun fell to the floor with a thud. There was blood on his wrist, running down his hand, along the end of his fingers.

"Tough break, Mandozza," Brown said simply, as he crossed the room and kicked Mandozza's gun into a far corner. "Now —pick up that phone and call this Benson at forty-seven—wherever that is. Tell him the girl's to be let go at once."

But Mandozza crouched back against the brick wall and cursed.

I don't remember the full details of those terrible minutes while I counted the seconds off. The seconds that might bring death to Una Coles. But I do remember Vee Brown's words, and do know that even to me they rang with a terrible truth.

"You've got less than five minutes— less than five minutes." Vee laid his watch upon the table. "Then—I swear to God I'll put my gun against your head and give it to you as I gave it to Capollo."

"That," said Mandozza, and his thick tongue came out and licked at dry lips, "would be murder."

"Murder or not, you have my word— and you'll be dead."

"All right," said Mandozza, and he straightened and stood with his back against the wall. "I'll—well—I'll die before I'll take the rap. You'll even hang the Quinley kill on me."

"Yes," said Brown slowly, "I was thinking of that—if you're alive."

There was more to it, of course, as I struggled frantically against the handcuffs that held me to the back of that chair. But I do know that Mandozza refused absolutely to save the girl until Brown struck a bargain with him, and I do know that time was quickly passing while Brown argued and threatened. In a way, I suppose, Mandozza won out. For I heard him say as he crossed to the phone: "I'm to leave the city, and as long as I stay out of it you are not to use that tax-fraud evidence nor attempt in any way to get me."

"That is right," said Brown. "And the moment you stick your face back in New York I use this evidence." He took the papers from the table and stuffed them into his pocket. "You are to be out of the city in two hours."

"Just as soon as I get this wrist fixed up. Your word of honor!" Mandozza picked up the receiver.

Brown hesitated a long moment. "I hate like hell to do this," he muttered, half to himself. "I might even hang the Quinley murder on him." And then to Mandozza, "My word of honor."

MANDOZZA called a number—and the brace of the chair broke off, and I was free. That is, free to be on my feet and move, for the cuffs still held my wrists tightly together behind me.

"Is the girl there, Benson? Good! Wait!" And putting his hand over the mouthpiece, Mandozza said to Brown: "Want her brought here?"

"No." Brown was emphatic. "Have him call her to the phone. I'll speak to her. What's this phone number here?"

And Brown did speak to her as he sat there with his gun jammed hard against Mandozza's stomach.

"Vee Brown speaking," he said abruptly. "Benson will let you go. Take a taxi straight to Dean Condon's apartment on Park Avenue. Wong will let you in. Then call this number." And he gave her the phone number Mandozza had told him. "Don't forget the number, and call at once. Put Benson back on the wire."

Mandozza spoke to Benson a minute.

Then they noticed me—for all the good it did. Mandozza had no key to the cuffs.

"Never mind, Dean." Vee grinned. "Wong will file them off. And if he can't we'll have an expert up from headquarters."

"But, Una!" I demanded. "Why not go to her now? Why wait?"

Vee laughed. "If she calls from the apartment and Wong speaks from the apartment we'll know she's safe. Mr. Mandozza and his friends do not exactly inspire me with confidence."

He was right, of course, and we waited. But the call came—and Una was safe.

At Brown's suggestion—or rather, insistence—for he jabbed a gun into Mandozza's ribs, Mandozza saw us to the taxi. Just as we climbed into it Mandozza spoke for the first time since he called Benson, to set the girl free. "It's over and done with," he said, somewhat bitterly and somewhat in resignation, I thought. "Will you tell me, Brown, where you got that gun?"

"Oh—that!" Brown said lightly. "Dean will tell you that I always manage to get a gun when I need one. That's my stock in trade, Mr. Louie Mandozza. Good night." And the cab pulled from the curb.

"Brown," I said as we sped uptown and I made myself as comfortable as possible in the corner of the cab—which was anything but comfortable, with those damned handcuffs biting into my wrists, "I don't know how to thank you. I know you don't like the girl. But I know, now, that friendship comes first with you. You had Mandozza and you let him go. I've misunderstood you. It was a great thing to do for a friend—to do for me."

"For you!" Brown peered at me in the darkness. "You flatter me, Dean—or maybe you flatter yourself—or maybe I would have done it for you. But—God in heaven man—didn't you see me searched? Didn't you see them go over every part of me? Are you so in love with the girl that your brains have stopped working? Don't you wonder where I got that gun —that gun which I held in my hand a good ten minutes before Mandozza had me turn around and I got my chance?"

And when I would have asked him: "Don't apologize; don't look so cowlike. Una Coles is a rather remarkable young lady. When she escaped from that window she came back into the house again before she finally fled." He grabbed me roughly by the shoulders and his voice broke. "Don't you understand? She came into the cellar and saved your life—and my life. So you've got it at last. Yes— it was Una Coles who shoved that gun into my hand. It couldn't have been anyone else."

FORGED KILL

A Dick Bentley Story

by

Erle Stanley Gardner

Author of "The Crippled Corpse," etc.

Silent lay that little graveyard, the ghostly tombstones looming through the fog. And silent, Dick Bentley kept his lonely danger-vigil there. Kept it while murder was being planted—at his very feet!

CHAPTER ONE

"It's Your Funeral!"

DICK BENTLEY, free-lance body-guard, was down in the basement, shooting from the hip, when the summons reached him. Miss Greer, his secretary, held her fingers to her ears and screamed the message at him.

Bentley didn't even try to listen.

A moving target the size of a man, was swinging between two steel plates, back and forth, back and forth. Dick's left gun was trying for the head. The right-hand gun tried for the heart. The roar of the weapons punctuated each appearance of the moving target.

When the sixth shot crashed from the right-hand gun and the trigger of the left-hand gun snapped the hammer down on an empty shell, Bentley switched on the floodlights and regarded his secretary with quizzical humor.

"A client," she said. "She seems to be all agitated. You must come up right away."

Dick reached for cleaning rags, oil, and rod. "Can't come with empty guns," he said.

The girl looked at the target. It had slowed almost to a stop now, swinging gently back and forth with a motion so slight as to be negligible. It was of heavy steel, painted white so that the marks

As the figure stooped there was a spurt of ruddy flame.

of the bullets would show. The figure represented the silhouette of a man, and there was a spattering of black marks about the head, a similar grouping about the heart.

She shuddered and turned away. "Please hurry," she said. "I'm going. This place gives me the creeps!"

Bentley nodded, without looking up as the girl left. He cleaned and loaded his guns, spun the cylinders in a glittering circle, then thrust the weapons into twin shoulder holsters and washed his hands.

Bentley walked up a flight of steps, opened a door, nodded to a janitor who was playing solitaire in front of a furnace, then walked out another door into the lobby. He took an elevator to the ninth floor, walked into his office.

The young woman who stared up at him wore a tight-fitting little hat, a black coat with a fur collar that covered up her neck and chin. Her eyes were large, dark and pathetic.

Miss Greer half turned from the clacking typewriter. "This is Miss Ann Sherwood," she said.

Dick Bentley bowed. "Won't you come in?" he asked, and held open the door of the inner office.

The young woman was lithe, graceful. She had a boyish figure, a swiftly light-footed step, a little lilt to the head, a swing to the shoulders that told of a freedom-loving disposition. She was about twenty-four.

Dick Bentley closed the doors, offered her a chair, took out a package of cigarettes, and went through the formality of offering her one. She reached for it with an eager hand. He noticed that the hand was trembling as she conveyed the cigarette to her lips. He held a match and studied her face by the light of the flame.

The private office was filled with shadow. Dick switched on the lights. The young woman sat down. She kept herself snuggled into the fur collar of the coat.

She sucked in a great lungful of smoke, exhaled appreciatively through her nostrils, sighed, and said: "I want you to help me."

BENTLEY nodded and regarded that fur coat again. The afternoon had not been particularly chilly. San Francisco's usual afternoon fog had been rolling in since three o'clock, but the office was warm.

"Well?" asked Bentley.

The words came with a rush. "I want you to go to a certain place tonight, as soon as it gets dark, and protect a young man who will be there. That young man will be in danger. I'm not going to try to disguise the fact that it's very, very dangerous."

Dick Bentley's slow smile was strangely matter of fact. "All my work is dangerous," he said.

She nodded, a swift nod of nervous acquiescence. "Of course. This is particularly dangerous. You will be well paid."

"Does the young man know I will be there to protect him?" asked Bentley.

"Yes."

"Where is the place?"

"One of the cemeteries."

Bentley raised his eyebrows.

"You will enter the place," she said, "without anyone knowing you are there. You will wait in a certain spot until you see the young man. He will signal you by striking a match and lighting a cigarette. When you see him do that, you will give a low whistle. That will be the signal that you are on the job."

"Then what?" asked Bentley.

"That's all."

Bentley raised his eyebrows.

"After that," she said hurriedly, "you'll just guard him. See that nothing happens to him, protect his life."

Dick nodded. "After he leaves the cemetery," he said casually, "or just while he's there?"

She paused for a moment before replying. "I think," she said slowly, "that just while he is in the cemetery will be long enough."

"O. K.," said Bentley. "What's the story?"

"Story?"

"Yes. You understand, Miss Sherwood, that in my capacity as bodyguard I frequently have to use weapons. A man can't run about using weapons unless he knows something about whom he's shooting at, and why. A person might get into serious trouble taking the wrong side of a case. I want to know who my clients are. I want to be certain that my activities are on the right side."

She bit her lip. "I hadn't thought of that," she said, and there was a quaver in her voice.

Dick Bentley's tone was kind. "Many people don't think of it," he reassured her. "They come to me when they're frightened. They can't think of details during such times of emotional stress. That's why I'm calling it to your attention now."

It was a moment before she spoke. Then she took another deep inhalation of the cigarette, fidgeted uneasily in the chair, and said: "The young man is Paul Sherwood, my brother. He's become rather involved in—in an affair with a married woman. He has to surrender money. It's got to be delivered at a certain place. I think they may mean trouble—"

Dick Bentley laughed. "Shucks, Miss Sherwood, you don't need me. Probably your brother has got tangled up with a bunch of blackmailers. Have him go to the police, or have him come to me himself. I'll talk things over with him. He shouldn't pay money."

She shook her head vehemently. "No, no! That's why I didn't want to tell you. I was afraid you'd say that. This is different. He's got to pay the money.

He's got to go and put the money by a certain tombstone. There can't be any delay, can't be any question. You'll have to guard him. That's all you're hired for. Here—here's some money."

SHE groped in her handbag, brought out a roll of bills. The roll was fat. Dick Bentley caught a glimpse of two ciphers after the figure "one" on the outside bill. She handed over the roll.

He touched her hand as his fingers closed about the money. Her hand was ice cold. The fingers were so clammy, so corpselike that Bentley almost dropped the money.

"Look here," he said, "you're under a terrific strain. How about a little brandy?"

She shook her head, glanced at a wrist watch. "No, thank you. I'm all right. It's five o'clock now. Do you suppose you can be ready in time? You can't afford to miss this, you know. It's got to be handled right on the minute."

Dick nodded, half absently. He finished counting the roll of money. There were eight hundred and fifty dollars in the roll.

"See here," he said, "this is too much money, if this thing's on the level; too little if it isn't."

"No. I want you to be well paid. You're risking your life." And she shuddered.

Dick Bentley snapped his jaw in a sudden decision. "O. K.," he said. "It's your funeral."

"No, no, no!" she screamed. "Don't say that!"

He looked at her, puzzled, then comprehension dawned upon him. She was livid, wild-eyed, hysterical. His words had, somehow, started a train of thought that had snapped her self-control for the moment as one snaps a thread.

"I'm sorry," he said. "I only meant it as a slang expression. You mustn't feel that—"

She smiled wanly. "I'm all right now. It was my fault. Not yours."

"I'll give this money to my secretary and get you a receipt," said Bentley, rising. "What's your address, please?"

She hesitated for a minute. "Seventeen hundred and three Stanyan Street," she said.

Bentley made a note of the address, walked to the outer office. Miss Greer was putting on her hat.

Dick Bentley sat down at the desk. "Look here, Stella," he said in a low voice. "Get me a receipt will you?"

The girl came over to him.

Dick Bentley thrust the money in his trousers' pocket. The girl opened a drawer in the desk. As she did so her face was very close to Dick's. Dick spoke in a low tone.

"Don't move. Keep your ear right close. That's it. Now when that jane leaves the office I want you to follow her as far as you can without attracting attention. Make a note of where she goes and how she gets there."

Stella Greer nodded. "O. K. It's not dangerous?"

"I don't think so, or I wouldn't send you. Go on out now so you can spot her when she leaves the building. Telephone to me when you have the information. Take some money for expenses if you need a cab."

"I've got a dinner date."

"O. K. Don't miss it. Just give her a little once-over when she goes out. Quit when you have to. It's probably not important."

BENTLEY made out the receipt. The girl walked out of the office. Dick blotted the receipt, walked back to the inner office and handed the receipt to Miss Sherwood.

"My secretary was leaving for the evening. I had to scrawl this out myself. I guess you can read it."

She nodded, thrust the receipt into her purse without reading it, got up. Her cold fingers thrust a folded paper into Dick Bentley's hand.

"Here's a map of the cemetery. Go out as soon as it gets dark. Stand somewhere in the shadows. My brother is going to deliver the money back of the tombstone that's marked. Be where you can protect him."

"What time, exactly?" asked Bentley.

"When it gets dark," she said, and moved toward the door, as though she was in a panic to leave the place.

"There are some other details," said Bentley, very courteously, considerately, "that—"

"No. I think not!" snapped Miss Sherwood. She jerked the door open, walked swiftly across the outer office, twisted the knob of the outer door, and pulled it open. She was running by the time the door-closing device had clicked the latch.

Bentley pursed his lips, studied the diagram the young woman had given him. It was a printed plat of the cemetery, one of the sort that are put out to show the location of various lots. There was a lot marked with a cross. It was lot number one hundred and seventy-three.

Dick Bentley slipped some extra shells for his guns into his pockets. He put on a hat and coat, pulled the hat low down on his forehead, lit a cigarette, looked at his strap watch, and waited.

Ten minutes and the telephone rang.

It was Miss Greer on the line.

"I can't tell you much, Mr. Bentley. She walked around the corner to a parking station and got in a Buick coupé. I tried to follow in a taxicab, but she was going too fast. I don't think she saw me, but she was driving like the wind."

"Did you get the number of the car license?" asked Bentley.

"Yes . It's 3M 14 17."

Bentley jotted down the number. "O. K., Stella, thanks."

He hung up, walked across the outer office, slipped a flat automatic from a drawer in a chest of drawers, dropped it in the side pocket of his overcoat, added a couple of extra clips of shells, switched out the lights and went out.

He got in his car, drove up to Van Ness, turned left on Van Ness and paused when he was well out on Mission for a sandwich at a little restaurant which promised to make up in speed of service what it lacked in style.

CHAPTER TWO

Terror of the Tombs

IT WAS still daylight when Bentley parked his car a couple of blocks from the cemetery. He moved unobstrusively through the half light of the foggy dusk, esconced himself in a thick hedge and waited. He was still some distance from the place which had been marked on the map.

As soon as darkness descended the night became cold. Bentley wrapped his coat around him, started picking his way among the somber tombstones, moving like some stealthy shadow along the winding paths.

The fog was thicker here, swirling in, sweeping along the moist grass, clutching at the cold tombstones with twisting tendrils of beady moisture. He could feel the surge of the little fog particles as an almost imperceptible wind swept them onward.

The spot was lonely. It was in an unfrequented section of the cemetery, isolated by hedges. Far down the slope, there was a main highway running to San Mateo. Cars going along that highway gave forth snarling noises of speeding tires and pulsing motors. Aside from that there was utter silence.

Dick Bentley was marooned, alone in a fog-swept city of the dead.

Once he heard a machine turn up the hill. He could hear it grinding up the slope on the other side of the hedge on the opposite side of the cemetery. It was more than two hundred yards away.

Bentley heard the motor stop, thought he heard the sound of voices. He dared not leave his post lest he should miss the young man whom he had agreed to protect. But the sound of that motor made him grasp the automatic in the side pocket of his overcoat, and his eyes were narrowed as they peered into the murky, moist darkness.

After some ten minutes he heard the motor start again, and the car wound its way around a loop in the road, then ran down the hill. The fog swallowed up all sound.

Bentley crouched down so that he would not be silhouetted against such light as came from the sky. He listened intently, but could hear nothing. The fog managed to blanket sound effectually. Then he heard the crunch of steps along the gravel of a pathway. They were quick, short, nervous steps and they were coming his way.

Dick listened, made certain that there was but one person walking toward him. Then he dropped down back of a cold marble tombstone, all slimed with beads of moisture, and waited.

The steps paused, uncertainly, as though the person were listening. Then they came on again, faltering somewhat. The figure loomed up in the darkness, coming along the pathway Bentley had selected as the most probable means of approach.

He could see it, vague and indistinct through the foggy darkness. Then, abruptly, it was upon him, looming unexpectedly large, out of proportion, as is always the case with things seen in fog on a murky night.

Dick tried to make it out.

It was attired in an overcoat that seemed baggy. It wore a cap that was pulled down on the head, and it was walking with nervous short steps. More than that he could not tell, save that he had an impression of slightness of build, despite the distortion of the fog and the bagginess of the overcoat.

THERE was a moon somewhere above the fog, not a full moon, but one which would give some light if it were not for the fog. But that particular section was always foggy during this season of the year. Dick wondered, idly, if it had been selected because it was usually fog-covered. Certainly, a person who wished to make an attack upon another could pick no more appropriate place to lure his victim. That particular section of the cemetery was isolated, quiet, gruesome.

Then the figure paused and lit a match, held it to a cigarette. But the head was bent down, the hands were cupped, and it was impossible to catch a glimpse of the features.

The match was handled inexpertly. It went out before the cigarette tip glowed into red light.

Dick Bentley watched with anxious eyes, tried to shift his position somewhat. If the cigarette had been glowing he would, perforce, have had to give the signal. But he was not to give the signal until the cigarette had been lit, and that would mean another match.

He waited.

The figure seemed uncertain, seemed to waver between flight and going ahead. Then it awkwardly struck another match. This time the cigarette glowed into a red spot and Dick's nostrils caught the aroma of the fragrant tobacco smoke.

But the match had been held in such a manner that he had not been able to see the features .There had been just the red glow of the flame.

Dick gave a low whistle. The figure straightened, paused with head held on one side, listening. Bentley repeated the signal.

The figure walked forward now, and seemed to have suddenly regained its courage. It went unhesitatingly between the tombstones, leaving the walk, stepping over the moist grass of the well-kept lawns, moving toward a definite objective.

Bentley, crouched over, moved from tombstone to tombstone, keeping out of sight himself, but keeping the figure in sight. A sense of impending disaster sombered his thoughts. Perhaps it was the chill of the fog, perhaps the environment, but this city of the dead seemed strangely threatening in its quiet way. It was as though some whispered menace moved through the fog upon silent feet.

The dark blotch of the moving figure paused before a tombstone. It seemed to be making certain of the location. Yet it was not the tombstone that the young lady had checked on the map. It was a good hundred yards away, farther up the hill, nearer the place where that machine had stopped.

The figure stooped.

Dick Bentley closed the distance, moving upon silent feet. The distant moon, seeping stray rays of light through the fog, gave a sort of half illumination sufficient to disclose substantial objects.

The figure deposited something, a small satchel or a dark package, upon the grave, behind the tombstone. Then it straightened, took the cigarette from its lips and tossed it to one side. The figure turned, took one step toward the place where Bentley crouched.

Off to the left there was a stabbing spurt of ruddy flame. The fog boomed with the noise of a revolver shot. The figure doubled, swung to one side in a running half circle.

The place on the left where the flame had showed gave forth additional spurts of fire. Three more explosions boomed through the night. The running figure uttered a sharp scream, shouted words. "Shoot! Shoot!" it said. The voice was high-pitched, shrill with terror.

BENTLEY raised his automatic and fired, once. He shot blindly, into the fog. There were more shots. He fired again.

The shots ceased. There was nothing save chill silence. After the roar of the guns, that moist silence seemed gray and ghostly, utterly unreal. The tombstones showed like silent specters of the night, rising up in ghastly array.

Dick listened and could hear absolutely nothing. The figure in the baggy overcoat had vanished, as utterly as though the ground had swallowed it. There were no more shots, nor was there any noise of running steps from the direction in which the shots had come.

Bentley knew that his first duty was to that overcoated figure. He started back the way he had come. Once he thought he heard feet moving surreptitiously across gravel. He grasped his gun, waited. The sound was not repeated.

Then he decided to chance attracting the fire of the persons who had shot, and gave a low whistle. It was not answered. On the other hand, there were no more shots. He whistled again, louder. There was no sound whatever.

The fog curtain clasped the graveyard to its bosom. The bristling tombstones were as moist fingers clutching at the drifting fog tendrils.

Bentley ran down the hill, keeping to the grass as much as possible. He worked over toward the hedge, waited, listened. He could hear nothing for some two or three minutes. Then he heard the sound of a starting motor, the whir of a machine purring into smooth power. Then the fog swallowed even that noise.

Bentley made a thorough search of the graveyard, moving about the tombstones, automatic clutched in his right hand. From time to time he gave low whistles, but received no response. Regardless of what else might have happened, he realized that the person he had been employed to protect had fled from the scene; fled, also, from his protection, since the flight had taken place while he was shooting at the mysterious assailant who had opened fire from behind the curtain of foggy darkness.

Dick Bentley had a knack of remembering locations. Now he retraced his steps toward the place where the mysterious figure had stood when the shooting started. He found the spot, went to the grave over which the figure had stooped. There was a bundle lying there, a dark, bulky bundle. Bentley picked it up. It consisted of oblong articles wrapped in a rubberized, waterproof cloth. There were elastics snapped about the ends of the bundle.

Dick opened the end and used a pocket flashlight to illuminate the contents. He found slips of paper, blank and unprinted, held together by paper bands. Save for one fact that there was no printing upon the papers, they might have been bank notes, fastened together in bundles of tens, twenties and fifties. He noticed that the sizes of the bundles varied. It was as though a man had been ordered to bring a sum of money in bills of various denominations, and had used these blank paper oblongs to fool someone who would have tested the package in the dark.

Bentley faced the direction in which he had seen the flashes. He was using his pocket flashlight now, and the beam sent weird shadows moving over the graveyard. It also illuminated the drifting particles of moisture which swirled about on the wings of the wind.

He had moved some thirty or forty yards when something attracted his attention. He shifted the beam of the light, then whipped his automatic around so that it was pointed toward the object. For a moment he stood motionless, waiting. Then he moved cautiously forward.

THE object which was thrust out into the beam of the flashlight was a foot, clad in sock and shoe, with the edge of a cuffed trouser leg protruding from around the edge of a tombstone. Dick moved around that tombstone and saw the man.

He was seated against a marble shaft, his face the unmistakable color of death. The eyes were partly open and glassy. The arms hung limply at the side. Near the right hand was the gleam of blued steel.

There was a bullet hole, drilled neatly in the center of the forehead, looking small and round, blued along the edges.

Dick bent over the weapon on the ground. It was a thirty-eight, Smith & Wesson. There was still a bit of heat about the barrel, as he ascertained by placing the back of his hand against the metal. Bentley whistled. Here was something he hadn't bargained for.

He had been guarding the mysterious figure of the young man. There had been shots. Dick had fired into the darkness, and his fire had taken effect upon an adversary he could not even see. Shooting in that dark, at that distance, through fog at an invisible target over an uncertain range, he would have considered the chances more than ten thousand to one against hitting his mark. Yet he had fired twice, and the bullet of one of those shots had, apparently, made a dead-center shot.

Bentley switched out his flashlight and considered the situation. It needed no extended examination to show that the man was dead. It also needed no particular thought to convince Dick that it was highly inadvisable for him to loiter around the place, leaving tracks which could be measured, perhaps, if the ground were soft enough to retain impressions of footprints.

Dick turned, started walking through the darkness, avoiding tombstones and graves, moving, however, with great caution. Then, suddenly he stopped.

The man must have been shot as he was in the act of firing. The natural position for such a man to shoot from would be from behind a tombstone, crouching, just his head protruding over the marble. Yet here was a man who had, apparently, seated himself, back propped against a tombstone, and started firing.

It was incredible.

Dick Bentley went back. He bent over the quiet form, stooped, touched the skin of the face. It was as he had commenced to suspect. The man was cold.

He tried the wrist, lifted the arm. The man had been dead for some four or five hours. . . . But the gun that was on the ground beside this still figure was still warm!

Bentley took a deep breath. After a moment he spat out an exclamation of disgust.

He retraced his steps and paused over the black rubber-covered package. Then he switched on his flashlight again and started making an examination of the ground, searching to find something that would give him some clue as to the identity of the person who had deposited that dark package upon the grave.

He found a place where the soft turf had been pushed down into two little depressions, more than an inch deep, very small and round, hardly more than three quarters of an inch in diameter. Then he found the cigarette end which had been thrown away.

It was a Marlboro, and the white tip was stained with a red smear. It had gone out when it had hit the damp, fog-soaked grass. The part which remained was about two thirds of the length of the cigarette.

Bentley picked up the package of rubberized cloth, opened it again, abstracted some of the paper oblongs, used them to wrap up the cigarette. He slipped the folded papers in his pocket, the cigarette wrapped in them, and walked out of the cemetery. He gained his car, stepped on the throttle, and headed for Stanyan Street.

CHAPTER THREE

Murder Plant

AT number seventeen hundred and three, Bentley parked the car, walked up a flight of steps and rang a bell. A radio was playing loudly, blaring forth a jazz number. There was a child crying somewhere within the house. Steps sounded in the hallway, and a matronly woman with steel-rimmed reading glasses hoisted up on her forehead, surveyed him with kindly eyes through the glass. She opened the door.

Dick Bentley raised his hat. "Do you," he asked, "happen to know a Miss Ann Sherwood who lives here, or somewhere in the neighborhood?"

The blank surprise in the woman's eyes could not have been simulated. "Not here," she said. "She doesn't live in this house. I don't even know any Sherwoods here. There was a family back east we knew years ago. . . . And they didn't have a daughter named Ann. Her name was Shirley."

Dick Bentley smiled, bowed again. "Sorry," he said, "to have disturbed you. Pardon it, please."

The woman watched him down the stairs. "I wish I could help you," she said.

Dick Bentley drove to a telephone, called up a friend at police headquarters. "I want the owner of the car with the license number 3M 14 17," he said.

The voice over the telephone made a jesting remark and asked whether he wanted it right then or when he could get it. Dick grinned and said that he'd take the information when he could get it. He left a number at which he could be called, the number of the drug store at which he had placed the call.

He purchased a newspaper, had a malted milk, and waited.

The bell rang. He went into the telephone booth.

"Buick coupé?" asked his friend at headquarters.

Dick Bentley was mildly surprised. He had rather expected that the license number would have turned out to fit some other car.

"That's the one," he said.

"O. K. The address is ten fourteen San Anselmo Drive, and the name's Lois Wheaton. Sounds like a nice girl, Lois. She didn't run into you, or anything, did she, Dick?"

Bentley felt in no mood for chaffing. "No," he said, "she just planted a corpse on me." He muttered a word of thanks, then hung up the telephone, clamped his lips into a thin line of determination and made for his car.

He was in the general direction of San Anselmo Drive, and he tore through the park, cut across to the south and found the street he wanted. It followed the contours of a slope, and the houses were expensive dwellings set in wide lots.

Dick found the number, a three-storied house with shrubbery around it, and a wide driveway leading to a quadruple garage. There were lights on the lower and third floors. The second floor was dark.

Bentley drove his car a few yards up the street, turned it so that it was on a downhill slope, got out and walked up the steps of the porch. He jabbed a viciously indignant finger into the button which was on the side of the door.

A bell jangled. Steps sounded inside and a dour-faced individual opened the door and regarded him most uncordially.

"I want to see Miss Lois Wheaton upon a matter of grave importance," said Dick Bentley.

The dour-faced individual regarded him with even less cordiality than he had shown upon opening the door. "You have a card?" he asked.

Dick Bentley reached in his side pocket. He took out one of the oblong blank papers which he had extracted from that rubberized package which had been laid on the grave.

"Tell her this is my card," he said.

THE man could not have been more astonished had Bentley slapped his face. He gasped. The eyes blinked rapidly, seemed unable to tear themselves away from the oblong of paper. He tried to speak, and was only able to make an unintelligible sound on the second attempt.

"I say, sir . . . I say . . . Where did you get this?"

Bentley was sure of his ground now. He pushed forward. "Kindly take that to Miss Wheaton, and tell her to see me at once."

The man nodded. "Come in. Be seated," he said. He indicated a reception hall, started to say something, changed his mind, retired abruptly.

Dick lit a cigarette. His eyes were cold and hostile. He fell to pacing the length of the reception hall, puffing smoke as he walked.

There were running steps, the click of heels on stairs, and the girl who had been in his office, who had given the name of Ann Sherwood, came down the wide sweep of stairs. Her face was drained utterly of color. The dark, tragic eyes looked at Dick as though he had been a ghost.

"C-c-come in," she said. "Come into the library . . . please."

The dour individual moved forward. The girl turned to him with a gesture of regal command. "Parker," she said, "take Mr. Bentley's hat and coat."

The dour-faced individual, who looked for all the world as though he had taken a lemon in the dark in place of a piece of candy, and his organs of taste were just apprizing him of the mistake, bowed, extended a hand, took Dick's hat and coat. Dick followed the girl into a spacious living room where a fire blazed in a grate, where deep chairs stood invitingly.

The girl motioned him to a seat, sat down. "I'm sorry I had to give you a false name," she said, slowly. "How did you find me?"

"I'm a detective," said Bentley. "Where's your brother?"

Her face showed startled surprise. "Didn't you stay with him? Isn't he with you?"

"No," said Bentley.

She caught her lip between her teeth, looked at the floor for several seconds, then reached for a cigarette. Bentley made no effort to light it for her. She struck a match, held the flame to the tip of the cigarette.

"I thought I hired you to stay with him and see that nothing happened to him!" she said.

"You did," agreed Bentley, "up to the time he deposited his package. After that your instructions were rather indefinite, as though you rather expected that I wouldn't be seeing your brother after that."

She frowned. "Was there trouble—shooting?"

"Yes," he said, his eyes staring moodily into hers, "there was shooting."

"Was anybody hurt? Tell me, was anyone hurt?"

"One man, killed," said Bentley.

She gasped. "You're sure?"

Bentley nodded. "Quite sure. He was shot through the head. The remarkable part of it is that if I'd gone on about my business, and hadn't searched until I found this man, I'd have read of the body being discovered sometime tomorrow and thought that I'd killed him."

The girl's lips were almost white now. "You—you—mean that you didn't kill him?"

Bentley smiled, shook his head. "No. I think you killed him. At any rate he was dead when you and your friends took him and parked him against the tombstone. Then one of your friends bang-banged a gun and left it beside him. As soon as I fired, that was a signal for you to beat it. You thought you'd framed the murder on me. You thought that I'd think I was the guilty party."

Her dark eyes were wide, staring with a fear that amounted to hysteria. "You mean—I—accuse me—me—"

Bentley nodded, casually. He took the cigarette from his pocket, held it out to her on one of the oblongs of blank paper.

"The brand you smoke," he said quietly. "You lit it, rather clumsily, too. A man would have lit it the first time. You tossed it away when you came to the place where you knew your accomplices could see its red end twisting and turning when you tossed it. That, I suppose, was the signal for the shooting to start. You knew I was there then.

"You'll notice there are some red stains near the end of the cigarette. That's lipstick. You'll also notice that you were your own high-heeled shoes with your masculine costume. That was what made you walk so funny. The marks of your heels are very plainly imprinted in the soft soil near the grave where you deposited the package of oblong papers.

"You told me you were going to put them near one tombstone which you marked on the map. You didn't ever intend to put them there. You only said so so that I wouldn't be near the other end of the cemetery when your friends arranged the body by the tombstone.

"Now I haven't notified the police—as yet. I wanted to hear your story. I knew you were agitated about something when you came to my office. But I didn't think it was a murder. And I didn't think you and your friends would figure me as much of a sap as to think I'd fall for the corpse. It would have been nice to lead me to believe that I'd done the killing— and in self-defense at that. But, unfortunately, the corpse remains your responsibility, Miss Wheaton."

Dick Bentley took a cigarette from his pocket, lit it.

Lois Wheaton's eyes roved helplessly about the room, as though seeking some avenue of escape. It was the look which a trapped animal gives to his surroundings when he hears the footsteps of the approaching trapper.

"I'm sure," she said, "you're mistaken. I gave you a false name and address. There my responsibility ends."

Her voice was flat, wearied.

Dick Bentley shook his head. "I can't take responsibility for the corpse. That's your funeral."

She swayed as though she was going to faint. Dick suddenly became friendly. "Look here, Miss Wheaton. You're not a murderess. You're carrying too big a load. You came to me in the first place because you wanted my help. You've given me your money, you're entitled to my help. Whoever killed this man, it couldn't have been you. Won't you please—"

He saw her eyes widen with alarm, heard a cautious motion behind him. His right hand whipped to the shoulder holster.

"Freddie, don't!" screamed the girl.

DICK BENTLEY felt something cold on his neck just above the collar. It was circular in shape. He knew what that was without the necessity of hearing the voice of the man behind the chair. Slowly, reluctantly, he raised his hands.

He did not take his eyes from the face of the young woman.

"It's about your last chance," he said, "to come clean and get my help instead of fighting me."

The man behind the chair grunted a command. "Shut up talking to her. Stick your hands down behind the back of the chair. Don't try to make a squawk. I'd just as soon blow the back of your neck out as not."

The voice was that of a young man. Dick felt that there was a resemblance between it and the voice of the young woman. "Your brother, I suppose," he said.

"Shut up!" snarled the voice behind him.

"Freddie," pleaded the girl, "that's not the way to get out of this thing. Let's try putting our cards on the table—"

The young man interrupted her. "Sure," he sneered, "and get hung for murder! A fat chance!"

Dick Bentley lowered his arms as he had been commanded. A bit of cloth whipped around them.

"Come and tie him, Lois," ordered the young man.

She hesitated for a moment. The dark eyes glistened with tears. Then she moved over behind Dick's chair. He felt the bite of the cloth, the tug of tension, the slight vibration of the taut cloth as knots were tied in it.

"Now get some rope or tear up a sheet or something. We can't take any chances of his getting loose. Hurry!"

"But, Freddie, what are you going to do? You can't—"

"Don't argue," he said. "Leave this thing to me."

She went from the room. Dick Bentley addressed the young man who kept out of sight. "If you love your sister you—"

Something struck him on the side of the head. It was the barrel of the revolver. He tried to fight off the wave of nauseat-ing darkness which threatened to engulf him. For a moment he succeeded. Then the wave moved upward and caught him.

IT SEEMED like it had been some appreciable time that he was fighting off that darkness. Yet he realized, subconsciously, that it had been almost instantaneous.

He seemed to be coming out of the darkness, but he could not tell how great a length of time had elapsed since he had been bound. He felt the pain pulse in his head. The lights were shining in his eyes, and they seared the dazzling illumination into his very brain. Then he came up out of the haze, and realized what had happened.

He took a deep breath, shouted.

Almost at once there were steps. He heard a door open. A voice said: "Did you call?"

Then there was an exclamation of surprise. He heard the feet break into a half-running shuffle. A shadow fell over his eyes, and the dour-visaged butler was standing over him.

"Good heavens, sir! What is it, sir? Tell me what happened."

Dick Bentley grunted a command. "Cut my hands loose," he said.

The butler bent over the bound wrists. "It's a handkerchief, or a bit of sheet, knotted around the chair, sir. Just a moment. I think I can untie it."

His fingers struggled with the knot, then the cloth loosened. Dick worked his left hand free, then his right. He reached at once for his shoulder holsters. His guns were there.

He got to his feet, fought off a spell of nausea and giddiness, stared at the butler. "All right," he said, grimly, "I'll hear your story."

"My story, sir?"

"Yes. What do you know about all this?"

"Nothing at all, sir. I let you in, and

there was nothing else for me to do unless I was summoned. I heard the sound of people moving around, and then a door banged. I thought you had gone, sir. I thought Mr. Wheaton had let you out without troubling me. He does that sometimes at night, sir. Then I heard your shout. That's all I know."

HE looked Bentley straight in the eyes. His face seemed almost pathetic in its eager anxiety to convey an honesty of expression. "What happened, sir—if you don't mind telling?"

"Freddie Wheaton stuck a gun in my neck, tied me up."

"A gun, sir! Good heavens, there must be some mistake, sir."

Dick Bentley was grim. "Yes," he said, "there was a mistake all right. That lad made the mistake of his life. Come on, we're going to look this place over."

The butler stepped back. "Look it over? The place, sir! You don't mean a search! You can't do that!"

"The hell I can't," said Dick Bentley. His hand flashed to the holster, ripped out a gun. He looked into the astonished eyes of the butler and said: "I don't know how you fit into this picture, but I've played Santa Claus enough for one night. Get started ahead of me, lead the way through the house. Go into every room. Switch on the lights. Don't try anything funny or I'll blow you apart. Get going!"

The butler turned about. "I protest, sir—"

Dick jabbed the gun into his back. "Protest and be hanged. Get going!"

The butler led the way. They went through the ground floor, through conventional rooms, furnished in a conventional, although expensive manner. They climbed stairs, went through upstairs suites of sitting rooms and bedrooms.

"This is Master Freddie's suite, sir," said the butler, switching on the lights as he had in the other rooms, making the an-nouncements in a dull, lifeless tone of voice. "This is his study and sitting room. There's a bedroom, dressing room and bath in beyond."

"Let's take a look at it," said Bentley.

"Yes, sir. It's the same as the other—"

"Go on. I'll do the looking. Never mind telling me what it's like. Turn on the lights."

The butler switched on the lights. The bed looked strange. Dick looked at it. "No sheets on the bed," he said. The butler's tone showed surprise! "Great heavens, that's so, sir!"

Bentley pushed the butler on before him, toward the bathroom. The butler opened the door, clicked on the lights, recoiled. "Good heavens!" he exclaimed.

There on the floor were the sheets from the bed. It needed but one look at them to tell that they had figured in tragedy. Some one had mopped up gruesome stains with those sheets, and now they reposed on the floor of the bathroom, stiff and red.

Dick Bentley paid but little attention to the butler. He stooped, examined the sheets. From the manner in which the stains were smeared, it appeared that the sheets had been used as mops, to wipe up telltale pools from the floor.

Bentley moved into the bedroom, examined the hardwood, waxed floors. Then he went into the study and examined those floors. It was when he reached the outer corner of the room, the one that was on the west and nearest the street, that he found what he sought.

There had been a diligent attempt made to eliminate all the stains, but enough remained to tell the story. There was a stiff, red spot on the edge of the carpet. The back of a chair showed where it had been scrubbed in a futile attempt to remove every trace from it.

"He was shot here," said Bentley, "and then toppled to the floor."

"Who was, sir?" asked the butler.

Bentley stared at him. "You know

him," he said. "You must know him. He's about forty-five or six, partially bald, has a deep cleft in his chin and a mole on the left side of his forehead. He's about medium height, broad-shouldered, and—"

It was evident from the butler's face that he recognized the description.

"O. K.," snapped Bentley, "spill it!"

The dour-faced butler cleared his throat, shifted his eyes. "I'd rather not, sir."

BENTLEY'S hand shot out, caught the man by the collar of his shirt, held him out at the end of a rigid and menacing arm. Bentley's right hand made a fist. "I didn't ask you what you wanted to do. I told you to spill it. And your time's short."

The butler collapsed into wheedling acquiescence. "Please don't drag me into this, sir. That is, don't tell my employers that I gave out any information. But it's some sort of blackmail, sir. I don't know what it's about. But they're both mixed in it, both Master Freddie and his sister.

"And this man that you mention, sir, and his partner, sir, are the ones who have been getting the gravy. I don't know how much they've collected, but it's a good deal. They come and get money every once in a while. Sometimes they get it from Freddie, sometimes from Miss Lois."

Dick Bentley's brows were level, his eyes stern. "So they try to drag me in on a murder to get rid of blackmailers, eh?"

"I don't know, sir. I'm sure I don't know!"

"O. K. Who is this man, who's his partner?"

"I'm sure I couldn't say, sir. I only know that he gave the name of Gregory. His partner is a tall man, over six feet, very slender and quite dark. He may be foreign. He usually comes with Gregory. Sometimes he doesn't come, but he never comes alone. I've never heard his name.

When they are at the door it is always Gregory who does the talking. But I couldn't tell you anything else about either of them."

Bentley pursed his lips. "Payments made in cash or by check?" he asked.

"I'm sure I don't know, sir. And I wouldn't want to be quoted in the matter at all, sir. You see, I have—er—that is to say, sir—some of my information has been obtained surreptitiously, sir."

"Yeah," said Bentley, "I know." He looked around him at the room. "Tell me if they've taken anything, suitcases or anything like that."

The butler opened drawers and the door of a closet, surveyed the clothes which were hung there. "Yes, sir. Master Freddie has taken a suitcase, sir. He's evidently packed it with a supply of clothes."

Dick Bentley grunted, squinted his eyes in thought. He crossed the room to the telephone, thought better of it, turned away. "Stick around where you can hear the telephone," he said. "I'll give you a ring after a while. If they come in I want to know it."

The butler fidgeted. "I'll do my best, sir. But I'm a dreadfully sound sleeper, sir. When I once get to sleep I never hear the doorbell or the telephone. I'm sorry, sir."

"Don't go to sleep then," said Bentley.

"I'll try, sir. But sitting up alone, you know, sir, one sometimes starts to doze, and if I ever close my eyes I'm gone."

Bentley stared at him meditatively. "I see," he said. "Can you guarantee to keep awake for an hour and a half?"

The butler nodded.

"O. K.," said Bentley. "I'll call you a couple of times during that hour and a half. If Freddie and his sister come back tell them that I've got to see them. Tell them they're making fools of themselves. I'm the best friend they've got, see? I've taken their money to give 'em protection, and there's no reason not to accept it."

The butler wet his lips. "Protection from murder, sir? Surely, sir, you don't mean that message in just that way, sir!"

Dick Bentley stared at the butler. His eyes were dark and moody. His jaw was thrust forward. "You give 'em my messages," he said. "That's all you need to do."

CHAPTER FOUR

The Man in 19

AFTER the butler had let him out, Bentley jumped in his car and raced to police headquarters, went into the identification department, cornered a man he knew there.

"Listen, Pete, I want some dope on blackmailers. You got a file?"

"Yeah, sure. Know anything about the guy you want?"

"A tall man with a dark complexion."

The officer laughed. "You're a hell of a detective. Help yourself. They're classified according to fingerprints, and there's an index of methods of operation. There's a file of photographs. Look 'em over. You'll find it's pretty well thumbed up. We have more people sneak in here to look over this file than almost any other."

"Uh huh," said Bentley. He went through the photographs, looking, not for a tall man, but for a photograph of the man he had seen in the fog-drenched cemetery. He found him at last. The name was not Gregory, but Rankin, Frank Rankin. There was considerable information about him, including the names of known associates. Bentley ran down the names of the known associates, and found a man named "Slim" Spinale, who had been christened Tony. This man was dark, spare, tall, listed as a suspect. He had been arrested three times, had been released twice when the case blew up

because of missing witnesses, and acquitted by a jury once because of insufficient evidence.

Bentley secured a list of addresses where this man might be found, also a list of aliases under which he was reputed to have worked. He was a man who kept much in the background, usually working in connection with, or through others.

Bentley put in a call for the Wheaton residence, heard the voice of the butler.

"Anything new?"

"Not a thing, sir."

"Do you know where Freddie or his sister keep their check books?"

"Yes, sir."

"Look them up. See if there's been any big withdrawals within the last few days."

"Yes, sir. Shall I do it while you wait, sir?"

"No. I'll call back."

"Yes, sir. Where are you now, sir? That is, are you near the house?"

"Within a few blocks at a drug store," lied Bentley easily. "I'll have to go uptown in a few minutes, though, so I'll give you a ring from town."

"Yes, sir. Thank you, sir."

The receiver clicked. Bentley left headquarters, jumped into his car and made speed for San Anselmo Drive. It was still foggy. In the downtown district the fog was high, reflecting back the lights of the city in a red glow. As he got out to the western district, the fog hung lower, formed globules on his windshield. He had to keep his wiper going, continually.

There was a drug store a few blocks from the house. It was open. Dick Bentley parked the car, telephoned the house. Parker's voice answered the telephone at once.

"Yes, sir. I've found the books, sir. There was a withdrawal of ten thousand dollars in cash, sir, in Miss Lois's book, sir. It almost wiped out her account, sir. You see, their father left them the principal of the estate in a trust. They can get the income from time to time, sir."

"O. K.," said Bentley, "stay awake as long as you can. I'm going to town. I may call you later on."

HE hung up, got in his machine, ran a few blocks up the street, turned it, parked at the curb, got out and walked to a place from which he could see the three-storied house. He waited, his coat huddled about him against the chill of the fog.

He had but ten or fifteen minutes to wait. A door closed somewhere in the rear of the house. There was the noise made by a garage door sliding open. A coupé slid smoothly down the driveway. The lights switched on. The form of the butler was outlined against those lights.

Dick Bentley waited until the car had passed him, then he ran to his own car, got in, took off the brake, coasted into motion, slammed the clutch in and turned on the ignition. His car roared into instant speed. He ran without lights, sweeping down the contours of the drive on the trail of the coupé.

The coupé ran at high speed. Dick switched on his lights after he had reached the intersection of the main boulevard. He had no difficulty whatever in trailing the car. Apparently the idea of being shadowed was the last thing which had entered the head of the butler.

The coupé ran down Geary Street, slowed when it got to the outskirts of the fashionable hotel district. Evidently the butler was looking for a parking space. He failed to find one, circled a block twice, and then stopped the car directly in front of a hotel.

A uniformed footman opened the door. The butler jumped out, went to the back of the car. They raised the cover of the rear, started dragging out suitcases and hat boxes. The space had been crammed with baggage. The butler gave

it to the doorman with instructions, handed out a coin, jumped back into the coupé, and slid once more into traffic.

Dick followed, sliding in behind the coupé. He followed for half a dozen blocks, saw that the coupé was headed back toward San Anselmo Drive. Then he swung off to the right, drove to the right, up to Bush, down Bush to Kearney, over to Columbus Avenue, and started a round-up of the places where Slim Spinale might be found.

Time was too precious to waste on the mere chance of running into his quarry. He had to make judicious inquiries from men who might or might not be "safe."

He obtained half a dozen blind leads, finally got a whimpering stoolie in a corner of a dance-hall joint. The stoolie's eyes betrayed that he was in a panic. "Honest, Mister Bentley, I ain't seen 'm for a month. What you want with him?"

"Just want to talk with him."

"About what?"

"About a murder, 'Dopey.' You wouldn't want to give me a false steer on a murder rap would you, and get your own head in a noose?"

"Geez no!"

"Well, kick through then. Where is he?"

"Cripes, I don't know. You ain't a bull. You ain't got the right to shake me down like this and threaten to give me a murder rap if I don't squeal. I've told you ten times I don't know—"

The words were blocked by the impact of Dick Bentley's open hand as it smashed against the weak mouth of the stoolie.

Dopey fell back against a chair, crashed the chair to the floor, tugged at a table cloth, pulled the salt, sugar, ash tray over on top of him. A broad-shouldered bouncer started moving toward the commotion. Dance-hall girls paused to stare. The stoolie crawled from beneath the table cloth. His face was dead white. His eyes were glittering with rage and fear.

It was a look such as a cornered rat might give to a terrier.

"Hey, what's this. Out with you!" roared the bouncer.

Dick Bentley met his eyes. "Oh," he said, "yeah?"

"Yeah," said the bouncer, and made that swift motion which would have caught the arm of an ordinary man, twisted it up behind his back, giving him the proper position for the bum's rush.

But Dick Bentley moved just far enough to avoid that clutching wrist. His left snapped up. "Starting anything?" he asked.

The bouncer whirled back on balance. "Get out," he said.

"O. K.," said Bentley. He walked out, people staring at him, the bouncer walking a pace or two behind, evidently debating the advisability of saving his face by some show of violence, and deciding against it.

BENTLEY pushed aside the swinging doors, moved out to the street. He crossed the street, eased his way into a cigar stand, and waited. It was less than three minutes before Dopey came sliding out of the swinging doors, glanced about him, started going along the sidewalk, hugging the doors.

Bentley let him get a lead, then followed.

The chase led for a matter of three blocks. Then Dopey oozed through a door and disappeared. Dick squared his shoulders, moved forward until he found a dark doorway within a few feet of the place where Dopey had disappeared, and waited.

Within five minutes Dopey was out again. Bentley heard the sound of the door opening and closing, then the shuffling feet on the sidewalk. Dopey was coming back the way he had gone, and he was following his habit of hugging in close to the doorways, ready to duck for cover at the first sign of danger.

Bentley reached out with his hand, caught Dopey's coat by the shoulder, jerked him back and around, snaked him into the dark doorway almost before Dopey knew that he had been grabbed.

"So," said Bentley, "you do want to hang, eh?"

Dopey stared up at him with wide eyes. His white lips moved but he made no sound.

Bentley shook him. "Spill it," he said.

Dopey found his voice. "Geez, leggo! You ain't got nothin' on me. You ain't nothin' but a private dick. You can't pin nothin' on me."

Bentley grinned. "Yeah," he said, "maybe up to ten minutes ago I hadn't. But then I told you that Slim was wanted on a murder rap. You knew it then. And, just because you got peeved at me because I popped you one, you had to run up and tell Slim. That makes you an accessory after the fact. You're just as guilty as Slim is, right now."

Dopey writhed under the firm grasp of Bentley. "Geez!" he sniffled, "Give a guy a break won't youse?"

Bentley shook him again. "I'll give you just as good a break as you give me," he said.

Dopey whimpered, sniffled. Then he raised his eyes. "Up the stairs, second floor, room number nineteen," he said. "For God's sake don't tell him I squealed!"

Bentley released his grasp. "On your way!" he said, and pushed Dopey out onto the sidewalk. Then he moved out of the doorway, walked boldly to the doorway from which Dopey had emerged, pushed the door open, and walked in.

There was a little oblong of hallway, then a flight of stairs, very narrow, very dirty, and very steep. They stretched upward into a mysterious gloom. But Bentley did not concern himself with those stairs. He merely waited in the little oblong of smelly half light until he was satisfied Dopey had disappeared, convinced that Slim Spinale was receiving visitors.

Then Dick opened the door again, walked out on the sidewalk, moved purposefully to the corner, looked up and down the street. He walked a block, paused on the next corner, looked and waited. On the third corner he found a uniformed officer.

Bentley introduced himself, showed his credentials as a private detective. "I think I got something on Slim Spinale for blackmail," he said. "Slim's holed up in a rooming house three blocks from here. I'd like to have you go up with me. It won't take five minutes, and I think I've got the deadwood on him. The department's been anxious to hang something on that baby for a long time.

"If I've got the stuff, you make the pinch and get the credit. If I haven't, there won't be any harm done. I'll just ask him a couple of questions."

The officer accepted a cigar, nodded his acquiescence. Dick led him down the side street to the door, opened the door, started up the flight of steps.

"Number nineteen it is," he said, "on the second floor."

THEY went up the stairs. Dick found number nineteen, the dirty door having a chalked number on it. The door was closed, but a ribbon of light came through the bottom.

"Tough neighborhood," said the officer.

"Yeah," said Bentley, made a fist of his right hand and banged peremptorily on the panels.

"Who is it?" asked a voice.

"Dick Bentley, private detective. Want to talk with you. Open up!" said Bentley.

There was a moment of rustling activity from the other side of the door.

"I ain't got nothing to talk over with you," said the voice from behind the door.

"Going to open up, or shall I get it open?" asked Bentley pleasantly.

There followed more rustling sounds.

"I'll open," said the voice.

Dick Bentley abruptly crouched down on his heels, motioned the officer to one side.

The door flew open. Light glinted from nickeled steel. A gun roared twice. It had been thrust out, waist high, fired with the same motion that pushed it out.

Bentley reached up. The gun was within six inches of the top of his head, spitting lead, the explosions booming through the smelly corridor. Bentley's fingers closed over the wrist that held the gun, twisted. The gun roared once more, then thudded to the floor. Bentley heaved his weight against the door. The door crashed inward, sweeping the man on the inside off his balance. He fell with a jar that shivered the cheap building with vibrations. He was mouthing curses, kicking.

Dick Bentley jumped over the kicking feet, avoided a knife that glittered through the air in a sweeping arc. The uniformed officer grabbed a foot, swung the slim body of the struggling man away from the door, crashed a nightstick down on the wrist that held the knife.

As the knife dashed from the nerveless hand, the officer pulled out handcuffs. Slim Spinale lay very still, staring up at them with a white face.

The room was a cheap affair, the walls littered with pictures of women cut from the artist-model magazines. There was a pine bureau, the drawers open, a few ash trays, well filled with butts, a bed that sagged in the middle, covered with grimed blankets and a comforter that was slick with dirt. A couple of cane-bottomed chairs and a frayed rug completed the furniture. There was a cheap pasteboard suitcase half filled with clothes on the bed.

"What you got against him?" asked the officer.

Dick Bentley grinned. "Assault with a deadly weapon with intent to commit murder," he said.

The officer stared. "That all?"

Bentley shrugged his shoulders. "Ain't it enough?"

"Didn't you have something on him when you came in?"

Dick nodded. "I wanted to talk with him, about some blackmail."

Slim Spinale took heart. He spoke up. "You birds ain't got nothing on me. I was within my rights. You can't come bustin' in here that way!"

The officer grunted. "Yeah," he said, "what was you doin' with that gun, and where did you get that knife?"

Spinale lapsed into silence.

BENTLEY walked to the suitcase, examined the contents. Then he walked to Spinale, bent over the man's middle. His questing fingers touched something bulky. He ripped open the man's vest and shirt, disclosed a leather money belt next to the undershirt. He opened one of the pockets.

It was crammed with twenty-dollar bills. The bills were new. He opened another pocket. That held ten hundreds. There were other pockets. He motioned to them. The officer felt with his fingers, grunted.

"Sure as hell dough heavy," he said.

"Yeah," observed Bentley, "hoarding."

"You birds ain't got a thing on me," said Spinale, more as a matter of formula than with any hope.

Bentley regarded the handcuffed figure, seated on the floor, looking strangely frightened and woebegone. Here and there in the rooming house were signs of motion. Occasionally furtive footsteps went past the door and sought the street. There was no other indication that the

revolver shots had been heard. It was a crook rooming house. The occupants were creatures of the night, softly gliding into its shadows.

"Maybe," said Bentley, "if you'd tell me exactly what happened to Frank Rankin, I might be able to make things easy for you."

Spinale closed his mouth, tightly.

"Try and make me talk," he said.

Bentley grinned. "Take him away, officer. The charge is assault with a deadly weapon. You're a witness."

The officer grunted. "There's more to this than assault," he said.

"Is there?" asked Bentley innocently. "He's a blackmailer, but the D. A. would rather put him over on assault. It's easier to get witnesses to testify."

The officer tugged Spinale to his feet. "Come on," he said.

"I'll report later," said Bentley. "You take the credit of the pinch. Throw him in. Maybe he'll talk by morning. How much has he got on him?"

The officer nodded. "Better count it while we're here together. He might claim I rolled him."

They counted the money, spreading it out on the bed. Spinale watched them with black, furious eyes. He was silent. There were five thousand dollars in the belt.

Bentley nodded. He looked at Spinale and said: "How come it's an even five?"

"What'd you think it'd be?" asked Spinale, "a hundred grand?"

Bentley shook his head. "A two-way split," he said.

Spinale spat out an epithet, said to Bentley: "If you're so damned wise go out and find out what you want to know."

Bentley nodded. "I will," he said, and took to the stairs.

CHAPTER FIVE

Two-Way Split

DICK BENTLEY slid his car to a stop out on San Anselmo Drive once more. He adjusted a black leather mask over the upper part of his face, wrapped himself in an overcoat. He had changed his hat for a cap, and he pulled that cap down low over his eyes.

He moved through the foggy night with the purposeful certainty of a man who is going about a task that has been thoroughly rehearsed. He went around the back of the residence that loomed dark and mysterious, tried a window. The window was fastened. Bentley used a jimmy, and the window came open. He crawled in, paused to listen. The house was dark and silent save for a rhythmical *creak-creak-creak* which came from a room on the second floor.

Bentley moved softly and cautiously about the lower floor. He did not take anything, but disarranged everything. He opened drawers, lifted out their contents, spilled them on the floor. He opened a writing desk, strewed the papers all about, as though there had been a hasty search for some particular paper. Then he eased his way up the stairs, went toward the sound of the creaking. It was in a back room. He cautiously opened the door.

Parker, the butler, was sitting in a rocking chair, gently rocking back and forth. He was in slippers, and shirt sleeves. He was smoking a pipe, and there was a look of serene self-satisfaction on his features.

Dick Bentley moved into the room.

The butler detected the motion, glanced up, saw the masked man, holding a gun in front of him, the barrel pointed directly at his face. He lost the look of serene complacency, made a dive for his pocket, thought better of it, and elevated his hands.

"What the devil?" he asked.

Bentley prodded the gun into his ribs. "Get up," he husked.

The butler got up.

"Upstairs, into the attic," ordered Bentley.

The butler started to argue, received a jab of the gun in his ribs, and became docile. Bentley herded him up the stairs, into the attic, found some old rope around a trunk, tied him up.

He tied him with loose knots, but used lots of rope. Within a matter of a few minutes the butler could free himself from those knots. But Bentley pretended an amateurish awkwardness about the tying process. He inserted a makeshift gag, searched the butler's clothes, took out a key ring and a watch, some few dollars in small paper currency, and some loose silver. Then he left the attic, padded down the stairs.

On the second floor he worked with the same efficiency of disorder that he had used on the lower floor. He jerked out drawers, spilled contents, even ripped open two of the mattresses, spilled their contents. He did the same on the third floor.

Then he went down to the garage, slammed open the garage door, found the Buick coupé. He stepped on the starter, raced the motor, crawled out of the driveway in low gear. Then he drove the car half a block down the street, shut off the motor, walked back to the house on noiseless feet.

He took off his shoes, climbed the stairs until he was in the hallway at the foot of the attic stairs, looked about for a closet, found one, left the door slightly ajar, and waited.

The big house was uncannily silent.

After a few minutes he heard the sound of motion from the attic. It was as though a big body were rolling and twisting, writhing and kicking. After five or ten minutes the sounds ceased. Then there were feet on the stairs. Through a small crack in the closet door, Bentley could see Parker, the butler, slip out of the attic stairway, survey the disordered confusion of the upper floor.

The butler ran from room to room. He returned to the corridor, started down the stairs. Dick glided out and followed him silently. The butler ran down to the lower floor, back through living room, dining room and serving pantry into the kitchen.

BENTLEY followed him upon feet that gave forth not the slightest sound. He found the butler in the kitchen, frantically pawing in a flour bin, arm up to the shoulder.

He could see the expression on the man's face, the worry, the agony of uncertainty, then the flood of relief which suffused his countenance. He withdrew his arm. In his hand was clutched a package, wrapped in a white dish towel.

Bentley stepped out from behind the door, into the room. "O. K., Parker," he said. "I'll take it."

The man gave a yell of surprise, of rage. His hand flashed around to his hip pocket, paused as he realized he had taken out the gun. He spat forth expletives, looked about him for a weapon, then, with the courage of desperation, flung himself upon Bentley.

Dick raised the hand which held the gun. He brought it down sharply upon the skull of the butler. The man quivered, gave a whooshing sigh, and slumped to the floor.

Bentley slipped a length of rope about his wrists and feet, bound him, this time securely. He took the package which had been in the flour bin, beat the surplus flour off the cloth with his hand, removed the cloth, and found a package wrapped in paper, tied with a string. On top of the package was another little package, fastened with a rubber band. Taking off

that band, Bentley gazed upon a sheaf of bank notes.

He grunted his satisfaction, pocketed the currency, took the paper package, put on his shoes and left the house. He drove at once to the downtown hotel, walked into the lobby, looked at the registrations of the evening.

There was one registration of a brother and sister. The names were not Wheaton, but Dick was sure enough of his ground to go to the house phones and ring the room.

The voice which answered, tremulous with fright, was the voice of Lois Wheaton.

"I'm coming up," said Bentley. "Open the door."

He hung up the telephone, went up on the elevator, found the door of the suite, knocked on it. After he had knocked the second time, the door opened, and the white face of Lois Wheaton stared into his.

"Freddie in?" asked Bentley.

She gulped, hesitated, shook her head.

"Forget it," said Bentley, walking into the room. "You don't need to be afraid of me. You should have called me sooner, that's all." He kicked the door closed behind him.

The room was a sitting room of a suite, a bedroom opened off on either side. Bentley walked to the table, pulled out the package of currency.

"Here's the five thousand dollars that Parker got as his cut," he said. "Slim Spinale has got the other five. He's in jail. I'll make charges against him in the morning. You can get the money back through the D. A.'s office, but you'd better hire a lawyer to see that you don't have too much delay in getting it. There'll be ambulance chasers hanging around first thing in the morning, smelling a fee.

"O. K. for that. Here's a package that I s'pose has got the papers in it that you were being blackmailed over. Being a gentleman, and knowing it's none of my business, I'm turning 'em over to you unopened.

"Come on out, Freddie. It's O. K. I ain't got any hard feelings. It's all in the day's work as far as I'm concerned. And I know you got a little panicky. Can't blame you."

The door of one of the bedrooms opened. Freddie Wheaton came out. He was in pajamas and dressing gown. He was two or three years younger than his sister. His face was soulful, impractical, the face of an artist or a poet. He had his sister's large, dark eyes, and his face was very, very white.

Bentley sighed. "Just about as I figured," he said. "These two guys were shaking you two down. The butler was in with 'em all the time. You didn't know it. You trusted the butler. Then the guy you knew as Gregory tried to cross the others. He offered to get you all the proofs for ten grand. You didn't have that much coming in under the trust, but you borrowed it.

"Gregory came up. The butler wasn't to know about it, but he found it out. You paid over the ten grand to Gregory, and then something happened. What was it?"

He paused, peering sharply at Freddie.

FREDDIE gulped. "I stepped into the bathroom. There was a shot. I came out. Gregory had been shot through the head. The papers were gone and so was the ten thousand."

Bentley nodded. "About the way I figured it must have happened. I couldn't figure you being so dumb as to pay over the ten grand and not get the papers, though."

Freddie flushed. "I took the papers and put them in a drawer in my desk. When Gregory's partner killed him he must have known right where the papers were."

Bentley yawned. "Yeah," he said, "Parker killed him. The butler found out

about the cross. He couldn't bear to see those papers get away. They'd been a source of income. So he shot Gregory and then I s'pose he was the one that hatched up the plot about having the girl go to my office, retain me to snoop around the graveyard.

"Then they'd plant the corpse, trick me into shooting, dust out, and when the stiff was found the next morning, I'd think I'd done the job. He was a known blackmailer, so the butler suggested that you leave some blank paper on one of the graves. The cops would find it, figure that some one had been ordered to deposit some coin on the grave as blackmail, that they'd taken blank paper, that there was a gun fight and Gregory got rubbed out.

"Knowing Gregory as a crook, they wouldn't bother too much about the murder. I'd think I was the guy that did it, and keep quiet because I had some coin and didn't want to mix a client in it. Having given me a phony address, you thought I couldn't come back on you.

"The butler pretended to be sort of a father adviser to you, and you did as he said. Whatever's in that package, you didn't want it to come out, and you knew it would if there was an investigation over a murdered man found in your home.

"You also probably had the assurance of the butler that the police would claim Freddie was guilty, seeing the guy was blackmailing him.

"Well, it's all over now. You'd better burn these papers and get indefinite about the blackmail. I know Slim Spinale. He's yellow. He'll squeal to save his neck. I think your butler will, too. They'll probably both try to frame the other."

Freddie nodded, looked at his sister. "The papers concerned an indiscretion of mine—"

"What the hell do I care what they concern?" said Bentley. "Ain't I working for you? Didn't I take your sister's money. Here, let me have 'em."

He crossed to the fireplace, tossed in the crumpled remains of an evening newspaper, struck a match, put the papers on top of the flame. "They'll burn," he said.

"How did you know?" asked the girl.

Bentley laughed. "A cinch. You kids were babes in the woods. You weren't the kind that could have engineered a cold corpse on me as a victim of my gun. It took a hardened, resourceful crook to think up that fast one. I knew, therefore, some one had your confidence who was a crook.

"When I showed the blank paper to the butler as a calling card I knew at once he knew the game was up, as far as the corpse business was concerned, and that I'd traced you. That meant the butler either had to be a real friend or a crooked one. When I found only five grand on Spinale and knew that ten had been paid, I knew there was a two-way split. If Spinale had a partner it was bound to have been one who was on the inside. That meant Parker, the butler.

"Shucks, that case was a cinch. What makes me sore is that damned Parker trying to frame me with a cold kill. I might have fallen for it."

Lois Wheaton's eyes filled with tears. "Oh, you're wonderful! I'm so glad we called you!

Bentley's eyes were moody. "If I'd been able to play it a little different," he said, "I might have coaxed those two into a gun fight and rubbed 'em out, so there wouldn't have been any notoriety. But you keep indefinite about that blackmail, and I guess I can work it so you won't be bothered."

The fire on the grate blazed merrily. The papers sputtered and crackled. Dick Bentley crossed to the telephone. "Gimme police headquarters," he said.

It's bad enough to have to handle lawyers, crooks and frantic parents in a snatch-gang set-up. But all that didn't faze Cardigan. It wasn't until a lot of job-minded cops started in to gum the works that he really began to worry. Then it was red rage and flaming lead in the fastest clean-up of his thrill-packed career.

Cardigan grabbed the shotgun—leaped through the window.

Rogues' Ransom

A Cardigan Story

by

Frederick Nebel

Author of "Tailormade Clue," etc.

CAPTER ONE

Snatch-Racket Stuff

THE toll-bridge made a black fret-work against the setting sun. The wheels of the train clicked more leisurely and the Pullmans had a lazy side-to-side heave. The hills beyond the Ohio were burned brown and the river itself was flat and copperish.

"Wheelburgh!" intoned the porter.

Cardigan needed a shave and a clean shirt. The ride had been hot. His shaggy crop of hair was damp; it looped wetly around his ears, down his forehead. He shoved it back with his left hand, used his right to yank on a faded gray fedora. As he rose, towering, the porter came along with a whiskbroom.

"Nix," Cardigan said, and flipped him a quarter.

He had a brown Gladstone that was new years ago. He picked it up and went down the aisle; reached the vestibule and pushed on into the next Pullman. Half-way down the aisle, a girl sitting alone dropped a handkerchief. Cardigan stooped, picked it up and thrust it into her out-stretched hand.

He muttered: "Not too close, Pat."

"O. K.," she said.

He rolled on to the next vestibule, set down his bag and drew a packet of cig-arettes from his pocket. They were damp and crumpled and he lit one and it didn't taste good. The Pullman sloughed over switches. The *bong-bong* of the loco's bell was more resonant as the train moved past outlying freight sheds. A porter hauled bags into the vestibule, raised the metal leaf in the platform and opened the door. The train slid into the station and stopped.

Cardigan swung down the steps, barged through a flock of red-caps and lugged his bag up the platform. Going into the waiting-room, a newsboy shouted in his face: "Read all the latest news about big kidnaping!"

"Here, kid."

He bought a paper, dropped his bag, snapped the paper open and down with a loud report.

POLICE FOLLOW NEW CLUES IN MILBRAY CASE

"Cardigan, ain't you?"

Cardigan looked over the top of his paper; saw first the baggy knees of black alpaca trousers; next, the tarnished buckle of a broad belt that girded a generous paunch. The black alpaca coat was open and Cardigan followed the plain white shirt up to a black bow tie; then to a hard round chin, a humorless mouth, a scraggly mustache, a nose like a twist of rope—and China-blue eyes, steady, probing.

He said: "Selling something?"

"Advice, maybe."

Cardigan regarded him for a brief mo-ment, then bent down, scooped up his bag and started past. A big freckled hand closed on his left arm. He looked at the hand and then at the man's China-blue eyes.

He said: "Take your advice and that hand, stranger, and go places."

The man didn't say anything. He smiled humorously and turned back the lapel of his coat.

"Badge 'n' everything, huh?" Cardigan said.

"And the name's Michaels." He lifted his thumb. "There's an empty office down there. I want to talk to you."

Over Michaels' head Cardigan saw Pat Seaward. She was standing just inside the platform entry holding a black patent-leather suitcase and watching him with a cool, quiet look. He made no gesture.

"Sure," he said to Michaels.

THEY went down past the baggage room and entered a small cubicle of an office furnished with two chairs and a roll-top. The office was hot as an oven and smelled of coal dust. Michaels closed the door, turned sluggishly, took off his hard straw hat and mopped the sweatband with a handkerchief. His hair was dry, thick, reddish; it bunched down over a low forehead, overlapped the back of his collar. He fanned himself with his hat.

"Now get this, Cardigan," he said. "We know all about you. We know you're an A-1 dick. But we don't need you here. We don't want you clowning around Wheelburgh. He spoke in a throaty monotone, thick and harsh. "That train east is a nice one. Grab it and give New York a break. We don't need you."

"Is that all?"

"That's all."

Cardigan picked up his bag again and started toward the door. Michaels put his broad bulk between.

"Where you going?"

"Hotel," Cardigan said. "Bath, shave, drink, meditation."

"You can do all that on that train."

Cardigan dropped his bag and jammed his fists against his hips. "Copper, I'm going to a hotel. For a few days I'm going to live in your lousy city, not because I like it, but because I've got a job here. All this bright conversation on your part is just a lot of bushwa."

"It's worth its weight in gold, Cardigan."

"I'm off the gold standard." He picked up his bag and walked around Michaels.

Michaels grabbed him. Suddenly his big freckled hands slapped Cardigan's pockets.

"Cut it!" Cardigan snapped.

Michaels grabbed his wrists. "Where is it?"

"What?"

"Your rod."

"Fat-head, the Cosmos Agency has a license to operate in this state!"

"The license don't say anything about packing a gun."

Cardigan's eyes drooped. "Right away you're getting lousy, huh?"

"Where is it?" Michaels nodded to the Gladstone. "Open that."

Cardigan eyed him darkly. Then he swore. Then he took a ring of keys from his pocket, selected one and opened the bag. He shoved his hand down beneath his linen, drew out a gun and hefted it in his palm.

"I'll take it," Michaels said.

"O. K.," Cardigan said.

He half-turned, hurled the gun. It smashed a window pane and went outside into the yard.

Michaels reddened. "Tricks, eh?"

"You started it."

Michaels had his gun out. "Come on. We'll get it."

"You want it. You go get it."

"Get outside, Cardigan!"

Cardigan sat down. "Waving that rod don't kid me, Michaels. You want my gun. You go out and get it. I know a frame when I see it and you're trying to frame me."

Michaels went to the door, looked out. He called: "Hey, Brady!"

A uniformed cop came down from the waiting room and Michaels said: "Watch this guy, Brady. He's funny."

"O. K.," the cop said, and twirled his nightstick.

Michaels went on down the corridor, found a door near the end and shoved out into the yard. His heavy shoes crunched cinders. He reached the broken window, looked in and saw Cardigan sitting on the chair. Then he swung around and his eyes swept back and forth across the cinders. He saw no gun and he saw that there was no place where it might be concealed. The cinder field was flat and stretched to the nearest rails, fifty feet beyond. He cursed. He turned and saw Cardigan leaning in the window. He reddened. Then he crunched around on his heel and reentered the building, reentered the office.

"Things get funnier," he said, husky-voiced. Some of the red color of his face seemed to have gone to his eyes.

Cardigan picked up his bag. "Well, I'll be going."

Michaels' face looked bloated. He stepped in front of Cardigan.

"Get out, get out," Cardigan said.

Michaels stepped aside. The cop took this as a hint and lowered his nightstick. Cardigan swung out of the office and went hard-heeled toward the waiting room. He didn't pause once. He went straight to the sidewalk and climbed into a taxicab.

"The Wheelburgh," he said.

THE room was big, on the fifth floor. The hotel was on a grade. The fifth-floor window overlooked smoke-grimed roofs; and beyond these were warehouses, freight yards, and beyond all, the copperish river. There was a red haze in the air, the wake of a sun gone down. The hills made a bowl and in the center of the bowl lay the city; hot, smoky, unlovely.

Cardigan had shaved and put on a fresh white shirt, but it made him look no less shaggy. He was good to look at in a hard male way. He was cramming a pipe when a knock sounded on the door.

"Who's it?"

"Me, chief."

He let Pat Seaward in, closed the door, took her arm and led her to the window. He bowed, nodded: "Beautiful Ohio. Am I right or am I?"

"Here's your gun."

"What a pal, what a pal!"

She took a flat black automatic from the sleeve of her light-weight blue coat and slid it into his palm.

"How'd you know?" he said.

"Well, I saw him take you in the office

so I went around outside and crept up beneath the window. Incidentally, when you chucked the gun out, kind sir, you almost beaned me. . . . So I took it and said 'abracadabra' and—lo!—I vanished."

He muttered: "Little wonderful!"

She began fanning herself with a newspaper, and stared blank-eyed at the Ohio. "What was the matter with that dick?"

"Professional jealousy—maybe." He bent his wiry brows, warped his mouth. "Or something screwy. He burned me up, that baby!"

"Hear from Blaine and Stope?"

"They got in on the 4:30 bus from Harrisburg. They're in 209 awaiting orders. What are you in?"

"One floor down—412. The dick tailed you here. I tailed him. He got your room number from the desk and then went away."

"O. K. Now you go down to your room, wash the coal dust off your face and catch up on your reading till you hear from me. I've got to see Milbray. Scoot, chile!"

She smiled—that bright, certain smile he liked. Then she turned and went out, trim from white nape to bright patent-leather heels.

He put on a hat and a coat and caught an elevator down. Twilight was in the hilly streets, and the air hung motionless like a warm invisible cloud. He walked around the block, looking over his shoulder at each turn. Then he hopped a taxi and gave an address.

The cab climbed out of the heart of the city. The street lights were turned on and presently a broad avenue opened before the cab. It followed this for a quarter mile, turned right and followed a winding road past large, pretentious houses. It stopped before a stone gateway across which a heavy chain had been stretched. Cardigan got out, paid up, and went toward the chain. A short, leather-faced man appeared there.

"Who are you?"

"I'm Cardigan. Mr. Milbray's expecting me."

"Oh, yeah. I'm the gardener." He unhooked the chain. "Just follow the driveway."

It was a hundred yards to the broad veranda of the big white house. A dumpy old woman in a black dress and an Eton collar opened the door.

"My name's Cardigan."

"Oh, thank goodness you got here!"

He entered and she took his hat and steered him across a foyer, through a music room to the entry of a library. A lean man with white hair and a drawn face rose from a divan, drew shut the folds of a silk dressing gown and knotted a rope at his waist. Cardigan crossed the soft carpet with his right hand extended. They shook and stood for a moment looking at each other in silence. The old woman backed out, closed the door quietly, and the white-haired man sat down, sighed, laid a hand on either knee and stared morosely at the carpet.

"Please sit down," he said.

Cardigan turned, walked several paces, picked up a straight-backed chair and brought it over to face the divan. He sat down.

"Let's have it," he said in a low voice.

MILBRAY straightened, then leaned back in the divan and thrust his hands into his robe pockets. "She was abducted a week ago today. Right out of the garden."

"How old is she?"

"Three. At four o'clock Mrs. Floom, the woman who let you in, called the nursemaid from the garden. My wife is ill. Her fever was high then and she'd fallen out of the bed and it took her nurse, Mrs. Floom and the nursemaid to get her back. Little hysterical, you understand. When the nursemaid returned to the garden, ten minutes later, Gloria was gone. There was a note in the carriage. It said: 'Don't tell the police. You'll get a letter tomorrow.' But the women were all upset. Mrs. Floom called the police. I wasn't here, at the time. In Pittsburgh on business."

"Any of the help see anybody in the garden—before or afterwards?"

"No. There are woods behind the house. Whoever kidnaped Gloria could have gone that way, easily, and not been detected. So the police came, and the newspapers, and at nine there was an extra on the streets. I got home at midnight. The police were still here, droves of them, and the newspapermen—all asking questions. I was shown the note the kidnaper left. I—I told the police to get out. I—you understand, I wanted to get my baby back!"

"Naturally."

Milbray ground the heel of his hand on his knee, stared hard into space. "Next day—the letter. Twenty-five thousand dollars and instructions where to put it at nine that night. The police came again. The reporters again. It was like a madhouse. They wanted to know what arrangements had been made. I told them I would not tell them. The child was mine, the money mine, and all of it no affair of theirs.

"Well, this is the fourth kidnaping in Wheelburgh in five months and the three others were successful. The administration has been booed from all quarters and the police are desperate. They're determined to get the criminals in this case—even, I believe, at the risk of sacrificing my child. You see?" he cried out suddenly, shaking.

"Go on."

"Yes—yes of course. Well, I kept the letter secret. I managed to get twenty-five thousand cash. I was instructed to take it to the abandoned Marsh farm on the Hillside Road and to place it under the right side of the front porch. An hour later I was to receive Gloria. The letter explained that she would be left in some doorway with a note pinned to her dress explaining that the finder should notify me.

"Well, I started out for the Marsh farm. I placed the money under the porch and drove away. I came home. I was barely in the house when the telephone rang. A man's voice said: 'Not this time, Milbray. You might just as well go back and get that money. We told you not to bring the cops along. The ante is up another ten thousand. You'll get a letter in a day or so.' So I drove back there and sure enough the money was under the porch. As I took it out half a dozen plainclothesmen jumped on me. They apologized. Imagine!" he cried. "Apologized!"

Cardigan grunted. "I've had an example of this burg's gumshoe," he said. "The example was terrible. . . . So now what?"

"The kidnapers have got bolder. They instructed me to engage an agent to act as intermediary. They have named an attorney to act as their representative. You probably know what procedure to go through. You will meet their agent, talk with him and arrange matters. I have the cash on hand."

"Who's the shyster?"

"His name is Aaron Steinfarb. He has an office in the Metals Building. But, remember—this is in strict confidence. The police seem to have acquired a grudge against me simply because I refuse to take them into my confidence." He thumped his chest and his voice was clogged. "After all, my child is—my child!"

Cardigan stood up. "Been bothered to-day?"

"All day. If it's not the police it's the newsmen. Driving up. Ringing bells. Taking pictures."

"O. K.," Cardigan grunted and held his hands out, palms down. "I've got two

men assistants and a woman along. We'll keep these grounds clean. I'll see Stein-farb."

They shook and Cardigan strode into the foyer. Old Mrs. Floom got him his hat.

"You'll try your best, sir?" she pleaded.

"Madam—yes."

She opened the door and there was a man standing there. "I'm Casey of The Morning Trib and—"

"Oh, yeah?" Cardigan said.

He moved. He caught Casey by the nape with one hand, by the seat of the pants with the other. He heaved once and Casey never touched a step on the way down. Cardigan walked down the steps and reached the gravel as Casey was rising.

"You fell," Cardigan said, unpleasantly. "It breaks my heart."

"What the hell's the idea—"

"Blow, sweetheart, blow!"

CHAPTER TWO

Thirty-Five Grand

THE Metals Building was two squares west of the hotel. It was old. The elevator was old and looked like a tarnished brass cage. It wheezed up three flights and Cardigan got out. Night lights were burning in the corridor and down at the end glowed a frosted square of light that was a glass-paneled door. There were black letters on it saying: Aaron Steinfarb, Counsellor at Law.

"Phooey," muttered Cardigan.

He knocked and a voice said: "Come in."

"I thought I might have to look up your home address," Cardigan said, kicking the door shut behind him.

"Who are you?"

"Calm, counsellor."

Cardigan tipped back his hat and eyed the small, chubby-cheeked man behind a battered flat-top. "You're Steinfarb, huh?"

"Can't you read?"

"Now is that nice?"

Steinfarb took a couple of quick drags on a tremendous cigar. He stood up. He was a very small man, far below medium height. He was all white and chunky and looked like a flyweight boxer gone to soft weight and too much electric light. His black hair was combed back flat, but through it his scalp was visible.

"Spiel it," he said. "And be quick. I was just about to leave. Get it off your chest. Come on, come on!" He threw his hands up irritably. "You think I've got all night?"

Cardigan said: "I'm representing Mr. Milbray. You're representing the quantity known as X."

Steinfarb blinked, screwed up his white fat nose. "Oh, you're—then you're the rep—"

"Cardigan. . . . Please sit down, counsellor. You give me the heebejeebies ducking around like that."

"Well, well, of course, of course. Ah, yes, Mr. Cardigan." He smacked his white hands together, beamed, sat down in the swivel chair. "It is really lamentable that—"

"Quit it, Steinfarb. I'm no babe in arms. Quit the preliminaries. All I want from you is the dope on how we can put this deal through. I understand that these heels that snatched the Milbray kid engaged you as counsel. All right. Now just what is what?"

Steinfarb got up, went to the door, opened it and peered into the corridor. Closing the door, he locked it and returned to his swivel chair.

His voice, his manner ceased to be theatrical. His eyes took on an oblique slant, evading Cardigan's. His mouth jerked: "Well, the price is thirty-five thousand. It was twenty-five but the cops

got childish and my clients upped it ten grand. They've got the kid. The kid's unharmed, well and happy. If there's another fluke it'll be swan song."

"Have you seen the kid?"

"No."

"How do you know she's well and happy?"

Steinfarb's fingers drummed, his shoulders twitched. "I was told. When a guy walks in here with a proposition like that he's bound to tell the truth."

"How do I know the kid's not dead?"

"I'm telling you."

"And you were told by somebody else. How do you know the guy who walked in here and propositioned you wasn't some wise bunny that didn't kidnap the kid at all but is just muscling in on general principles?"

Steinfarb made a sour face. "Are you telling me my business?"

"No. I'm working for Milbray. You're working for these kid-snatchers. It's my job to have my client's interest at heart and I've got to be sure of where this dough goes. It's not my job to pinch these guys. I'm interested only in getting the kid back. I've got to have proof that this client of yours has the kid."

SEINFARB drew on his cigar, rose and went to one of the windows. The shade was down, but he drew it gently aside and peered down into the street. In a minute he turned, came back to the desk and sat down. His eyes narrowed. He picked up a pencil, held it erect—then tossed it aside and laughed harshly.

"You can't talk to me, mister," he snarled. "I'm sitting on dynamite and I've got to be careful."

"What's eating you?"

Steinfarb nodded to the window. "Instead of leaving Lieutenant Michaels down under that street light, why didn't you bring him up with you?"

"Michaels?"

"Michaels!" Steinfarb barked. He picked up the pencil and threw it down again. "Michaels! Michaels!"

Cardigan got up and started for the window.

Steinfarb snarled: "Stay away from there!"

Cardigan turned and found Steinfarb holding a gun. Cardigan raised his shoulders. "You've got me."

"I just don't want Michaels to see where you are."

"O. K. Put that gun down."

The storm passed as quickly as it had risen. Steinfarb slipped the gun into his desk drawer and chewed petulantly on his big cigar.

Cardigan said: "Don't be a goof, Steinfarb. The bum ran into me as I got off the train today. He tried to make me take another train back east. I thought I'd ducked him but he must have picked me up again. I represent Milbray—not the cops. The cops want these heels. I want the kid."

"All right, all right. I got excited. I just got excited." He looked at the ragged end of his cigar. "The kid's all right. Safe. Sound. All I can do is carry on negotiations. You give me thirty-five thousand dollars. I give it—minus my commission—to my clients. The baby will be returned—automatically."

"Fair enough. But first—first, counsellor, I've got to be sure your clients have the baby."

Steinfarb flared up. "My God, do you think I can take you to these guys!"

"No. Take this." He pulled a small vest-pocket camera from his coat. "Have your clients take all exposures on this of the kid in various positions."

"Why?"

"So we'll know she's alive."

Steinfarb leaned back, drew one eye shut. He smiled—a bleak, warped smile. "You think of things, don't you?"

"I'm in 517 at The Wheelburgh."

"I'll see."

Cardigan turned and went to the door. "Is there a back way out?"

"Yeah. Downstairs, turn left after you get out of the elevator. At the end of the lobby there's a door. That leads down a flight of stairs to a garage. Go out that way."

CARDIGAN ignored the elevator in The Wheelburgh. He walked all the way around the lobby, stopped at the cigar stand, bought a paper and some pipe tobacco and used the mirror behind the counter to watch the lobby. Then he took the stairway to the second floor and knocked on 209. Blaine let him in and Stope lay on the bed in an undershirt kicking his heels up and laughing.

Cardigan shot Blaine a dark sidelong look and Blaine said: "What the hell, he said he was going out only for a paper."

Cardigan went over to the bed, drew a blackjack and smacked Stope on the soles. Stope's body vibrated as though an electric current had shot through it. He sat up, half laughing, half snarling: "What do you think—"

Cardigan laid the flat of his hand against Stope's cheek and knocked him spinning across the bed. Stope put his face in his hands and went into a crying jag. Cardigan crossed the room to a lowboy and picked up two pint flasks. They were unlabeled and contained a smoky white fluid. Cardigan uncorked them, sniffed.

"You try this, Blaine?"

"I've got kids to support."

Cardigan took both bottles into the bathroom and emptied them. He dropped the empties into a wicker linen hamper, reentered the bedroom rubbing his hands slowly together. Stope was sitting up, cross-legged like an Indian. He wore a silly grin and kept hiccupping regularly. Cardigan suddenly shot across the room, grabbed Stope by the throat and shook him violently.

"Listen to me, you dirty bum! What the hell do you think you are, a traveling salesman?"

"Jus' little drinky—"

"By cripes, you're working for a tough agency, Stope. You got kicked off the cops for boozing. I don't care how much you drink when you're not on the road with me, but when you're out with me—Ah-r-r, you sap!" He flung him across the bed. Then he began tearing Stope's clothes off.

"Come on, Blaine. We'll sober him."

They stripped him and held him under an ice-cold shower. He moaned, groaned, prayed. They turned the shower off, hauled him out of the tub. Cardigan threw him a towel and motioned Blaine into the bedroom.

He said: "You and Stope go out to the Milbray place pronto. Bum's-rush anybody who doesn't belong there. Leave your rods here. The cops in this burg are funny that way. Ask Milbray for a room. Let this honk-out sleep a couple of hours, then you catch shut-eye—and so on, alternating."

"O. K., chief."

"Now open the door and see if anybody's in the hall."

Blaine looked, said: "O. K."

Cardigan went out and climbed to 412. Pat had on black pajamas and a mandarin coat.

He began: "I'd climb the highest mountain and swim the broadest river—"

"Be your profession. I hate mountain climbers. Always make me think of yodeling."

He spun his hat on a forefinger. "Milbray's all broken up. It must be tough on a guy when they snatch his kid. . . . Well, look. You be down in the lobby bright and early in the morning. I figure Michaels still might try to pick me up for packing a gun. You pack my gun. You follow me wherever I go and if I get in a jam, pass me the gun and then get to hell out of the way. Savvy?"

"Little Chinee girl savvy."

He raised his hand. "Stop that!" And grinned. He turned and said: "Take a look in the hall."

She opened the door, looked out, stepped back in. "Scur-ram!" she said.

"Happy dreams!"

IN a minute he was in his room. Five minutes later he was in blue cotton pajamas, his big feet thrust into worn-down slippers. He crammed an ancient briar and opened both windows wide. Night brought fewer sounds, but each of these was clear, resonant; the drawn-out rattle of a trolley crossing switches, the toll of a freight engine in the railroad yards, the sad hoot of a river boat. He drew on his pipe, cuddling the smoke behind his lips in the manner of the true pipe-smoker. Darkness had a way of making the unlovely city romantic—and of making him feel acutely lonely.

He chuckled to himself: "Sentimental Mick!"

Knuckles rapped his door. He scowled at it, his face a hard network of shadows. He crossed and put his ear to the panel.

"Yeah?"

"Cardigan, this is Kittles, city editor of The Trib."

"I'm not interested in subscribing."

"Listen, Cardigan, I've got news for you!" the voice hissed.

Cardigan let him in, eyed him with a calloused stare. The man was scrawny, wore spectacles that looked like thick magnifying glasses. He had a confidential air, rolling eyebrows, dry wrinkled lips. He started off by tapping Cardigan's chest.

"Now don't do that," Cardigan said. "It makes me fidgety."

"Of course, of course," Kittles' low voice raked on in a cracked whisper; and his eyebrows rolled. "Cardigan, we're glad to see you're here. I, personally, am glad to see you here. Oh, I've heard of you. Remember the time you were head of the St. Louis branch? Yes, yes, indeed! Ah, yes. Great work, great work! . . . Can I send you up a case of nice liquor, the real McCoy?"

"Thanks—no. You can tell me what you want, though."

He huddled close to Cardigan. "We'd just like to know, old man, what progress you've made since you came here. What transpired between you and Milbray? Have you made contact with the kidnapers? When do you expect to have the child back? Just a few words, old man —just a hint, here and there."

Cardigan rolled a harsh laugh between closed teeth.

Kittles raised a finger. "Oh, of course, we expect to make you a little present. Little pin-money. Five hundred, say."

Cardigan repeated the laugh, raked Kittles from head to foot with a sardonic smile, turned and crossed to one of the windows. Kittles blinked, looked at the ceiling, at the floor, then at Cardigan's back. Then he crossed the room, moistening his lips.

"Of course, old man—"

Cardigan swiveled. "Of course, old man!" he growled. He tossed his thumb. "I don't like your groceries. Blow!"

Kittles wore a quaint, hurt expression. "But, gosh, old man—"

"Yeah, a swell chance Milbray has of getting his kid back when you newspaper guys and the cops clown all over the city. What about those other three kidnapings? What good are they? You print a lot of crap in the papers. You scare the heels. You're no help and you're a lot of nuisance. Now get out of here. And stay away from Milbray's place. And don't bother me. And go to hell."

Kittles pouted. He turned and scuffled to the door. He paused to blink at Cardigan through his heavy glasses. Then he scowled petulantly and went out, slamming the door.

CHAPTER THREE

Kick-the-Wicket

CARDIGAN went downstairs at eight next morning and had breakfast in the coffee shop. The headlines went far toward spoiling his appetite. They made him curse; made him glare at the waitress, through her, beyond her; until she began blushing and backing away.

"Baked apple," he said. "And eggs, three, three minutes. Rolls. Coffee."

"Y-yes, sir."

He crackled the paper and glared at it

POLICE PROMISE ARREST
IN MILBRAY CASE

"Horsefeathers!" he muttered.

New Clues Indicate Early Arrest Of
Baby Milbray Kidnapers

He tossed the paper to one end of the table, ran his hand across his cheek, up around the back of his neck. He rushed through his breakfast, ate too rapidly, and left the table with a stuffed, unpleasant feeling. And in this condition he ran into Michaels, in the lobby. Michaels had a couple of boys with him. At the same time Cardigan saw Pat watching him from the depths of a leather chair.

Michaels took his arm. "We wanted to wait till you ate, Cardigan. Come along."

"Where?"

"Headquarters."

"What for now, pitching pennies?"

Michaels moved his head. "Come on. No use stalling."

"What for?"

"Little talk."

Cardigan shook his head. His voice was low, quiet, but dynamite was in the background. "I'm busy, Michaels. I can't go." He put his left hand on Michaels' right and wrenched it from his arm. "Grow up, copper." His dark eyes were steady, sultry.

"No wait, Cardigan," Michaels said, blocking him. "We're going to have a talk with you. There's three of us and if you start to get rough we'll jump you and beat hell out of you and fix you for a three-months' spree in jail. Use your head. Use your head. Come on before we get sloppy."

Cardigan looked at the other two men. They were big, bigger than Michaels, and looked like hard parties. He shrugged. "O. K., let's go."

THEY went outside. The street was already hot, the air motionless and soggy, the sun hidden behind a dull haze but nonetheless felt in the narrow street. The two bruisers walked beside Cardigan and Michaels walked in front, led the way around the corner to a parked sedan. They got in and one of the bruisers took the wheel.

After five minutes Cardigan said: "Headquarters, huh?"

"Sit tight," Michaels said.

Cardigan turned and punched him in the jaw. "You crummy bum, I know where headquarters is!"

The bruiser on his right grabbed him and then Michaels had his gun out. "Easy, Cardigan." His face looked red and bloated and somehow desperate.

Cardigan put his hands on his knees and stared straight ahead. The car left the suburbs and went down the other side of the mountain. It passed a glass factory; went on downward toward the coal mines; cruised along the outside of a husky settlement drenched in coal dust,

sooty and tatterdemalion. It entered a clump of trees and stopped before a board-and-batten shack. A gaunt man with one eye missing came out and unleashed a slow tobacco shot.

The two bruisers hustled Cardigan inside. The place smelled of raw corn liquor. He got one arm free and took a smack at the nearer face and then Michaels came in and helped crowd him into a chair.

"Now use your head, Cardigan."

Cardigan hit Michaels in the stomach, rose wheeling the chair with him and let it fly. It missed both bruisers but stopped the one-eyed man in the doorway. It was a heavy chair. It knocked the man cold. Cardigan had a stone jug in his hand by this time, but Michaels clipped him with a blackjack and Cardigan leaned against the wall, shaking his head. They shoved him into another chair.

"Be your age!" Michaels cried hoarsely. "We don't want to kill you, dope!"

Cardigan walked across the room and sat down heavily, his arms hanging, fingers touching the floor. He addressed Michaels in colorful if unprintable idiom.

"That won't get you anywhere," Michaels said. He planted a chair in front of Cardigan and sat down solidly. He looked serious, worried, desperate. "I've got to know how things stand," he said. "I'm going to break this case. I've got to. I've got to get this kid-snatching crowd. I've got to. There's no halfway measure about it. Get me, Cardigan. I mean it. There's no out for me. None. I either crash this case or I'm all washed up. All washed up."

"Good. I hope you get all washed up."

Cardigan—" Michaels leaned forward. His stomach bunched, overlapping his tight belt. He looked red hot, sweaty, and there was a fierce glow way back in his China-blue eyes. "There's been a kidnap gang systematically working this city for six months. Three times they got away from me. I'm on the carpet now. If I flop this one, I'm out—out. Broke. Out on my pants! I can't afford it." He made a fist, looked at it, then laid it on his thick knee.

Cardigan said: "You'll flop this like you flopped the others. Why? Because you're dumb. Because you're the kind of cop that went out of style when I wore diapers. Because you're a louse. You couldn't even get a job sweeping out our agency's office."

"Cardigan, I am going to get the low-down on this. Milbray won't even talk to me. He's talked to you. You've made contact. You were in the Metals Building last night. Who'd you see?"

"That's my business."

"That building is full of lawyers. You saw a lawyer. Who is he?"

"Again—my business."

Michaels thumped his knee. "I'm telling you I'm serious. There's nothing going to stop me. I'm going to get these heels. Where are they? When is the money to be turned over—and where?"

Cardigan said: "My job is to get the kid."

"Mine is to get the gang."

"Even if it costs the kid's life?"

"I tell you, Cardigan—I've got to break this, one way or another, and I don't care who pays."

CARDIGAN raised his foot, planted it on Michaels' chest and toppled him to the floor. The two bruisers grabbed Cardigan as he rose and slammed him down again. They held him locked in the chair. Michaels got up, replaced his hat and jammed his hands into the pockets of his alpaca coat. Red color swam in his eyes and sweat poured down his face.

He said: "You may as well come clean, Cardigan, because if you don't you'll stay here till you rot. You'll be no good to Milbray or anybody else."

Cardigan shook his head. "I'd rot before I'd tell you anything."

Michaels hitched his shoulders. "Give it to him."

The two bruisers landed on Cardigan and spent five minutes tossing him around the shack. In the end, he sat in the middle of the floor, tie and collar gone and a stupid look in his eyes. Then very quietly, as though no one were watching him, he got on his hands and knees and began crawling toward the door. One of the bruisers took half a dozen easy steps, braced himself in the doorway, and when Cardigan arrived reached down and cracked him between the eyes. Cardigan fell flat and lay very quiet.

The bruisers looked worried. One said: "Hell, we might kill this guy."

"No fear," Michaels said. "But we've got to make him talk."

The one-eyed man came to and sat up. Michaels got him a drink and the man said: "What hit me?"

"A chair. There it is. Now sit on it till you feel better."

Cardigan began coughing. He rolled over on his back.

"Be sensible," Michaels said.

"Nuts," Cardigan said.

A voice screamed from the woods: "Help! Police! Help!"

Michaels started. "What's that?"

"A woman," one of the bruisers said.

"Oh-o-o-o! Help!"

Michaels snapped at the one-eyed man. "You all right, Jake?"

"Sure, I'm all right."

Michaels took down a shotgun from a rack on the wall, thrust it into the one-eyed man's hands. "Watch this guy! . . . Come on, boys. We'll see—"

"Help!"

The three men barged out and Jake stood up gripping the shotgun and peering after them. Gradually his gaze lowered to Cardigan. He saw Cardigan's mouth fall open. He saw a fixed, wide-open stare. He shuddered, moved a step closer.

"Hey," he croaked.

He saw that not a muscle twitched. He saw that Cardigan's chest was motionless. And the eyes stared at the ceiling, the mouth was lax, deathly.

"Jeepers!" he croaked. He started for the door.

Cardigan heaved and floored him. Jake hit hard and his head bounced against the floor. A blow ripped to his jaw and moved his entire body several inches across the boards. Cardigan grabbed the shotgun, went out through a back window and lunged along the woods road. A figure leaped from the bushes. Cardigan almost struck.

"How was that?" Pat asked.

"Little wonderful—step on it!"

She had a gun of her own—and his gun. She thrust it into his hand and he tossed the shotgun away. They reached the hill road and there was a taxi parked a few yards away. He bundled her into it.

"I fixed their car," she said.

"What'd you do?"

"Broke their carburetor."

The taxi was speeding past the Hunky settlement. Dust billowed in white clouds behind.

Cardigan looked at her. "Do you know what Michaels is?"

"Don't," she said. "I hate language."

CARDIGAN entered the hotel by way of the garage. He found an open unattended service elevator. He ran it up to the fourth floor and left it there. Pat's key was in his hand and he went to her room. Five minutes later she came in with some packages. She opened them and displayed absorbent cotton, salve, antiseptics.

"Sit on that chair by the window," she said.

"Yes, mama."

"And don't be funny."

She had small hands, white hands, neatly pointed at the tips. She washed his face with a soft sponge, did some cauterizing.

"Ouch!" he said.

"Don't be a baby."

She washed and cleansed a broken welt on his back where a hard shoe had torn his flesh.

"Boy oh boy," he said, gazing out of the window, "what names I could call Michaels!"

"Don't." She sighed. "Some day you're going to discover that while you're a pretty hard hombre you can't lick more than double your weight. Sometimes I think you're a case of arrested development."

"A few more cracks like that I'll recommend your discharge."

"Yes, you will! . . . There milord, except for five tiny bits of tape on the face, you look presentable."

He shook her hand. "Thanks, trainer."

"What now?"

"Well, for the time being I think Michaels will lay off me. I've several calls to make. You stay here, right at the telephone, until further notice. I'll go up to my room and put on a shirt and tie."

"Wait till I brush your suit."

She whiskbroomed it thoroughly. Then she looked into the corridor, nodded, and he went out and climbed to his room. He put on a white shirt and a blue tie, looked at himself in the mirror, said, "Humph!" and left the hotel.

AARON STEINFARB was dictating to a gum-chewing stenographer when Cardigan looked in. The lawyer shooed the girl into her own little office and waved a tremendous cigar. It said 11:25 by the clock on Steinfarb's desk.

"I phoned you this morning," Steinfarb said.

"I wasn't in."

"No."

"I took a ride out to the mines to see some country. I fell in some broken glass."

"It's tough, falling in broken glass."

"Yeah. Well?" Cardigan said, lifting an eyebrow.

Steinfarb reached into his desk, brought out the little camera. "There. All exposures made. You can get 'em developed."

"Thanks."

Steinfarb screwed up his white pudgy face. "Listen . . ." He chewed one corner of his lower lip, scowled sidewise at a blank wall. "Listen, Cardigan. I think I ought to tell you. It's going to be tough getting that kid."

"Why?"

Steinfarb made a sour face. "Oh, the cops. Not all the cops. Some. One or two or three. They're sore. They hate private dicks in this town. They hate anybody who tries to butt into their bowl of cherries. Just be careful."

"Thanks. Is everything set?"

"Thirty-five thousand bucks."

Cardigan said: "C. O. D."

"Huh?"

"I've got a girl with me. She'll go with you. She'll carry thirty-five thousand dollars. The cops don't know her. They don't know she's with me. She'll take the thirty-five thousand and she'll turn it over on receipt of the baby. If," he added, "these pictures satisfy me."

"*B-r-r!* They'll shy at that."

"Listen, Steinfarb. I'm on the level. If I'd been hired to get these guys, I'd get them. But I've been hired to get that child. This mug of mine, well—" he shrugged— "some cops tried to play kick-the-wicket with me. But they don't know this girl. She's an agency operative. Do you know why the cops kicked me around?"

"No."

Cardigan pointed. "They wanted to know who I came to see last night in this building."

"Oh," Steinfarb nodded. "Oh, I see."

Cardigan walked to the door. "Get in touch with these kid-snatchers and talk turkey. I'll be seeing you."

CHAPTER FOUR

Plate Glass—and a Punk

THE roll of film gave up four good exposures. The others were blurred or blanks. Cardigan got the pictures at 3:30 that afternoon and hopped a cab. Blaine was on the Milbray grounds.

"Where's Stope?" Cardigan said.

"Snoozing."

Cardigan went on through the grounds and Mrs. Floom let him in. Milbray was fully dressed. He looked not as depressed as he had on Cardigan's first meeting with him. He had a grip on himself, chin up, jaw tight.

"Well?"

Cardigan took the four snapshots from an envelope. "That her?"

"Yes! But where—how—"

"I don't know where, yet. I made Steinfarb get pictures of her. She's alive—"

"Thank God!"

Cardigan tapped the pictures. "You can see. Here she's looking scared. Here she's smiling. Here she's looking down and here she's looking to one side. That's swell."

"This is a great load off my mind, my heart. But I say—your face!"

"Slipped getting out of the bathtub this morning. Now—" Cardigan dropped his voice— "the money. Have it ready at a moment's notice."

Milbray's chest swelled. "Your confidence, sir, makes me feel that the worst is past!"

"Good! It is, I'm sure." He looked around. "Where is Mr. Stope's room?"

"Up that stairway—at the rear of the corridor."

Cardigan climbed the staircase, strode down the upper corridor, knocked. He opened the door and found the room empty. His lips tightened. He went downstairs again and into the kitchen. No one there had seen Mr. Stope. He returned to the library.

"I ought to be back about five," he said.

He went out like a blast of wind and found Blaine at the gate. He gripped Blaine's arm. "Stope's not there."

"Oh-oh."

Cardigan made knots of his fists. "Sure you didn't see him outside?"

"Left him in the room, last."

"When?"

"Hour ago." Blaine began swearing, then stopped and said: "Do you think he slipped out for a drink?"

Cardigan turned on Blaine and yelled at him: "I told Hammerhorn he should never have sent that booze hound with us! I told him! You heard me tell him!"

"Well, why take my head off?"

Cardigan shrugged. "Sorry, fella . . . O. K., you stay here. If he turns up, phone Pat and I'll connect with her later. That bum!"

AARON STEINFARB lit a large cigar and whipped smoke out of one corner of his mouth. "Jake, Cardigan. It's all set. You get the dough and give it to the jane and the jane and I will go and meet my clients. There's four of them, Cardigan, and I'll be frank with you—two of them are real hot hoods. So don't double the cross."

"I'm no gofor."

"I don't think you are. I just said that—well, to convince you that only the up-and-up will get that kid. You may think I'm a louse for representing these guys. Maybe I am. Only if I didn't they'd have got someone else. And besides, louse or not, I'm being partially instrumental in the attempt to get the kid back. Don't get me wrong—I'm not grabbing any glory. Don't want it."

Cardigan said: "You don't have to alibi your motives."

"Am I? Excuse me!"

"That was no crack, Steinfarb."

Steinfarb cackled. "O. K., boy, O. K.!" He picked up a pencil, twirled it. "Pictures good, eh?"

"Swell."

"I'll meet the jane at Windsor and Pellman—northeast corner—at nine tonight. And for crying out loud, don't let Michaels or anybody else see you with her or they'll catch on. Michaels will crab this if he can. He's got a lot at stake."

Cardigan said: "The girl will have the dough when she meets you. Stand on the corner whistling something—say, *Sweet And Lovely*. Know it?"

"Yeah."

"Goom-by!"

CARDIGAN entered Pat Seaward's room at 8:30. He took from his pocket a long flat package wrapped in brown paper and bound with ordinary twine. She was sitting in an easy chair reading a magazine which she lowered when the package struck her lap.

"Thirty-five thousand," Cardigan said.

She hefted it but didn't say anything. Cardigan sat on the edge of the bed. He looked at her a few times in silence and then looked at the floor. He was chewing on his lip. He looked dark and worried.

"Penny for your thoughts."

He said: "They're worth thousands, little wonderful." He scowled down at his wrist watch, still wore the scowl when he looked at Pat. "No word about Stope, huh?"

"No."

He rose, smacked fist lazily into palm and took a few exasperated turns up and down the room. Then he stopped and extended a hand toward her. "Can you imagine a guy like that?"

"Do you suppose he's on a drunk?"

"Of course."

"Well, that ought to make him harmless."

He growled, paced the length of the room, stopped and said: "Do you think I like having that drunk wandering around town on a night like this? Anything can happen. He might take a pass at some guy and get pinched. Then what? Then they'll find his identification in the station house. Then what? Well, if Michaels happens to be around . . ." He swore under his breath and heaved his shoulders.

"What does Steinfarb look like?"

"Little guy. Dark clothes. Derby. Very white face—sort of too white. You'll know him by the song."

"Should I carry a gun?"

"You'd better."

She stood up and stretched her arms. "Well, here's hoping."

"If we win, Pat, hike the kid right to home. Don't bother phoning me until you've got the kid home. Only—" a shadow passed his eyes and his mouth hardened— "if that bum Stope were only where I could lay my hands on him!"

She smiled. She had a rather soft smile at times. "Don't get all steamed up, chief. You might get rash."

He muttered: "Better get started, Pat."

She made a trim figure on her way through the lobby, ten minutes later. She had a smart, straight-legged walk and a fine eyes-front way about her. She looked white and cool and clean in the hot street. Lobby loungers looked after her.

The street climbed upward here. No matter their original state, the buildings, one and all, were made dusky brothers by the everlasting coal dust. Neon lights looked red and swollen in the warm night haze. Pat reached the top and flicked a glance at the signpost there. She went on past the bleat and blare of a radio store. Corner loafers whistled at her. One wise guy tried to take her arm. She gave a backward kick, expertly, and the man fell down huddling his shins. She went on.

A block behind, on the other side of the street, Cardigan drifted past shop windows, took a passing interest in their contents, followed with intermittent glances the progress of Pat. On the next corner was a large weighing scale surmounted by a large mirror. He stopped before it and in the mirror he was able to see a block ahead. Remaining there, he saw Pat cross the street, saw her linger on the corner and, after a moment, turn toward a small man. Cardigan kept his gaze fixed on the mirror. He saw Pat and Steinfarb start walking.

"Gain any weight?"

Cardigan knew the voice. He didn't turn. "I've all the weight I need, Michaels. I suppose it'll get to the point where I won't be able to take a bath without having you pop in. How do you like my face?"

"What happened to you?"

Cardigan turned slowly and made a sarcastic grimace.

Farther up the street there was the sound of glass crashing. Pedestrians stopped, turned. A police whistle blew. Cardigan stiffened.

MICHAELS raised his chin, started off on the run and Cardigan followed at a fast walk, joining the crowd. Then he too broke into a run. People began shouting and, beyond the next corner, a crowd was gathering, bunching on the sidewalk. Cardigan elbowed his way ahead roughly. In a minute he saw what had caused the sound. A plate-glass window had been smashed. Heels were grinding glass to powder on the sidewalk and a cop's red face was working.

Michaels broke through. "What's up, Finn?"

Cardigan saw the cop holding Stope by one arm. Stope was drunk. His hat was on the back of his head and his hair was in tatters down on his forehead. He was swaying on his feet and complaining.

Steinfarb was holding Pat. He was saying: "The guy's drunk. I didn't strike him. He tried to get smart."

Stope said: "F'r Gawd's sake, ossifer, I tell you I know the lady. Old pals. Yeah . . . I jus' said hello and wanna shake hands and she high-hats me. And the bozo shoves me and this here glass window kind of bends out and smacks me and breaks. 'S 'onest trut'."

Pat was white-faced. "I'm sorry, officer. I never saw this man before. He must be mistaken."

"What's your name?" Michaels butted in.

Steinfarb said: "My name 'll do. The lady's a friend of mine. Pinch this punk if you want to. He took a swing at me, missed and struck the window."

"Stay there," Michaels rapped out; spun on Stope. "What's your name?"

"Harvey M. S-Stope."

"Where do you live?"

"N' York."

"What are you doing here?"

"Sh! Mustn't tell, commissioner! 'S trut'—hic—I'm private detective. Like you—only ver' private. I—I—"

Cardigan came through, glitter-eyed. "I'll take him, Michaels. The fat-head works for me. We'll settle for the window."

"Oh, yeah?"

Cardigan grabbed Stope by the throat. "For two cents, I'd push in your mug.

Stand up! What's the idea of insulting strange women on the streets? Every woman you meet you think you've met before. Stand up!"

"See here, Cardigan," Michaels broke in.

But Cardigan thrust him aside, said to Pat: "I'm sorry, madam, my friend did this. He's drunk. I'm sorry. I'll fix it for this window."

"O. K.," Steinfarb said.

He turned Pat around and marched her off. Michaels looked after them. He started to say somehting several times. His face reddened. Then he turned to Cardigan.

"All right. Beat it. Take this guy home."

The storekeeper cried: "But what about my window?"

Cardigan thrust an agency card into his hand. "Send your bill there, mister."

He wheeled Stope across the street, and when he looked around he saw Michaels stretching his legs up the street. Cardigan stopped, watched him for a split-minute, then shook Stope violently.

"Listen, you. Go back to the hotel—" It was useless. Stope couldn't stand up. Cardigan walked him to a taxicab, opened the door and pushed him in. He gave the driver a dollar. "Take this stew to The Wheelburgh and drop him in the lobby."

"O. K."

Cardigan stepped back, turned, and went sloping up the street. He saw Michaels climb into a taxi beneath a corner street light a block beyond. He ran a hundred yards, caught another taxi making the turn. He flagged it and climbed in.

"Follow that white cab."

CHAPTER FIVE

Blond Piccaninny

THE white cab jounced over broken pavement. Sparks showered from Steinfarb's cigar to the floor. He stamped them out.

"That chump Michaels," he said, irritably.

Pat said: "Stope, you mean!"

"You used your head, little girl." He reached over and patted her hand. "I could go for you in a big way."

"Pul-lease."

"Honest, I could—"

"Stop that!" She bit off and threw his hand back across his lap. "Keep your mind on your business, Mr. Steinfarb."

He chuckled and leaned back in his corner, drew reflectively on his big cigar. The cab struck smoother pavement and rushed on through the dark streets. Presently Steinfarb leaned forward and tapped the connecting window, pointed ahead. The cab stopped at the next corner. Steinfarb got out, paid up, took Pat's arm and walked her down a narrow, deserted street.

They walked two blocks, turned into a main drag. It was a narrow, noisy street, lined with cheap novelty shops, cheap burlesque houses, open-faced soda-pop stands, sidewalk shooting galleries alive with the flat metallic rattle of 22 caliber rifles and revolvers. High-yellow girls sauntered with strutting black sheiks. Cheap perfume clogged the soggy air. Tough whites stood on street corners and cops traveled in pairs.

Steinfarb stopped Pat before the Old West Shooting Gallery. Twelve rifles and six revolvers lay on the platform. Behind it stood a mulatto in a ten-gallon hat and a lavender bandana. He looked at Steinfarb. Steinfarb nodded, then the mulatto nodded and went to the rear, disappearing behind a curtain.

"How's your eye, Miss Seaward?" Steinfarb smiled.

She picked up a nine-shot 22 revolver and knocked down eight moving ducks.

"Whew!" whistled Steinfarb.

"It's a cheap gun," she commented.

"As if you needed an alibi!"

The mulatto reappeared and jerked his thumb. Steinfarb took Pat's arm and guided her into a hallway. They climbed a narrow wooden staircase in which yellow gas light wavered. A man opened a door and looked at them with eyes that were yellow in the yellow gas light. They entered a drab sitting room and a second man stood leaning against the wall with his hand in his coat pocket. He had some nervous affliction and his lips, his nose, his brows kept twitching.

He said: "Happy to thee you. Thit down."

The man who had opened the door now closed it and shot a bolt home. His yellow hair was fine and shiny like corn silk, his neck rugged.

He said: "You got it?"

"I've got it," Pat said. She held up the brown paper package.

"Open it."

She opened it and thumbed the thick sheaf of bills. The yellow-haired man came toward her. She stepped back.

"C.O.D.," she said.

The man scowled.

Steinfarb said: "Don't get fresh now. Everything is on the up-and-up. Get the kid."

The lisper did not move from the wall. The yellow-haired man turned on his heel and went into another room, closing the door. When the door reopened a large black woman came out carrying a black child.

Pat frowned. "What's that?"

The black woman grinned. She drew down one of the child's stockings, showing white flesh. Only the arms and the face had been stained and there was a black knitted cap drawn tightly over the head. She lifted this, showing golden curls.

THE yellow-haired man came in and said: "There she is. We had a hell of a time getting that stain off to get those pictures. It was easier getting it back again." His eyes were hard as they moved from Steinfarb to Pat. "The nigger'll take the baby out. She'll walk two blocks down to Ennis Street with the kid. You watch her from the front window. You'll give us the dough and you'll stay in here till we go out. We'll go up the street. You can watch us. When you see us turn a corner you come out. Not before. If you run out right after us, the kid gets it. Right now we've got two guys stationed down the street. If something starts, these guys let the kid and the nigger have it."

Pat started.

The yellow-haired man said: "The nigger's deaf."

The negress kept grinning like a fool.

Pat threw the money on the table and the yellow-haired man scooped it up, counted it. He peeled off several bills and gave them to Steinfarb. Steinfarb pocketed them. Pat went into the darkened front room. The bay-windows were large. She had a full view of the street, both ways. She came back into the lighted room.

The yellow-haired man was telling the negress things with his fingers. She nodded and went over to the door. The yellow-haired man opened it and the negress went out. They all moved into the front room and stood by the windows.

They could not see Michaels. He was down leaning against the counter of the shooting gallery.

"A little guy," he was saying, "and a neat-looking jane. They came down this street and I lost track of 'em. Did you see 'em? Come on. I'm asking you!"

The mulatto looked innocent. "No, boss, I ain't seen 'em."

"You're lying!"

"Me lie? Shucks, I wouldn't lie!"

Michaels gnawed his lip. "They came down on this side of the street. You—"

He stopped and turned. A man had cursed out loud. Stope had reeled into the man. The man had shoved him and Stope had fallen down. Now he rose.

"Ah!" he said, spotting Michaels.

He started forward and began losing his balance. He came fast. Michaels, scowling, stepped aside and Stope hit the counter, bounced off, reeled on and collided with the negress as she came out of the door. Both went down. The negress yelped, clutching the child tightly as she rolled over. The black knitted cap fell off and gold curls burst into view.

"M' Gawd!" exclaimed Stope. "A blond piccaninny!"

Michaels' teeth clamped shut and he leaped forward.

Upstairs, Pat was the first to sense things. Her gun was in her hand and she whirled on the lisper and the yellow-haired man. "Beat it!" she said. "Get out the back way and run. The woman fell and there's a drunk and a cop down there!"

The yellow-haired man snarled: "A frame!"

"Get," Pat said. "I could hold you boys, but get while you've got time. We've been double-crossed! Go on, fools!"

Steinfarb said: "You heard her. Do you think I'd risk getting in a jam like this? It's a tough break. You dopes, scram!"

The two men turned. Pat was at their heels with her gun. She saw them through a rear window and watched them scamper down a fire-escape. She spun and Steinfarb was glowering.

He snapped: "That drunk didn't go home!"

"You're telling me!"

SHE flew across the room, out into the hall, down the stairway. She reached the sidewalk to find Michaels trying to tear the child from the negress's arms. Michaels struck with his gun and the black woman tottered, her arms loosened. Pat leaped and the force of her body staggered Michaels. She caught the child as it fell, as the negress went down.

Cardigan came bounding across the street, caught Michaels' arm as Michaels swung on Pat. He twisted Michaels all the way around.

'Michaels, beat it!" he rasped. "This is a hot spot!"

Pedestrians, loungers, began running away.

"Leggo!" Michaels roared.

The roar of a car gathering speed rose above the tumult in the street. Pat clasped the child and ran toward the open hall door. The black woman was up, wild-eyed, reeling about. Stope was up, teetering.

Pat flung a terrified look over her shoulder as she saw the car swing in toward the curb, speeding. She fell over the threshold, into the hallway. Guns banged and a bullet splintered wood near her head. She crowded her small body against the baby, protecting it. The guns banged again. Stope, staggering around, suddenly stiffened. He was directly in front of the door, in front of Pat and the child. His body stopped four bullets and then he turned around twice, sat down, coughed, and straightened out.

Pat couldn't seem to get up. Cardigan flung away from Michaels, leaped to the door, laid his big hands on Pat's shoulder.

"I'm all feet," she panted.

"Shot?"

"No—no."

Bang! Bang! Bang! The gunflame was red, spurting from the darkened tonneau of the car as it whipped past. One shot broke a window, one chipped pavement, the third hit Cardigan somewhere above the waist, behind, and he cursed and fell down. But he was up in a second, wheeling around, drawing his own gun.

"Put 'em up, you!" Michaels screamed, his gun leveled.

"Me? You fool, why don't you get that car?"

"Put 'em up or I'll— Put 'em up Cardigan!" yelled Michaels. He was red-faced. In his voice, in the blaze of his eyes, was madness.

The negress lolled against the counter, her eyes rolling. She looked mad, too, but in a dazed, dumb way. Her big black hands fell on two revolvers. She gripped them. They were 22's, nine shots each. She swiveled hugely and began pumping.

Michaels turned on her, his eyes widening as the small slugs drove into him. He fired. His gun shook in his hand and the negress went down to her knees; and while she knelt she kept on pulling both triggers. She cut Michaels down. They were all hits. His gun fell before he did. Then he fell on top of it. And then the negress fell, for Michaels' one shot had been well aimed.

The street was suddenly quiet. There was no one nearby. For two blocks, either way, the street was empty. Until a squad of cops came running on the double.

Cardigan ran a hand across his eyes, grunted and sat down in the doorway. Pat was sitting beside him. She held the child in her arms, rocking it gently saying, "Sh—sh; don't cry, don't cry, honey."

Then she put one arm around Cardigan's neck. "Steady, chief. Steady!"

"I'll be all right, little wonderful."

He woke up in a hospital several hours later.

Pat was sitting beside the bed.

He said: "I'd climb the highest mountain—"

"Please," she said, half smiling, and patted his hand. "Please, chief, don't yodel."

The Hooded Terror

by
Oscar Schisgall

Author of "The Death Scream," etc.

A dilapidated, gloomy pile it was—that old estate at Lakeview—but Kent Carmody bought it for his own. He never guessed his new home would be a murder mansion—its unkept grounds a slaughter garden for his closest friend.

He bent over her like some monstrous ghoul.

DOCTOR BARRY, the assistant coroner, rose from the body beside the hedge and daubed a handkerchief over his forehead. His big, strained face was very pale.

"Dead," he announced huskily. "Dead, all right. Shot through the heart!"

For a while the twenty-odd men who stood in the moonlight, tense and appalled, gaping in awe at the murdered remains of old Ben Hawkins, were silent. They exchanged stunned glances. A few fidgeted nervously and cleared their throats. Murder was not a commonplace occurrence in the village of Lakeview, and this was quite the most shocking thing that had happened locally in more than a decade. Nor could anybody in that crowd foresee that it was to be merely one in a series of stupefying horrors—a series that had begun just twenty-four hours ago with the disappearance of a girl . . .

"He must have died instantly," muttered Doctor Barry.

Pete Mesmore—who held the title of Police Chief, though he commanded only one subordinate—sucked in a sharp breath. He peered from the body to the thick-set physician.

"How long would you say he's been dead, doc?" he whispered.

"About an hour. No more."

"*Mmm.* Fits in, all right." Chief Mesmore anxiously plucked at his lower lip until, of a sudden, he turned to call, "Hey, Lu! Lu Flint! C'mere!"

A tall, gaunt man pushed his way through the group. He had the lanky figure of an Ichabod Crane and the bright, close-set eyes of a fox, agleam in the moonlight. Lucien Flint was well on in his fifties. But just now he looked like a badly frightened boy.

"Wh-what is it?" he asked.

"How did you come to find him?" Mesmore demanded.

"I told you that."

"The details, I mean. Come on!"

Lucien Flint's hand rubbed along the side of his shapeless trousers. An instant he scowled down at the body, then shuddered and lifted his eyes to Mesmore's.

"It was like this," he said hoarsely. "I was down to the lake, fishin' for bullheads like I do most every night. And all of a sudden I hear this here shot—and a yell. It—it kinda give me a chill. So I sat still a while, just listenin'. But there wasn't no other sound. Only the bullfrogs croakin' the dark. Well, I—I figured maybe I'd better go see what's what. So I come up here, and there's Ben Hawkins layin' like you see him. It didn't take me a minute to find out he was dead. Then I beat it into town to call you. That's all."

"You didn't see anybody around?"

"Course not!" Lucien Flint retorted. "I'd have told you, wouldn't I?"

At that Chief Mesmore uttered a grunt. In the crowd behind him a low, excited voice was whispering: "Things sure are happening in this town! Yesterday the Holmes girl disappears, and now this thing! I'd say—"

"Oh, shut up!" growled Mesmore. "Ain't things bad enough without hollerin' about 'em?" He paused to frown at a dilapidated old house looming beyond a curtain of elms and oaks. It was dark, having for many years been untenanted; and now it looked strangely ominous and forbidding. "Well, Lu," the chief mumbled, "this here killing lays on your property."

"It does not!" declared Lucien Flint.

"Huh?" Mesmore glanced at him in surprise. "You own the old place, don't you?"

"No," snapped Flint. "Sold it last week!"

That amazed everyone; somebody ejaculated softly. And twenty pairs of incredulous eyes swung toward the gaunt man, so that for a second even the body was ignored. In Lakeview any transfer of real estate constituted an important item of public news. The astonishing fact that Flint had not announced this sale was a sort of affront to the entire community. Certainly there could be no reason for secrecy in the sale of an ancient landmark.

"What do you mean?" challenged Mesmore, his eyes round. "How come nobody knows about it?"

Flint said testily: "The deal wasn't closed till yestiddy. I wasn't goin' to talk about it 'fore it was all settled. Besides, 'tain't nobody's business, anyhow!"

"Now it is!" declared the chief. "The owner of this place has to be notified. Who bought it?"

"Young feller from New York. Writin' man. Reckon you ought to remember him. Name of Kent Carmody. He spent all last summer over to Jim Honeywell's place, writin' a book."

There were murmurs of bewilderment. Doctor Barry, who enjoyed very little intellectual companionship in the village, said with a note of eagerness: "Of course! He's quite well known. Writes adventure stories. Is Carmody coming out here to live?"

"Sure," assented Flint. "He's coming up next week with some architect. They're going to remodel the place. Fix it up with plumbing an' all. But the point is, he owns this land now. The murder lays on his property, not mine!"

"Well," snapped the chief, "it don't really matter one way or the other. The thing that counts is that Ben Hawkins has been killed. And I aim to find out who killed him!"

On this grim declaration he kneeled again beside the body. The other men peered anxiously over his shoulders. It seemed a little absurd that anyone should have wanted to kill old Ben Hawkins. For Ben had been a harmless, genial derelict of almost seventy who had supported himself by doing odd chores around the village.

Yet there he lay, dead in the dark, with no clue to indicate the identity of the murderer; with nothing to suggest why he had been shot. There he lay in moonlight, beside the hedge—the first of the horrors that were to strike the newly acquired property of Kent Carmody . . .

WHEN that tragic drama pounced upon young Carmody himself, it came furiously, suddenly, without the slightest warning.

That happened five nights later.

It was ten o'clock in the evening when Kent Carmody reached the outskirts of Lakeview, after an eight-hour drive from New York. He brought his red roadster to a stop beside a low, untrimmed hedge and waved his hand toward the sprawling house visible beyond the screen of magnificent oaks and elms.

Apparently he was not thinking of the murder, for he said cheerily enough: "There she is, Jerry! My first estate. You can't tell much in the dark. But you'll find it beautiful in daylight. The lake is only a couple of hundred yards away."

Jerry Devere, who was much too plump and rosy and soft for his thirty-two years, regarded the house with frank skepticism. "So that," he said, "is the junk heap you paid good money for? Well, well—and another well."

"What's the matter with it?" Kent Carmody demanded.

"Everything. Whoever sold it to you must be chuckling up his sleeve."

"Why?"

"In the first place, it looks to be about a hundred years old—a home for decrepit ghosts."

"That," laughed Carmody, "is one of its charms."

"And you expect me to modernize a wreck like that?"

"You're an architect, aren't you?" Carmody demanded, still laughing.

"Yeah. But not a magician." Jerry paused to send an appraising survey over the trees. For a moment there was a hush challenged only by the croakings of distant bullfrogs. The night air was cool and fragrant, and both men drank of it deeply. "Well," Jerry admitted at last, "the grounds don't seem bad. Stately and all that. But pretty much neglected."

Carmody nodded. "The man who owned the place," he explained, "is a widower. Lives alone. It was too big for him. He's been staying at a small cottage in the village for the past few years, and nobody bothered about this place. But it's just the sort of home I've been hunting for!" He threw open the door of the car. "Want to have a look around?"

Jerry Devere, however, hesitated. He frowned faintly. After a few seconds he muttered: "Er—I don't know . . . By the way, Kent, where did they find that body?"

Instantly that query brought sternness to Carmody's lean young face. He shook his head. "I don't know exactly," he answered softly. "I haven't been here since. That's something I intend to look into; a murder on my property isn't the best thing to—"

And then, before he could finish, there came an astounding interruption—something that caused them both to sit up in abrupt tension, staring, rigid.

From somewhere on the other side of the house tore the screams of a woman!

Wild screams—frantic—they pierced the stillness of the night with terror. First they were meaningless. But they quickly became articulate: "No! Don't! Don't! Leave me alone! Do-on't!"

That was all.

They ended as suddenly as they had begun.

As the last sound ceased, Kent Carmody sprang out of the car. His face was gray. His eyes blazed. "Come on!" he whispered hoarsely.

From the running-board he leaped over the bridge and started a furious dash toward the other side of the house. Tall, lean, as lithe at thirty as he had been during college days, he ran with amazing speed. He darted among the huge trees like a shadow. Once he shot a swift glance back over his shoulder. Jerry Devere, he saw, was already following. But Jerry, being too plump for such exertions, was thudding along ponderously, panting, some thirty yards in the rear.

Kent Carmody circled a wing of the house. When he reached the back, he stopped. He was breathing heavily, and his eyes flamed as they swept about in search of the woman who had screamed.

But he saw no one.

Neither woman nor man! Nothing that stirred! Only darkness and crazy shadows in the moonlight and a background of black, silent trees . . .

For an instant he was too bewildered to think clearly. Someone had been here a few seconds ago; that was certain! Someone had screamed in terror and had vanished. Vanished where? In the house?

He spun around to gape at the old building. Its warped walls were gray in the moonlight. There was no hint of life in any of its bleak, broken windows. It stood there like the battered ghost of something that had once been dignified and splendid. It—

And then Kent Carmody heard a shot!

A single sharp crack from the front of the house—and after it—silence.

It was not the shot itself that paralyzed him momentarily. It was the thought of Jerry Devere . . . Jerry, lumbering on alone at the front . . .

With a cry stifled in his throat, Carmody turned and raced back around the house. His countenance was suddenly gaunt and colorless, the eyes haggard with unutterable fear. As he ran he shouted: "Jerry! Jerry!"

But there was no reply.

And the reason for that dreadful stillness he discovered soon enough—when he halted with a gasp to see Jerry Devere sprawling motionless in the grass!

Jerry's arms were outflung. He lay hatless, face down. From a hideous gash in his head, where a bullet had cracked the skull, poured a stream of blood!

"Good God!"

The whisper broke from Carmody on a note of stupefaction. He stood for a moment, horrified, then plunged forward to drop to his knees beside the plump figure. His face was as yellow as the moonlight. His whole being thundered as he lifted those limp, sagging shoulders out of the grass.

Jerry Devere was not dead.

Though his head lolled listlessly, though his arms dragged, fitful moans still flowed through his teeth.

Carmody whispered, "Jerry!" But there was no answer. He looked around in confusion, a thousand mad questions storming in his mind. Who had done this?

Who?

There was nobody to be seen in all that hushed darkness! Not even a shadow. Could Jerry have been shot by somebody in the house? Somebody even now peering out of a window? If so, would he perhaps shoot again?

CARMODY caught his breath, stiffened. This was no time for questions! Not while Jerry lay there unconscious, with blood pouring out of his head! He must be rushed to Lakeview, to a doctor. Nothing else mattered now!

Carmody thrust one arm under the wounded man's torso, the other under his knees, and staggered up with the weight. He reeled against the house. It was not going to be easy, this job of carrying a hundred and eighty pounds to the car. Yet, somehow, it must be done.

As he started toward the road with his burden, stumbling and swaying, a vast bitterness welled in him. He groaned. What if Jerry died? What if this were the end? He tried to crush the dreadful thought, for the physical task of bearing his friend demanded all his concentration. Time after time he had to steady himself against trees. But always that terrible thought returned to pound at his mind.

What if Jerry died?

It was he, Kent Carmody, who had brought Jerry Devere to Lakeview! He felt desperately responsible for what had happened. Jerry had a mother and a sister who would have to be told about this. Jerry had—

Carmody blotted the idea out of existence. He stumbled on, with sweat pouring from his forehead to blur his eyes. Fiery eyes. Often enough, in his tales of adventure, he had written of men who struggled to help wounded comrades; but his most vivid imaginings had never been as horrible as this reality.

His arms felt paralyzed. He went on half blindly and was in actual sight of the road when, of a sudden, he stopped. Stopped because he distinctly heard the thumps of approaching steps!

Running steps!

Carmody stood tense, his heart banging, his eyes flaming in the blackness under the trees. For a second he quite forgot Jerry's dead weight.

Was the killer returning?

Then, suddenly, he caught the glimpse of a shadowy figure no more than ten yards away. It halted. It stared. There was something familiar about that lean silhouette. And the voice, too, was recognizable when it gasped. "Carmody!"

"That you, Flint?" he shot back.

"Yes!" panted Lucien Flint. "Good Lord, wh-what's happened? Who you got there?"

Kent Carmody released a broken breath of relief. It was good to encounter a man he knew—the man from whom he had bought this land. Certainly Lucien Flint couldn't be standing there with murderous intent, else he would shoot immediately without pausing to ask these questions.

Carmody flung out hoarsely, "Give me a hand, will you? Hurry!"

Gaunt as a skeleton, Lucien Flint strode forward to help. His bony face was utterly colorless. He muttered to himself. He caught Jerry's legs in nervous hands and started backward toward the road. All about them was heavy silence, accentuated by the raucous croakings of bullfrogs.

"What's happened?" he whispered.

Carmody told him. He talked in spurts. By the time he finished the astounding report, they had propped Jerry into the seat of the roadster. Both he and Flint squeezed in beside the wounded man, to prevent him from toppling over.

"Take him to Doc Barry's!" Flint huskily advised. "I'll show you the way! Gosh, that—that's a terrible wound!"

Carmody said nothing. He started the car and sent it flying along the dark road at perilous speed. As his headlights split the blackness, he felt it would be worth a great deal now to explore the interior of his newly purchased home. He'd have given anything to put his hands on Jerry's assailant! His whole body blazed with the desire. But that must wait. Jerry came first; Jerry whose limp head still bleeding, dangled on Lucien Flint's chest.

They had been plunging along for several minutes, with the cool wind whizzing past them, when Carmody abruptly asked: "Flint, what were you doing there?"

"Me? I was down to the lake, fishin'!"

"At this hour?"

"Sure! I go down 'most every night. When I heard the screams and the shot, I come zipping up the hill to see what was happening. Gee Mr. Carmody, I don't know what's struck this town! Last week Ben Hawkins was killed, and tonight it's this! Both near the old house, too. How can you account for that? And those screams—Gee, I wonder—"

He hesitated; and though Carmody did not urge him on, he ejaculated softly: "You know, a girl disappeared hereabouts last week! Name of Catherine Holmes!"

Carmody whispered fiercely: "The devil with all that now! It's Jerry I'm worrying about!"

So they drove on in silence, spinning dangerously around curves, until at last they entered the village of Lakeview. When they stopped in front of Doctor Barry's house, Flint jumped out of the roadster and said: "Wait. I'll get the doc to help us."

He ran up a path and returned in a moment with the physician himself. A bald, thick-set man of forty, with incipient jowls, Doctor Barry might have been handsome, were it not for his inordinately prominent teeth. They jutted out far, making a snout of his mouth, so that he seemed always to be pouting.

When he saw Jerry Devere's gruesome head, his face became very grim. "Just a second before you lift him," he snapped; and motioning Carmody aside, he leaned into the car and pressed his ear to Jerry's heart. A moment he listened. Then he looked up with a peculiar expression, half doubtful, half puzzled. In that second he ceased being merely a village practitioner and became the assistant coroner.

"You sure he was breathing," he asked softly, "when you put him into the car?"

"Of course he was!" whispered Flint.

"Well—he's dead!"

HALF an hour later four cars raced out of Lakeview, bound for the desolate house that had witnessed so much tragedy. The first, Carmody's roadster, bore only him and the rugged gray-haired Chief Pete Mesmore. In the second came Doctor Barry, Lucien Flint, and three others. Jim Honeywell, the ponderous editor of The Lakeview Record, drove a black sedan crowded with five men. He never missed local excitement, and he did not intend to be absent from this investigation. The last automobile carried as many others as had already heard of this latest calamity.

As they swept out of town, Police Chief Mesmore asked, "You got the keys to the place?"

"Yes."

Kent Carmody's reply was almost curt. He sat very stiff. In the past thirty minutes he seemed to have aged ten years. His lean young countenance was gray and hard and haggard. Jerry was dead—dead —dead. He couldn't drive that terrible word out of his mind. Dead! Jerry, who had laughed so easily, who had been so plump and rosy and amiable, sitting here an hour ago, where Chief Mesmore sat now . . .

Carmody shuddered. And suddenly his face became indomitable, the jaws jutting. Whatever happened, he knew he could never rest again until Jerry's killer was caught!

He hadn't talked much since reaching Lakeview, save to report what had occurred on his grounds. Nor was he particularly anxious to talk now, until Mesmore muttered: "Queer about the screams you heard. Sure they were a woman's Mr. Carmody?"

"Positive."

"Lu Flint seems to think maybe it was this Catherine Holmes."

"What about her?" Carmody asked quickly. "I understand she disappeared."

"Yeah. Funny sort. She came to Lakeview about a month ago to recuperate from a nervous breakdown. Put up at Mrs. White's boarding house. And pretty soon Mrs. White had her hands full. The girl took sick again. Had fevers and delirium and what-not. But she pulled through, all right, and at the beginning of last week she was walking around town as healthy as any of us. Then—last Tuesday it was—she went out after supper and never came back. That's all anybody seems to know. She just disappeared. All her clothes and things are still at Mrs. White's."

"No explanation at all?"

"None," declared Mesmore. "I tried to trace her in New York, where she claimed she came from, but I couldn't locate any family. Mighty queer, the whole thing. I reported it to the New York police. They're trying to get a line on her."

Kent Carmody drew a deep, grim breath. His eyes narrowed as he drove around a sharp curve. Two murders and the screams of a woman—a woman who had cried: "No! Don't! Leave me alone! Don't!" All these centered about his newly purchased home, as if some nameless terror were making a playground of the old place.

His lips quivered. Of one thing he was doggedly certain. Before he started any work on the house, he must dig to the bottom of these mysteries. He must!

WHEN Carmody turned the key in the lock of the front door, he felt as though he were standing on the brink of some uncanny adventure.

Behind him a dozen men, equipped with lanterns and electric flashlights that illuminated their faces weirdly, stood ready to explore the house. No one spoke. A strained sense of expectation made them all tense. Chief Mesmore had a revolver in his hand, and four others had brought rifles. A lynching party could have looked no more menacing.

Carmody opened the door—to be greeted by the musty odor of rotting wood. Ahead of him was darkness; a darkness that seemed, now, vibrant with mystery. When the lights plunged into it, a dozen ungainly shadows crawled across the floor.

For a second nobody stirred.

Then Jim Honeywell, ponderous and red-haired and impulsive, snapped, "Let's go!" He would have stepped forward had not Carmody seized his arm in a detaining hold. They knew each other well, these two; it was at Honeywell's home that Carmody had spent his first summer in Lakeview. And now he said softly: "I wouldn't rush in, Jim."

"Why not?"

"There's probably a heavy layer of dust all over the place. Floors, window sills, everywhere."

"What of it?"

"No use destroying possible footprints."

Jim Honeywell, more eager than experienced, seemed slightly abashed by the admonition. But Chief Mesmore, with a sharp nod, promptly agreed: "Carmody's right! Look out, Jim. Let's have a peep at this. Lower those lights, will you?"

He knelt, with Carmody at his side, and keenly studied the floor beyond the threshold. A few lights were brought very close. And though he saw plenty of dust —a veritable carpet of it—he found no suggestion of a footprint. Obviously, if anyone had come into the house recently, it had not been by way of the front door.

And so the searching party entered.

They proceeded cautiously now, moving from room to room with eyes that stabbed the darkness, searched the floors. For fully half an hour the hunt continued. It encompassed every barren chamber. It went to the attic and it probed the cellar.

It dug into closets. Indeed, not a nook was neglected. But in the end a sorely baffled group congregated again on the porch and stared in wonder.

The house had not produced a single print!

Not a clue of any kind to indicate that anyone had of late been through those rooms! Even the window sills, which Kent Carmody himself had closely studied, showed coatings of undisturbed dust.

"Well, now!" muttered Chief Mesmore, scowling. "Looks like the killer didn't shoot from inside the house after all. I don't think anybody's been in there for weeks."

"And yet," insisted Jim Honeywell, "there's something mighty queer about this place. You can't put two murders and a woman's screams down to coincidence."

Kent Carmody stood still, frowning down at the floor. He heard little of what was said. His own mind was darting into a maze of fantastic possibilities. Something was wrong on this property of his; that much was clear enough. But what was it? And who was behind these horrors?

Suddenly he looked up at Mesmore. "Chief," he said decisively, "I don't think we'll find anything in the dark. I suggest you bring men out here first thing in the morning. In daylight we can go over the whole place, grounds and house. If we don't find the footprints of the killer, we may find some other clue. Some trace of the woman who screamed. Something to give us a lead!"

"He's right," Doctor Barry agreed. "We can't do much in the dark. Besides, if the killer was around, we've probably frightened him away by this time."

Mesmore considered, then nodded submission to this plan. He did not, however, see the curious gleam that flashed for an instant in Kent Carmody's eyes—a glint as brief as an electric spark.

A few minutes later, as the crowd started back toward the road, Jim Honeywell slipped his powerful arm through Carmody's. They were behind the others and out of earshot; and Honeywell invited in a low tone: "Kent, you come over and spend the night at my place. After what happened, you need a rest."

But Carmody grimly shook his head. "No, Jim. Thanks. I'm not going to sleep tonight."

"Huh?"

"Too much to do."

Jim Honeywell was frankly surprised. He had considered the search ended for the night, and said so. Carmody, however, peered at him keenly.

"Jim," he whispered, "can a newspaperman keep a secret?"

"If he has to."

Carmody shot a quick glance ahead at the others, then spoke in a swift, low voice. "Listen, Jim. I'm confiding in you so that somebody will know where to look for me—if anything unexpected should happen!"

"What the devil—"

"Wait. I asked Mesmore to call off this hunt tonight for a definite purpose. I've got some ideas."

"What do you mean? What ideas?"

"I think, for one thing, that the murderer is someone who belongs in Lakeview. The presence of a stranger in town would have been noticed long ago. Also, I think there's something around these grounds he doesn't want discovered. There must be! That's why he shot trespassers like Ben Hawkins and Jerry. Now, if my ideas are right, the killer will soon learn that the police intend to make a thorough search of the grounds in the morning; he'll make it his business to learn what Mesmore intends to do! And in that case, he may return tonight to re-

move or to conceal the thing he doesn't want discovered around here. Or else, he may come to wipe out any clues he may have left. One way or the other, I'll be here myself, watching for him when he comes!"

Jim Honeywell softly gasped: "But good heavens, Kent, do you realize how dangerous that is?"

Instead of replying Carmody inquired: "You own a revolver, don't you, Jim?"

"Ye-es, but—"

"I'll drive home with you, on the pretense of spending the night at your place; and you're going to lend me that gun."

"But look here," Honeywell protested. "Why do it alone? Why don't you get Chief Mesmore to go with you? After all, it's his job to trap the killer!"

Carmody earnestly shook his head. "I considered that," he admitted. "But it isn't very wise. I have an idea the murderer will be watching Mesmore pretty closely for the next hour or two. Just to be sure of what the chief proposes to do. It'll be playing the game more safely not to approach Mesmore at all. No, Jim, I'm going alone on this. It's my property; and —I brought Jerry to—all this."

"Suppose I go with you," Honeywell offered.

"Nothing doing! You've got a family, Jim. I'm not running any more of my friends into danger." As they reached the road, he patted the editor's shoulder reassuringly. "I'll be all right!" he whispered.

A ND so it was that at a few minutes after twelve on that unforgettable night Kent Carmody once more reached the desolate estate near the lake.

He stepped over the hedge, peered about cautiously for an instant, then darted as silently as a shadow into the blackness under the trees. He did not go to the house itself. Instead, he halted beside a huge oak, at a spot from which he could observe both the building and the grounds around it. And there, with his hand rigid on the revolver in his pocket, he waited.

His young face was hard, and his eyes were unnaturally bright. If his heart thumped too violently, that might be attributed to the fact that he had half walked, half run the mile from Honeywell's home. To bring his roadster, he had felt, might be to offer a warning to the killer.

If only he could catch a glimpse of that man!

Whether this fantastic plan would succeed, Carmody had no means of knowing. Quite possibly the entire notion would collapse. And yet it must be tried!

So he waited—and watched—and waited.

All about him hung a tense hush, save for the dolorous croaking of frogs; a sound so continuous that he soon ceased to notice it. Once he heard the melancholy howl of a distant train whistle, and its dying echoes. But that was all. The very darkness seemed to be holding its breath, waiting with him.

Minutes dragged into hours, and even the hours produced nothing. Carmody began to scowl. He grew tired of standing and sat on a stone, his back resting against a tree trunk. A dozen times he glanced at his watch. Two o'clock. Three o'clock. Almost four. . . Were all his hopes to be frustrated?

He tried to keep his thoughts calm. But again and again, in those silent hours, he had a horrible, sickening vision of Jerry Devere sprawling in the grass, his fractured head pouring out a stream of blood. The memory brought a deadly pallor to his face. And too, it brought a desperate resolve to see this thing through to its end! To identify and seize the nameless terror!

And then—

Suddenly, at almost four o'clock in the morning, Kent Carmody sprang to his feet. He stood very still, tense, listening. His eyes were afire, and his fingers curled around the revolver. Within him began a heavy pounding.

At the beginning he could not be certain of what he heard. Some prowling animal, perhaps? Or some prank of his tingling imagination? But the sounds became clearer, nearer, wholly unmistakable. They were soft footfalls!

Quick, furtive treads in the blackness somewhere to his right! Someone was hurrying toward the house! Someone still hidden by the trees.

Kent Carmody stood rigid as a statue. Tiny nerves were wriggling and zigzagging in his skin. His flaming gaze pierced its way under the trees, seeking, seeking —until, of a sudden, he found what he sought.

He saw the figure of a man!

A man who hastened out of the shadows to stride quickly toward the rear of the house.

Kent Carmody did not move.

It was not merely the sight of the man that stunned him; it was the incredible manner in which the figure concealed its identity. Perhaps this man had foreseen the danger of being spied. For he had thrown over his head and shoulders a sort of bag—a thing that served not only to hide his face but to mask even the shape of his torso!

TREMBLING despite himself, Carmody peered more keenly. The weird garment, he decided, must be a potato sack; something like that; with eyeholes and armholes no doubt, cut in the cloth.

The glimpse of that hooded apparition was so melodramatic, so unreal, that he gaped at it in a momentary daze. But he did not stir away from the tree.

It would serve no purpose, he warned himself, to rush out now and fight with that man. Even if he managed to overpower the fantastically attired creature, he could produce no adequate proof of guilt in murder. No, not yet. He must, he knew, wait and see what the fellow did here. He must crush every impulse until he understood the man's secret!

But, to Carmody's sudden dismay, the hooded shadow vanished around a corner of the house!

At that Kent Carmody no longer hesitated. It was from the rear, he vividly recalled, that the woman's screams had issued earlier in the night. The solution of this mystery, then, might lie behind the old building!

He slipped out from the concealment of the trees and lunged toward the house. When he was in the shadow of the walls, he advanced more cautiously, on his toes, with the revolver ready in his hand.

At the back corner he halted. He thrust his head forward carefully to reconnoitre—and saw the man again.

He was kneeling. Tugging industriously at something on the ground. Something that rose as he pulled. It was as if he were yanking up boards... And then, with a violent start, Carmody remembered.

That was the ancient well!

The well of which Lucien Flint had said: "She's been dry a good many years; reckon you'll have to rely on pipe water if you buy the place."

The well!

Why on earth should this man be opening the pit? What was in it? Was it there that he had hidden something?

The questions filled Carmody with electric tinglings of excitement. As he watched, perspiration oozed out of his forehead. He felt an almost irresistible urge to dash forward. To grapple with that hooded figure and overwhelm it. To see for himself what the well contained.

But mentally he rasped: "No! No! I've got to wait!"

For he felt that with every passing second the creature out there in the moonlight was moving nearer destruction. He was incriminating himself; possibly about to produce proof of his guilt as a killer. Certainly nothing could be lost now by watching him a little longer!

At last the well was open.

THE man peered down for a time, hanging over the pit like a gargoyle. When he rose, he held a stout rope. He parted his legs as if seeking a strong stance. He began to pull something up out of the well.

Whatever it was must have been exceedingly heavy, for the hooded man struggled mightily with the weight. Carmody could distinctly hear his grunts and pantings. He heaved like a fisherman hauling in a tremendous net.

Up, up, every pull a terrific effort. Carmody felt his own muscles quiver and tauten as though in sympathy with the other's. He watched... And suddenly the man brought his burden to the top.

He stretched it out in the moonlight, half on the ground half against the coping of the well where it squirmed and tossed feebly. Seeing it, Kent Carmody experienced so colossal a surge of horror that it threatened for an instant to overwhelm all discretion and sanity. He all but roared in outrage.

For the thing squirming there was—a woman!

A woman, bound hand and foot; gagged, helpless, her clothes in tatters! A woman whose fitful stirrings spoke of utter exhaustion.

"God!" hoarsely whispered Carmody. "He's kept her a prisoner in there!"

Then something happened to him that he could not control. A terrible, vicious rage began to boil in his very soul. The inhumanity of such torture to a woman was beyond credence. His lips drew back from his teeth in a savage snarl.

He saw things now. This was the woman who had screamed! She must have screamed just before being gagged and lowered into the well. And Jerry Devere must have caught sight of the fleeing man—only to be shot for having seen. Yes, that was it! Just as Ben Hawkins must have discovered something days ago!

And this woman—was she Catherine Holmes, who had so weirdly disappeared from Lakeview?

Carmody, beset by that seething fury, would gladly have run out to empty his revolver into that hooded figure. Yet, forcibly, he held himself in check. He wanted to see what would happen here. He wanted to hear that masked man's voice. He wanted to understand the purpose of this madness.

The man was kneeling beside the woman now. He shook her shoulder to command attention.

"Listen to me!"

His deep voice, though hushed, came clearly through the stillness of the night. Carmody, straining his ears as he leaned forward, could catch every syllable. Sweat poured from his whole body now. His chest throbbed; he actually trembled.

"Listen!" the hooded man repeated.

The huddle on the ground became still. He was bending over her like some monstrous ghoul.

"After tonight," he said, "I'm not coming again. This is your last chance. If you don't talk to me now, you'll stay down there—for good."

He paused. Then his voice rapped out harshly, bitterly: "Why can't you be reasonable? I didn't think you'd be such a fool! After all, I know all about you already, don't I? I know you're Catherine Wagner, not Holmes. I know your brother is in jail for the Chadwick Bank robbery. I know he hid $70,000 of the money before his arrest. And I know you can tell where he hid it—"

"In a moment," he went on, "I'm going to free your mouth. It's your last chance to tell me. If you don't, you go back—in there—dead!" He bent lower. "Do you understand? Dead!" One hand leaped to her gag; the other drew a revolver from a side pocket. "You'll have to decide—now!"

Then Kent Carmody knew he could endure no more.

If he could seize that hooded man and free the woman, her testimony would be sufficient to set any curt in turmoil! His hand tightened fiercely around his revolver. His eyes blazed. Softly, on his toes, he started out of the shadows of the house. He was approaching the man's back, unseen. He moved fully twenty feet through the thick grass. And at that moment the uncanny figure heard him.

THE man whirled around and sprang up with a cry. There was panic in his very pose. His revolver glinted in the moonlight. Though fifty yards still separated him from Carmody, he fired without hesitation, wasting a bullet on the darkness.

Then he swept the gun downward and fired again.

Two shots, two vivid flashes of flame—both aimed directly at the woman!

Witnessing that, Carmody roared in sheer horror. He knew exactly why the thing had happened. Trapped, discovered, the man had savagely murdered the only one who could testify against him! And now he turned and dashed toward the trees.

Carmody no longer shouted. His face was desperately strained. He ran with every ounce of strength in his long legs—and steadily gained. Twice he fired his own gun at the fleeing terror. But at forty yards he could not hit that figure, and the man continued his wild dash for safety. Halfway to the trees he turned just far enough to send back two answering bullets. Then he ran on, on, like a terrified deer, to bound into the black shadows under the trees.

And Carmody after him—

To swerve to the woman, he knew, would be futile. She was dead. This killer had fired point-blank into her body. The thing to do was to catch him! To kill him if necessary! To tear that hood from his head and identify him!

Plunging among the trees, Carmody thumped against them, scraping his hands on their bark, winding in and out to avoid collisions.

But he was gaining!

The killer reached the road and leaped over the hedge. Without a backward glance he dashed on to the grassy hill that sloped down to the lake. He raced on wildly, swishing through the grass. Ahead of him the lake glimmered in the moonlight, and he went toward it as if flying at a target.

Carmody was only thirty yards behind now. He knew he could win. He must win! Twenty-five yards behind. They were within a few feet of a little precipice that dropped to the lake now. And only twenty yards separated them. He raised his revolver, aimed. . .

Abruptly, then, the hooded man halted and spun around!

He turned like a beast at bay. A hoarse cry burst from him. Seeing Carmody's lifted gun, he dodged—just in time to avoid a bullet. And as he dodged, his own revolver roared.

Carmody felt hot steel rip through his right shoulder.

Something happened to his arm. It fell limp at his side. His fingers could no longer hold the gun, and the weapon dropped into the grass.

But that didn't stop him. He was beyond caution now, beyond all thought. He lunged straight at the killer. The man fired directly at his head, but only a metallic click resulted. He had spent his six bullets.

Kent Carmody's left fist, clenched hard as rock, swung out furiously. With all the power of his arm and shoulder and onrushing body it crashed squarely into that hooded face. The killer gasped. He went tottering back crazily, arms gyrating, to collapse in the grass.

Carmody leaped upon him. Leaped like a tiger springing to the kill. Though his right arm was useless, he still had that left. He seized the hood, ripped it off— just as the killer swung his gun up from the ground.

He drove it upward as though he were wielding an ax and brought the barrel crashing down squarely on Carmody's head!

Chaos, then.

Carmody groaned, swayed sidewise. Frantically he struggled to escape the blackness and explosive lights that stormed in his brain. But he couldn't. A pall swept over his senses. He fell limply over the edge of the eight-foot precipice and dropped into the shore-shallows of the lake with a tremendous splash.

The man in the grass rose dizzily, pulling the hood back over his head. For a moment he stood like a gorilla, arms dangling loosely, while he retrieved his breath in long, deep gasps.

Presently he went to the edge of the small cliff. He looked down at the unconscious figure below. Carmody lay half in the water, his head and shoulders still on the bank. Uttering a faint grunt, the killer glanced from left to right, seeking an easy descent.

But suddenly he heard a sound that made him straighten in new alarm. He spun around. Up near the road, still a hundred yards away, he saw two men— men already running toward the lake! Perhaps he recognized in them the rugged silhouette of Police Chief Mesmore and the ponderous bulk of Jim Honeywell.

Whether he did or not, however, he crouched and darted away as swiftly as a fox, to disappear among trees.

WHEN Kent Carmody regained consciousness, just before five o'clock that morning, he found himself stretched on a cot in Doctor Barry's office. Chief Mesmore and Jim Honeywell, both gripped by tense anxiety, sat beside him; and the physician, in striped pajamas and a dressing gown, was washing his hands in a basin, meanwhile eying his emergency patient over his shoulder.

Carmody lay pallid and disheveled, a battered caricature of himself. His memory, however, returned with a jolting rush. And when it came, he caught his breath on a little gasp and tried impulsively to rise. But a stab of pain in his wounded shoulder and redoubled poundings in his head warned him to remain quiet.

"Don't try to move," Honeywell worriedly advised. "You're pretty weak, Kent."

"What happened?" Carmody asked huskily.

"That's what we're waiting to hear."

"I—I'm afraid I can't talk yet. Better give me a few minutes to get my—my strength. Tell me—how did I get here?"

Honeywell cast an uncertain glance at the grim police chief. He sent hesitant fingers back through his red hair and muttered uneasily: "Maybe we ought just to let you rest a while—"

"No! I'll be all right," Carmody thickly insisted. "Tell me, Jim, What happened?"

"We-ell, it was like this. I was feeling pretty worried about you after you left. And when you hadn't returned by three-thirty, I decided it had been a mighty serious mistake to let you go alone. My wife thought so, too. So I phoned Mesmore and told him about it, and we rushed over to the old house. The minute we got near the place we heard those shots. We ran into the grounds and saw that—that girl, Catherine Holmes, stretched out by the open well. She was—dead."

Jim Honeywell paused nervously; but Carmody, closing his eyes, whispered, "Go on."

"Before we could so much as—as look around, we heard the other shots, down by the lake. So we raced down there. And we found you, with blood all over your shoulder, lying on the bank. That's about all there is to tell. We got you over here as fast as we could, and the chief has mustered up a posse that's down at the old house now."

And then, before Carmody could speak, Mesmore leaned forward and tensely gripped his wrist. The chief's narrowed eyes were flashing.

"Who did it?" he whispered. "Who was it?"

The hard, bitter ghost of a smile twisted Carmody's features. He looked at the chief obliquely.

"He had his face covered by a bag," he said. "I guess he thinks I didn't see that face—when I pulled the bag off him."

"Who was it?" Mesmore repeated hoarsely. His fingers actually squeezed into the wounded man's arm. "Come on, Carmody—who was it?"

The room was hushed. Carmody's mind raced. The three men all stared at him as if they expected him to scream. He answered in a low savage voice.

"It was he—Doctor Barry!"

Silence.

Ten seconds of absolute stillness during which not one of them stirred.

Then Doctor Howard Barry, his heavy face white as chalk, his eyes ablaze, seemed to suffer a convulsive shock. He caught his breath. He reeled back against a table.

"Me?" he gasped. "Are—are you crazy?"

"Am I?" Kent Carmody forced himself up on an elbow, his face afire with fury. Glaring at the physician, he shot out in a voice all the more terrible because of its passionate suppression: "When Catherine Holmes was sick here, in delirium, you treated her! You must have—you're the only doctor in town! She raved, and from what she said you learned she was Catherine Wagner—sister of a man in jail—a man who'd hidden $70,000! She recovered, and you kidnaped her. Tortured her brutally in an effort to make her tell where that money was concealed! Kept her a prisoner in that well! When you were spied near the thing by Ben Hawkins and Jerry Devere, you had to kill them so that you—and the kidnaping—wouldn't be found out! Then you dashed back here to your office and were ready when Chief Mesmore called on you as assistant coroner! You had nerve, doctor—and you were as inhuman as a devil! But this is the end for you! This—"

"You're mad, I tell you!" Doctor Barry roared.

"I saw you there, didn't I?" With the retort Carmody raised his head higher, challenging.

Both Mesmore and Jim Honeywell had risen in horror. They gaped from Carmody to the pallid doctor and saw that the physician's face was working wildly. Impetuously Chief Mesmore stepped forward, his hand darting to his pocket.

And an unexpected thing happened.

Beside Doctor Barry's hand stood a lamp. At the moment it furnished the only illumination in the room. As a gasp tore from his throat, he snatched up that lamp. He hurled it with all his power straight at Mesmore's head.

But the chief dodged, and the lamp shattered itself against the wall.

Darkness, then. Kent Carmody lay rigid, trembling. He heard oaths. Heard the scraping of feet, the bang of a door. Jim Honeywell found the wall switch and turned on the blazing ceiling lights—to reveal the fact that both Doctor Barry and Chief Mesmore had vanished from the room!

But the lights had scarcely flared when, from outside, came the sounds of shots. Two in quick succession. Then a third. A shriek of agony—and silence.

Presently Chief Pete Mesmore, very pale and very grim, appeared once more in the door. His right hand held a revolver. His left sought the support of the door knob. He looked from Carmody to Jim Honeywell. And very quietly he said: "The doc tried to get away in my car. But he wasn't fast enough."

"The truth is," muttered Carmody a minute later, when Honeywell sat alone with him, "that I didn't see his face at all when I yanked off that bag. He knocked me out before I could see anything."

"Wha-at!" Honeywell whispered incredulously.

"That's the truth of it, Jim."

"But for God's sake!· Then how did you know?"

"Well—" Carmody hesitated, half closed his eyes in a frown. "When we fought, I punched his face with my left hand. I hit him very hard—in the mouth. Look at this, Jim."

Carmody raised his left hand to display a curious V-shaped scar—or rather a series of tiny scars forming an acute angle. He regarded them grimly.

"The marks of the teeth I hit," he said simply. "They bit quite deep. Jim, do you know anybody else whose teeth jut out like that, to form a regular V? Doctor Barry was one in a million, I guess. When I found these marks on my hand, I built the rest of the story around them. But I couldn't throw a theory at Barry. So I made a direct accusation—and his reaction told the rest!"

What's In a Name?

LABELS are dubious things at best and all too often, unfortunately, completely misleading. We'd hate to admit the number of times we've been taken in by the catchy name or title tacked onto some product; been inveigled thereby into making the purchase, only to discover finally that we had merely proved vulnerable once again—the unwary victim of a facile blurb writer. It doesn't matter much whether it was a new brand of soap or tooth paste, some novel gadget for opening tin cans in a different way, or even the title of a movie or book—or magazine. Yes—even a detective-story magazine!

All of which brings us, at last, to the question. And, we hope, the answer too. It was Will Shakespeare (and after all he's the source of more titles, blurbs and catch words than are all the copy writers functioning today put together) who first popped the query: "What's In A Name?" But in answering he didn't go quite as far as he might have. He merely said, poetically enough, that roses would smell just as sweet by any other name. He could very well have added that onions would smell equally foul if labeled some other way, and in doing so have clinched his point beyond all bounds of argument. But maybe the bard liked onions—some people do—and possibly it wouldn't have made good poetry.

At any rate he made it pretty plain that names don't mean a great deal in themselves. It's what's back of the name that really counts. And that goes for 1932 just as truly as it did in 1632. Which is one reason why you don't see any sweepingly pretentious and magnifying adjectives attached to the name DIME DE-TECTIVE MAGAZINE. There isn't any superlative, three-ring circus termi-nology there. Just the three words of the title and the explanatory phrase "All Stories Complete." Simple—direct—and to the point. It's a magazine. It's a detective-story magazine. And it costs only a dime! Those three facts together with the statement that all the stories in each issue begin and end within that issue are all we feel warranted in telling you on the cover.

Perhaps, in the back of our minds—maybe not so far back either—we hold the belief that DIME DETECTIVE MAGAZINE really is the best buy in the detective-fiction field at any price. Perhaps we do feel that it publishes the most thrilling mystery yarns that are being published these days. But we refuse to be didactic about it in capital letters blazoned all over the cover. We are going to let the pages between the covers settle that for themselves and we have confidence that those pages aren't going to let the name of the magazine down.

DIME DETECTIVE MAGAZINE is the name. But the stories inside are what will continue to give it meaning, make it more than a mere label, keep it on the upgrade.

How about it?

AND while we're on the subject of names it seems a good time to mention one which has done more than a lot to make the magazine the thrill-special it has become. Erle Stanley Gardner. You'll find him clutching his trusty dicta-phone in the middle of the next page. If it were anyone else but Gardner we'd make some nasty crack about that book he's holding and begin to wonder just where he does dig up those master-mysteries he writes. However, we'll give him a break and call the tome a dictionary—or a law book. Before he turned to fiction he was one of the legal lights of California, his home state, so maybe the picture is an old one taken before he deserted the bar and he's merely preparing a brief.

Mr. Gardner is another one of those fictioneers whose life has been as varied and fraught with adventure as that of any of the characters in his yarns. He has lived in tough mining camps, been engaged in railroad construction work, been an amateur boxer, hunter, fisherman and flyer, has ranched in the mountains and traveled widely both for business and pleasure. He confesses to a love for the desert and when he gets fed up with civilization, which is often, he walks downstairs from his study, gets into his camp wagon, and heads for the waste places.

He says: "I like to poke along the Mexican border ports, too. Tiajuana's too civilized. Mexicali is where my beat begins. Mexicali, Los Algedones, San Luiz, Nogales . . . the old camp wagon's been parked at all of them for a day or a week or a month at a stretch. I like the mountains too, and have a little mountain ranch with saddle horses. Like archery, and have a whole side of my study filled with bows and arrows.

"That big camp-wagon affair of mine is a regular house on wheels. It has bed, bath, radio, cooking, heating, hot and cold water, typewriting desk. I keep it all equipped and in front of the house, filled with clothes, eats, typewriter, paper, and everything. When I get to feeling too routine-ish I don't need to do anything except walk up to the camp wagon, open the door and step on the starter.

It sounds like a fascinating kind of existence to us. And we're all for it if it makes for the great yarns Mr. Gardner gives us. We were relieved when he added:

Erle Stanley Gardner in the study of his California home.

"But mostly I like to write. I like to collect material from odd, out-of-the-way sources and put it on paper. I like to create characters and watch 'em do their stuff. No matter what else I do, I'm always writing. Whether I'm out in the desert, in China, or in a border port, I'm tapping away a little bit every day, and sometimes far into the night.

"Went to China a year ago, just to see if it was like I thought it would be. I've always been interested in the Chinese. Studied the language until I got to the point where I could kid the girls in their native tongue. And I don't know what more a man wants of any language. Came back with a swell collection of Oriental curios and weapons and the ability to handle chop sticks like a veteran, even unto the eating of rice."

And now keep your eyes open for the coming issues of DIME DETECTIVE. They will include more thrilling, more mysterious stories than ever before.

Half a Million People
have learned music this easy way

You, too, Can Learn to Play
Your Favorite Instrument
Without a Teacher

Easy as A-B-C

YES, over half a million delighted men and women all over the world have learned music this quick, easy way.

Half a million—what a gigantic orchestra they would make! Some are playing on the stage, others in orchestras, and many thousands are daily enjoying the pleasure and popularity of being able to play some instrument.

Surely this is convincing proof of the success of the **new, modern method** perfected by the U. S. School of Music! And what these people have done, YOU, too, can do!

Many of this half million didn't know one note from another—others had never touched an instrument—yet in half the usual time they learned to play their favorite instrument. Best of all, they found learning music **amazingly** easy. No monotonous hours of exercises—no tedious scales—no expensive teachers. This simplified method made learning music as easy as A-B-C!

It is like a fascinating game. From the very start you are playing **real** tunes, perfectly, by note. You simply can't go wrong, for every step, from beginning to end, is right before your eyes in print and picture. First you are **told** how to do a thing, then a picture **shows** you how, then you do it yourself and hear it. And almost before you know it, you are playing your favorite pieces —jazz, ballads, classics. No private teacher could make it clearer. Little theory—plenty of accomplishment. That's why students of the U. S. School of Music get ahead twice as fast—three times as fast as those who study old-fashioned, plodding methods.

You don't need any special "talent." Many of the half-million who have already become accomplished players never dreamed they possessed musical ability. They only wanted to play some instrument—just like you—and they found they could quickly learn how this easy way. Just a little of your spare time each day is needed—and you enjoy every minute of it. The cost is surprisingly low—averaging only a few cents a day—and the price is the same for whatever instrument you choose. And remember, you are studying right in your own home—without paying big fees to private teachers.

Don't miss any more good times! Learn now to play your favorite instrument and surprise all your friends. Change from a wallflower to the center of attraction. Music is the best thing to offer at a party—musicians are invited everywhere. Enjoy the popularity you have been missing. Get your share of the musician's pleasure and profit! Start now!

Free Booklet and Demonstration Lesson

If you are in earnest about wanting to join the crowd of entertainers and be a "big hit" at any party—if you really do want to play your favorite instrument, to become a performer whose services will be in demand—fill out and mail the convenient coupon asking for our Free Booklet and Free Demonstration Lesson. These explain our wonderful method fully and show you how easily and quickly you can learn to play at little expense. This booklet will also tell you all about the amazing new **Automatic Finger Control.** Instruments are supplied when needed—cash or credit, U. S. School of Music, 866 Brunswick Bldg., New York City.

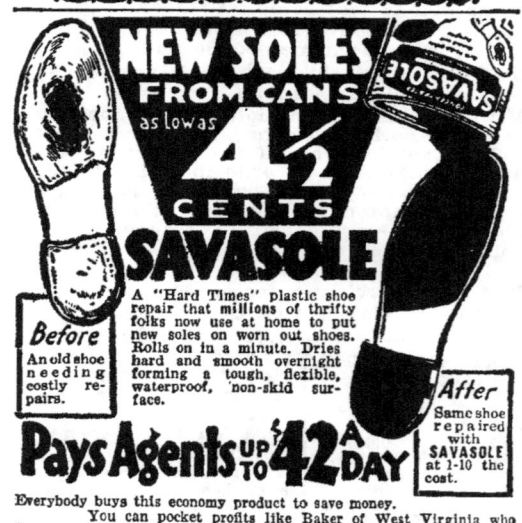

This Great Book

Now Only $1.00

"MARRIED LOVE"

A New Contribution to the Solution of Sex Difficulties

by

Dr. MARIE C. STOPES

OVER 800,000 COPIES SOLD!

100 Pages Finely Printed and Beautifully Bound.

THIS famous book, which only recently was made available to the American public by the decision of U. S. Federal Judge John M. Woolsey, is now offered at the *amazingly low price of only $1.00 per copy*. This edition of "Married Love" contains the text of the volume submitted to Judge Woolsey and upon which he based his decision.

Thousands of marriages end in discord and grief because of the ignorance in which most people enter the marital state. The primitive sex instincts are out of place in modern life. The youth and maiden of our time, if either is to find happiness in wedded life, must be instructed, must be taught, the supreme human relationship, The Art of Love. *This book gives this important knowledge in the frankest and clearest language.*

It has been said that if every couple who had to meet the tangled situations of wedded life could have the information given in "Married Love" their chances for complete happiness would be multiplied enormously.

If you are married or contemplating marriage you should own and read this valuable book.

"Married Love" has received the unqualified endorsement of leading authorities the world over, among whom are H. G. Wells, George Bernard Shaw, Havelock Ellis, May Sinclair and Dean Inge. "Married Love" is one of the frankest, most delicate and most helpful books ever written on the vital subject of the intimate contacts of sex love in marriage.

As there will be a tremendous demand for "Married Love" at this amazingly low price, we urge you to order your book without delay . . . at once . . . now . . . so as to be sure of securing a copy of this remarkable book before the special edition is exhausted and this low price offer withdrawn.

EUGENICS PUBLISHING CO., Dept. M-94
317 E. 34th ST., NEW YORK, N. Y.

In Lifting the Ban

on this famous book, Federal Judge John M. Woolsey said that it was "neither immoral nor obscene, but highly informative." He further said, " 'Married Love' is a considered attempt to explain to married people how their mutual sex life may be made happier.

"It also makes some apparently justified criticisms of the inopportune exercise, by the man in the marriage relation, of what are often referred to as his conjugal or marital rights, and it pleads with seriousness, and not without some eloquence, for a better understanding by husbands of the physical and emotional side of the sex life of their wives."

© E. P. C., Inc. 1932

In this FREE Book

a World-Famous Flier shows how *YOU* can get into *AVIATION*

40

Jobs on The Ground for Each One in the Air

Fliers are in demand—certainly! But for every man in the air, trained men are needed in over 40 highly-paid jobs on the ground. Hinton's training gives you your ground-work to earn real money as one of these:

Engineers, Designers, and Draughtsmen, Pilots, Engine and Plant Mechanics, Riggers, Electricians, Welders, Instrument Makers, Wood and Metal Workers, Plane and Motor Inspectors, Airport Operators, Radio Experts, Assemblymen, Aerial Surveyors and Photographers, Aerial Transport Managers, Salesmen.

HERE is the book that tells you straight from the shoulder what Aviation offers YOU. You've been wondering how to break into the field—wanting all the facts, all the information. Here it is! A story more exciting, more thrilling, more inspiring than fiction—yet a man-to-man message of FACTS from cover to cover. Walter Hinton—hero of history-making flights—gives you the brass tacks of Aviation Today. He shows you exactly *where* your opportunities lie—exactly *what* to do to make the most of them—exactly *how* to fit yourself for them. Here is a book for men with too much backbone to stay chained to a small-pay job—too much adventure in their blood for a humdrum grind—too much good sound business sense in their heads to let this opportunity of a lifetime outgrow them!

Walter Hinton

Trail-blazer, pioneer, explorer, author, instructor, AVIATOR. The first man to pilot a plane across the Atlantic—the famous NC-4—and first to fly from North to South America. The man who was a crack flying instructor for the Navy during the War; who today is training far-sighted men for Aviation. Hinton is ready to back YOU up to the limit. His Book is yours FREE for the coupon below.

The Richest, Fastest Growing Industry the World Has Ever Known

You haven't heard anything about this being a "bad year" for *Aviation!* Men like Ford, DuPont — *Millionaires* — are investing fortunes in the field. Cities everywhere are building more airports; 24-hour shifts are racing construction on new plane and equipment plants. Air lines, air service of every kind is doubling and re-doubling itself almost while you watch! There's no doubt about there being BIG PAY plus *a real future* for YOU in Aviation. Your one sure move is to get the *right training*-Quick!

Aviation Is Ready, Hinton Is Ready— Now It's Up to YOU

Right at home in spare-time Hinton will teach you all the essential facts about plane construction, rigging, repairs, motors, instruments, theory of flight, navigation, commercial Aviation. Whether you plan to fly, or to cash-in on one of the more than forty Big-Pay ground jobs, you must have this ground-work to land the job you want at the pay you expect. Learn just where you stand and what first steps to take. This Free Book tells how. Clip the coupon and send it TODAY. Hinton will rush your book by return mail.

You Must Be 18 or Over

To take an active part in Aviation you must be at least 18 years of age. If you are under 18, please do not ask for Lieut. Hinton's Book because it will not interest you.

Aviation Institute of U.S.A., Inc.

Walter Hinton, *President*

1115 Connecticut Ave., Washington, D.C

Rush Back to Washington!

Walter Hinton, Pres.,   675-R
Aviation Institute of U. S. A., Inc.
1115 Conn. Ave., Washington, D. C.

Dear Lieut. Hinton: Send me your FREE Book telling how I can train under you right at home for Aviation.

Name ....
(Print Clearly)

Street ....
Age ....
[Must be 18 or over]

City .... State ....